BRE.

AN ELA OF SAL ... EVAL MYSTERY

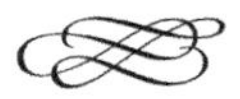

J. G. LEWIS

For my daughter, Mia Lewis, who would most definitely not have been satisfied with sitting quietly in her castle weaving and making polite conversation.

ACKNOWLEDGMENTS

I am deeply in debt to Betsy van der Hoek, Anne MacFarlane and Judith Tilden for their careful readings and excellent suggestions. Thanks also to Mark Armstrong for being my medieval sounding board on several occasions. Once again I am grateful for my fabulous editor, Lynn Messina. All remaining errors are mine alone.

CHAPTER 1

Easter Monday, Salisbury Castle, 1226

Everyone was surfeited by yesterday's feasting. Ela Longespée, Countess of Salisbury, sipped her watered wine and picked at her plate of leftover delicacies in the company of her sleepy children. For once the exhausted cook was allowed to sleep in. This morning even the hounds lolled at the fireside, too lazy to stir and beg for scraps.

Ela had insisted that her husband's recent death should not stint the festivities and she'd laid out a series of banquets for the noble families, the townspeople and the castle servants. Carved hams and roasted pheasants and fragrant lambs had weighed the silver platters. Cups sloshed and laughter filled the air of the great hall. The privations of Lent were finally over, and in this tenth year of King Henry III's reign they were blessed with peace and prosperity here at home.

If only William were there to enjoy it, too.

"My lady!" Albert, the stooped old porter, appeared in the hall door. "The hue and cry has been raised."

Already? Ela chastised herself for the slothful thought as she rose to her feet and excused herself from the table. Even before she reached the doorway she could hear a commotion outside the entrance. Gerald Deschamps, who marshaled the garrison troops, raised his voice on her approach. "Be quiet and attend your countess."

Two men paused in their argument and regarded her with curiosity. One of them was a tall, angular man whom she recognized vaguely as one of the hundred who could be called to serve as jurors. The other, a wiry, rather ragged man with weathered features and a limp, she didn't know at all.

"What's amiss?" she asked Deschamps, glad he'd come to her rather than taking matters into his own hands.

"Jacobus Pinchbeck found this man poaching in his woods."

"Bold as brass he was! Standing there before me with a fistful of my pheasants." The tall man's face was bilious with rage. "Luckily, I was out walking with two of my men so they were able to tackle him and bring him here." Two large men in rustic dress loomed behind him, one clutching a brace of limp pheasants. "I wish to see him tried as a thief."

"And what have you to say for yourself?" she asked the other.

"Very little, I'm afraid." His courtly French startled her. She'd expected him to have the speech of a villager. "Except that the land I hunted on has been in my family since the time of the conqueror."

"You claim you hunted those birds on your land?"

"He was in my forest!" Pinchbeck snarled. "I've owned it nigh on nineteen years, and every bird and beast in it is mine. It's fenced and ditched all around so there's no room for confusion."

Garrison soldiers bustled past them on the way to a

training exercise. Clearly Pinchbeck expected her to throw the other man in the dungeon.

"Your name?"

"Thomas Blount. They call me Drogo."

"Drogo Blount." Ela peered at him. The name was familiar, though the face was not. A Drogo Blount had fought in the Crusades with her husband and—if she recalled it right—even saved his life once by slaying a Saracen who held him at knifepoint. His grizzled hair, unshaven cheeks and weathered skin made him look more like a lowly serf than a valiant knight.

"Aye, my lady. I knew your husband once. A great man whose loss has rent all our hearts." He spoke like a knight. And his words touched her.

"My husband spoke of you. And told me he owed you the debt of his life." She frowned. "How do you find yourself poaching in another man's woods?"

"It's a long and lively tale, I'm afraid." His eyes were an odd green color, lichen pale. "Of a bold young man whose appetites exceeded his fortunes, and whose father lost the family estates to debt."

Ela turned to Pinchbeck. "You bought the manor from this man's father?"

"I had lent him money to finance a business venture. On finding that he'd squandered the money on horses and high living, I was forced to take his estate as my repayment. You'll find it was all legal. Your husband presided over the transfer."

"Indeed?" She looked at Blount. "Is this your understanding of how matters were settled?"

"It is." He looked apologetic, yet somehow arrogant at the same time. "My father traded a lifetime interest in the property for the payment of his debts. The manor will revert to my family on Jacobus Pinchbeck's death."

"That was the original arrangement, but I suppose his father never told him I later paid him a sum to secure full freehold rights to the property. So now he's scuttling around, stealing my stock and hoping for my death." Pinchbeck spat the words. "If he's abroad I fear to be murdered in my bed!"

"I'm not a killer, my lady." Drogo Blount stood with such confidence that she could almost picture him as a knight rather than a vagrant. "Well, in fact I am a killer. That has been my trade, fighting for king and country. But as a man in middle age I seek a life of peace. Injuries ended my career some years ago. Broken and penniless I find that I've returned to my old hunting grounds like a dumb beast." He executed a deft little half bow that complemented his humble speech.

Had a valiant knight, a close compatriot of her beloved husband, truly been reduced to poaching in the manor where he grew up? His fate tugged at her heartstrings.

"Knight or no, he deserves to hang for poaching!" Perhaps Pinchbeck saw her soften. "Is there to be no justice in Salisbury now that your husband is dead?"

"I shall dispense justice as I see fit," she said coldly. She wasn't sure what Jacobus Pinchbeck did for his living, but he wasn't a farmer. No doubt he had a burgher's arrogance and disdain for aristocracy as well as contempt for her as a woman.

Perhaps he'd deliberately swindled Blount's father out of his property in a calculated maneuver, which the books might reveal. "What is your business, Mr. Pinchbeck?"

"My business? What do you mean? I'm not on trial here."

"Answer my lady," growled Deschamps.

"I'm a merchant. A respectable merchant."

"What is your trade in?"

"In goods." Pinchbeck looked flustered. "Items of a decorative nature."

"Tapestries? Candlesticks? What exactly?"

"Those items and other...notions. Ribbons, gold thread, gemstone beads. Whatever is fashionable with the ladies in any given year." His beaky face creased into a disastrous attempt at a smile.

Ela found him evasive and likely dishonest.

"He cheated my father out of the property," said Drogo Blount. "He lent him money to bring a cargo of goods from Venice. My father was coerced into offering the manor as collateral, and then, when the ship was lost in a storm off the coast of Spain—"

"It was fair and square. Look at the contract!"

"My father died a broken man. I've stayed abroad most of my life," said Drogo softly. "I've lived by my sword and my wits, and now I find myself longing for my childhood home that was taken from my family nineteen long years ago."

Ela felt herself being manipulated. Still, if what he said was true— And he had saved her husband's life. Surely that deserved consideration? "Where are you staying, sir?"

Blount bowed his head slightly. "In the greenwood, my lady. I have no other—"

"My bloody greenwood," interjected Pinchbeck. "And stealing my bloody pheasants."

Pinchbeck's bad language further irritated Ela. She knew that the men expected her to throw Blount down in the dungeon, but that didn't feel right to her. "Master Deschamps, please show Sir Drogo to the tower rooms."

"What?" Pinchbeck looked like he might explode.

"He will be under guard while we investigate this matter, Master Pinchbeck."

"What if he escapes?"

"This is the king's garrison, Master Pinchbeck."

Deschamps simultaneously snapped at him to be silent. Ela nodded her thanks to him then turned a stern gaze on

Pinchbeck. "You'll be summoned when I have more information about the matter. Guards, please escort Master Pinchbeck to the gates."

Pinchbeck looked like he wanted to protest but wisely held his tongue—and left with the pheasants—because at this point it wouldn't have taken much for her to put him down in the dungeon.

THAT NIGHT, washed and dressed in borrowed clothing, Drogo Blount joined the family for dinner. He regaled them with tales of William's exploits in the Holy Land that made Ela laugh and weep for her husband's courage and high spirits.

He told them of the time William had been knocked from his horse by the thrust of a Saracen lance and knocked to the ground, unconscious. The Saracens seized him and debated whether to take him prisoner or slay him on the spot. Drogo, seeing his beloved lord captive and helpless, had become so enraged that he'd jumped from his horse in the heat of battle. He slayed three Saracen warriors with his hatchet, then heaved William onto his horse and carried him to safety.

Although Drogo sustained a nasty cut to the arm from a Saracen scimitar—he showed them the pale scar—William had survived without a scratch and recovered to resume the fight the next day.

The tale matched William's account—what she remembered of it—in all details, and Drogo's telling was both spirited and humble. Will, her eldest, sat riveted, quizzing Blount for details that brought the distant scenes of valor and camaraderie to life. "Your father was a true hero, my son. A man whose like is rarely seen on these shores or any other. No doubt you'll do his memory honor. You're almost the spit of him, tall as you are."

Will beamed. He was gangly and awkward, still growing into his newly tall frame. "Would you hunt with me tomorrow?"

Drogo looked both delighted and taken aback. He looked at Ela. "I believe I'm supposed to be under guard."

"Bill Talbot can accompany you." She glanced at the loyal knight who'd lived in her household for many years and taught Will much of what he knew of the manly arts. For the first time she realized that Bill hadn't been laughing and exclaiming along with the rest of them at Drogo's stories.

Did he know something about Drogo Blount that she didn't?

That night, after Blount had been escorted back to his chamber and Will had bedded down with his siblings, Ela took Talbot aside. "Did you know Drogo Blount?"

"I've never met him before." Bill's kind face was more furrowed than usual. He was a man of three score years and she'd known him since she was a child. "I've heard your husband mention him on several occasions, but I don't know him myself."

"What do you think of him?"

Talbot hesitated. "He's a good man and a brave one—but there's something...odd about him."

"Odd how? He has a limp from his battle injuries, but he has no strange accent or mannerisms. He talks and gestures like a knight of the realm. He's spent many years fighting the king's battles overseas." Ela was surprised to hear herself defending him so energetically. "Do you mistrust him?"

"I have no grounds to mistrust him, but there's something about him that sets the little hairs on my neck on their end." His pale blue eyes shone. "The way they did when I came upon the high tower where you were secreted away from the world."

"Your instincts are not to be trifled with." Ela smiled. After her father's death, Ela's family worried that, given her vast estates and inheritance, she'd fall prey to schemers or even be killed by a jealous relative. Talbot, sent by the king, had found the remote Normandy castle where her mother hid Ela. He'd entered the castle disguised as a traveling troubadour and rescued her from years of exile. She'd returned to England and married William and trusted Bill Talbot with her life ever since.

"Keep a close eye on Drogo Blount tomorrow, while I look into the sale of the Fernlees estate where he was poaching."

"Fernlees is close by. Do you remember Blount from when you were young?" asked Bill.

"No, but I was only nine when we left for France. Likely our paths never crossed."

"He looks a score or more years older than you, my lady," Bill protested. "Though I suppose that could be due to the harshness of his life."

"And of the hot desert sun. Besides, I am thirty-nine, don't forget." She was no fresh-faced girl and she didn't want to be. Being a wise older widow suited her fine. "Talk to him tomorrow. Get to know him. And give me your opinion then."

"Yes, my lady."

THE NEXT MORNING, while the men hunted, Ela summoned the clerk who dealt with matters of property to look up all documents relating to the transfer of Fernlees manor from Blount's father to Pinchbeck.

At midday, the same clerk returned with his master, both of them agitated. "There's nothing to be found, my lady," said the older man, wringing his hands. "No deed, no survey, no nothing. Nothing about a lifetime-only transfer of property, and nothing about a permanent one."

Ela sighed. "Could it have been a private treaty that wasn't recorded?"

"Then the sale wouldn't be legal. It seems official in that Pinchbeck has paid the taxes on the property since the reign of King John."

"But it's possible that Pinchbeck obtained the property by illegal means?"

The old man shrugged. "I was in this office myself at the time, and I didn't see or hear a word about the matter. The transfer seems to have been silent and secret."

"Under these circumstances, who then owns the property?" She knew the older man had studied the law at Oxford and had decades of experience with matters of property.

"The manor was given to the Blount family three generations ago by King Henry I as a reward for military service, according to our records. There's been no official transfer since."

"So Pinchbeck is the impostor." Ela's chest filled. This certainly complicated matters in a most interesting way. Drogo Blount would be pleased for sure. She thanked them for their time and asked Deschamps—without filling him in on this new development—to summon Pinchbeck to the castle.

Will returned, flushed and damp from the rain, with Drogo in tow and with tales of a freshly killed boar. "Finally, Lent is over and we can cook and eat our meat!"

"We'll have the cook prepare a great feast for dinner with it." Ela smiled. Will enjoyed the pleasures of the hunt as much as his father had. "But now come sup on the cook's meagre fare and hear the news I've found."

The cook had prepared a delicious meal rich with all the eggs and meat they'd pined for during Lent plus a salad of the new spring greens starting to grow in the castle garden.

After the meal Ela sat in her chair on the dais and summoned Jacobus Pinchbeck and Drogo Blount to attend her. She laid out the facts as the law clerks had described them and asked Pinchbeck for an explanation.

Pinchbeck immediately pulled a folded square of parchment from a leather scrip slung over his shoulder. "This contract details our agreement."

She gestured for him to bring it to her, and she studied it. "Whose seal is this?" The wax was broken.

"The elder Blount's," said Pinchbeck.

Ela summoned Drogo Blount. "Is this your father's seal?"

"It is." Curiosity burned in his eyes, and she could tell he'd like to read the contract.

Ela opened the parchment, which was crisp and clean and must have been locked away somewhere in the nineteen years since its creation. The writing was black in a clear hand and did promise Fernlees Manor and all is appurtenances to Jacobus Pinchbeck "for as long as he shall live." At that time it was to return to Blount's heir, who was detailed as his son Thomas. Drogo had previously explained that Thomas was his given name.

Now it was time for things to get complicated.

"Not only did my husband not preside over this property transfer—as far as I am aware—but it was not recorded legally."

"I've paid my taxes!" protested Pinchbeck. "I also gave him more money five years later to secure permanent ownership for my heirs. My son has the contract—still sealed!"

"That may be so, but your legal ownership of the property is in question."

"I brought him here for poaching! He's not even trying to get the property back."

"I would like my property back," interjected Drogo Blount, looking both stunned and intrigued.

"I'm afraid you unleashed the hounds with your poaching accusation, Master Pinchbeck. Now they must find justice."

"But the property has been mine, fair and square, for nineteen years! He came back hoping I'd be dead, and unfortunately for him I'm still kicking." Pinchbeck glared at Blount but was starting to look nervous. As well he might.

"I propose a wager of battle," said Drogo boldly. He appeared to have grown a full foot taller. "The winner takes the property, and the loser relinquishes his right to it."

Ela stiffened. Trial by combat was an old-fashioned way to solve issues where right and wrong were in the eye of the beholder. Neither of these men seemed well suited to a fight. Although Pinchbeck was a few years older, Blount had obvious physical deficiencies from his injuries. He stood a little crooked, with one shoulder higher than the other, and walked with a pronounced limp. Unfortunately, their respective frailties meant that the contest was feasible. She inhaled a slow breath and looked from one to the other. "Do you both agree to the test?"

"Absolutely," said Drogo with enthusiasm.

"I do not." Pinchbeck's face had grown pale.

"Why?" asked Ela. "You're not over sixty, or lame or blind." Those—and female sex—were the only legitimate reasons to bow out.

"I am lame. I have...spurs of bone in my right heel," spluttered Pinchbeck.

"You walked in here without a limp," observed Ela.

"I'm in pain with every step. This is preposterous! I found him poaching on my land!"

"Except that it doesn't legally appear to be your land. It seems to be his land." Ela thought him a coward. What world would they live in if any man could refuse to wield a sword to defend his own property?

On the other hand, she didn't believe that fighting skill should be the full measure of a man. Where did that leave clerics and scholars?

"Either man could choose to use a champion in his stead," suggested Deschamps. Ela felt a surge of irritation. She didn't like this relatively recent rule that allowed the rich to triumph over their adversaries with ease. Any man of honor would choose to fight for himself. She knew it would give the advantage to Pinchbeck because he had the funds to hire the strongest knight in Wiltshire, whereas Drogo would be forced to fight for himself.

Clearly Deschamps favored Pinchbeck in the conflict. And she realized with chagrin that she favored Drogo Blount. She was supposed to be an impartial dispenser of justice. She would have to pray for her own judgment.

"I accept the challenge if I can choose my own champion," said Pinchbeck finally. The gleam in his eye suggested that he'd warmed to the idea. As well he might.

"You shall have twelve days to choose your champion," said Ela. "The fight will take place in the castle courtyard at midday on Monday week."

Pinchbeck left looking satisfied with the arrangement. Ela's heart felt heavy as she wondered who he'd hire and how quickly Drogo Blount would be killed or gravely wounded.

"Have no fear, my lady," said Drogo, as soon as Pinchbeck had gone. "I have plenty of fight left in me."

"He has the coin to hire the best."

"I was once the best. Your husband knew it. I shall call on

my inner strength to defeat the usurper and reclaim my home."

"May God be with you." She sighed. "In the meantime you must eat and sleep well to conserve your strength. You may move freely within the outer walls of the castle but don't leave the castle mound."

Blount bowed deeply. "Your trust honors me, my lady."

"If you're willing to work in the armory honing the weapons, you shall earn money and the right to borrow armor for the battle."

He bowed deeply. "I'm grateful for the opportunity."

William had always put great importance in the constant inspection, sharpening and polishing of even the least-used weapon. *Strength lies in readiness* was one of his favorite mottoes. She was sure he'd approve this plan to employ his former savior and help him survive the contest.

"I never thought I'd see a female sheriff in my lifetime," said Drogo, as she rose from her chair and walked toward the fire to warm herself.

She wasn't officially sheriff yet, but she'd been acting in the role since her husband's sudden death and simply awaited the official warrant from the king. "I won't be the first. Nicola de la Haye has served as sheriff of Lincolnshire." His forwardness surprised and slightly irked her. In truth, her own husband was so disturbed by Nicola's boldness that he had himself taken and held the post of sheriff of Lincoln to rein her in.

The fire guttered as the hall doors swung open with force. "My lady," called the porter. "A messenger from the king."

This was it. Her commission as sheriff of Wiltshire. It was to be official, and she could command the role with confidence and all the wisdom and fairness that God chose to give her.

A mud-spattered messenger approached her with a sealed

scroll. She took it with thanks and broke the seal, her heart beating like a drum.

But as she read the words on the scroll she had to struggle to keep her face steady and rein in a heartfelt howl of injustice.

CHAPTER 2

Ela's hands started to tremble and she knew she couldn't command her features much longer. "Please take food and drink while I prepare a response for the king." Sibel, her lady's maid, hurried forward to take charge of the messenger. Ela turned and almost ran toward the solitude of her solar.

Up the stairs and with her door closed and bolted behind her, she finally let a low keening sound rush from her mouth.

How could he?

She opened the scroll again, still hardly able to believe what she'd read. "By the order of His Royal Majesty King Henry III"—more ceremonial blather—"the new sheriff of Wiltshire is Simon de Hal."

Tears blurred the words. There was no mention of her at all, as if she didn't exist and was never under consideration. It further elaborated that since the sheriff must inhabit the king's garrison, she and her family must repair forthwith to one of her many fine manors.

She wanted to growl with frustration, but sound might carry even through the stone walls of the castle and she did not intend to give anyone cause to call her weak or emotional. She'd summon her wits and prepare a response that the king couldn't ignore.

If only she could stop her hands shaking long enough to do it. She wished she could go down into the storeroom for a sheet of the finest vellum but didn't trust herself to be seen in company just yet.

She laid a sheet of workaday parchment on her desk and ran her fingers over it. She wished she could pour out her heart, bemoaning the death of her husband, which she still blamed on the king's closest friend and adviser. But that would gain her nothing.

Instead she picked up her quill, dipped it and wrote a forceful—she hoped—description of her own experience with public affairs at her husband's side, her commitment to peace and justice in the shire, and her successful resolution of the recent case involving two murders with multiple suspects.

As far as she knew, Simon de Hal was a minor noble with limited experience in public affairs and tastes that stretched the limits of his income. He might be tempted to usurp the position to enrich himself and possibly pervert the course of justice to win bribes. She did not spell this out but simply made her own aversion to such behavior clear as the black ink on the page.

She signed it with a flourish, folded it and dripped red wax onto it. It was a shame her new seal hadn't yet been delivered. It had more authority than the girlish one she'd used all her married life. Still, it was better than a thumbprint and she pressed it into the warm wax.

She studied herself in the mirror at her dressing table. Fortunately, her tears had not reddened her eyes with their salted misery.

One more obstacle. Another mountain to climb. She was

her father's daughter, the Countess of Salisbury, and this minor setback wasn't going to unseat her.

She hurried back down the stairs, forcing a smile onto her face as she entered the hall. She strode over to the messenger and placed the sealed document in his hands. "I thank you to deliver this to the king today."

His face fell. No doubt he'd hoped for a night of rest before starting the long journey back to Westminster or Windsor or wherever the king was. He might even have to hire a horse if his was too tired from the journey. But no matter, she didn't want King Henry to think this was anything less than a matter of burning importance to her.

Drogo Blount sat there in the hall, playing a game that induced one of the hounds to jump up and touch his hands, while the children gathered around and laughed. In her current mood she saw the dark shadow of everything. For all she knew he was a blackguard whom she'd welcomed into her home, and when he was found out she'd be the object of mockery and scorn for that as well as being passed over for sheriff.

She approached Deschamps and instructed him to keep Blount busy and also under watch. He might as well earn his keep and stay out of trouble. He might be a hero and an old battlefield companion of her husband's, but he had a ragged edge to him and she didn't want him honing it on her children and servants, or even her dogs.

THE KING'S written response three days later stung like a slap across the face.

He did have the decency to apologize for disappointing her in her ambitions. He even held out the hope that she might be sheriff on some future occasion, but Simon de Hal was to move into the castle on Thursday of the following week.

He wants money. A lot of money.

Most things could be bought in this day and age, even from the king, who always needed funds to finance whatever campaign of conquest made his heart beat faster that year.

How much, though? Should she offer a figure—say, a hundred marks—or wait for him to suggest one? It was clear she'd have to move out for now and plan her own campaign of reconquest.

The prospect of removing her entire household even just a few miles away seemed exhausting and onerous but it wasn't as if she'd never done it before. She could retreat to the manor at Gomeldon and enjoy the spring flowers in the deep woods that lay behind the house.

But she'd be back. She decided to leave the figure up to the king but made it clear she understood that there would be a payment. She enjoyed the subtle insult that came with implying that he could be bought. He wouldn't argue. Most men could be bought, and probably most women, too.

As she sealed the second letter she muttered a vow to herself that she would gain the role of sheriff. In the meantime she'd participate in the pursuit of justice in Salisbury in her role as countess.

Gomeldon was barely three miles away. Simon de Hal would see more of her than of his own wife.

THE FOLLOWING day was taken up with a reconnaissance trip to the manor at Gomeldon, where they made a long list of work needed to render it habitable. The house was more than seventy years old, built from sturdy wood beams arranged in a decorative pattern and filled with wattle and daub. It was picturesque, nestled in a small, wooded valley, and recalled an earlier and simpler time.

Unfortunately the house was damp from disuse, the paths were overgrown, the chimneys needed cleaning, the exterior needed whitewashing, the cellars had rats, and the thatched roof had fallen in at one end of the stables.

It would take a miracle to get it ready for occupation within a week, but she gave the orders and told everyone she expected to move in on Thursday. She fully anticipated her chests of blankets bumping up against de Hal's in the castle courtyard.

THE NEXT MORNING, Nicholas was crying over the move—and how he'd miss living in the great castle like his daddy—while Stephen tried to console him by pointing out that Gomeldon had a stream to sail boats in, when the hue and cry was raised again.

Deschamps marched into the hall and approached Ela. "I'm afraid there's disturbing news." He spoke quietly, then looked at the children.

Ela rose from the table and hurried to a spot away from the table. "What's happened?"

"Jacobus Pinchbeck is dead." He paused. "Under suspicious circumstances."

Ela stared. "How?"

"Crushed under the wheels of his own cart in the courtyard of Fernlees manor."

"Who found him?"

"His manservant. Apparently he dressed and prepared to leave for Exeter this morning, and his servant thought him an hour or more on the road. But at dawn he was found dead in his own courtyard with the horse still hitched to the cart and grazing nearby."

"Has the coroner been called?"

"Giles Haughton is on his way there."

"Where is Drogo Blount?" she whispered. He must be the first suspect since he stood to regain his family estate without fighting if his opponent was dead.

"In the armory, my lady, honing the blades. Trust me, he was the first person I looked for once the news broke."

She heaved a sigh of inward relief. "Let us ride there at once before the evidence gets disturbed."

Deschamps hesitated for a moment, as if wanting to say something. Did he think that—because Simon de Hal would soon be arriving to take over the role of sheriff—she should mind her own business?

"Until Thursday the peace of Salisbury is in my care," she said curtly.

"Yes, my lady. I'll bring four guards so we can send two to make an arrest if needed."

She thanked him and gave some instructions for the children's tutor. She also found Bill Talbot mending a piece of his own armor and quietly asked him to keep an eye on Drogo Blount. The death of his rival just days before their contest was a little too convenient for comfort.

FERNLEES, the disputed manor, was a short ride away by a well-worn cart road. The morning was brisk, spring flowers bursting from their buds as the earth warmed under a misty sun. The manor itself sat directly on the London road but set back down a long lane. Two stone posts marked the entrance to the manor, and Ela asked all but one guard to wait there so as not to mar the site.

Coroner Giles Haughton was already there, bent over the body, and he looked up as she climbed down from her horse and handed it to the soldier. "How long has he been dead?"

"Two or three hours only. His manservant says he left just before dawn."

"I wonder why he would leave in the dark, rather than waiting for morning." She moved closer. Her gut seized when she saw the way his chest was caved in under his blue tunic, the lower part of his rib cage crushed. "Why is there no mark of the cartwheel on his chest?"

"The mark is on his cloak." Haughton flipped the gray cloak back over him, and she could see the muddy track over the rumpled cloth.

"How is his manservant sure it was murder and not an accident? Was anyone out here with him?"

"Apparently not. The ostler prepared horse and cart for him. Pinchbeck mounted up and left. No one knows when or how he returned."

"He must have returned home to retrieve something he forgot. Then perhaps his horse startled in the darkness and upset the cart, then he was knocked down and run over."

Giles Haughton looked at her. His knowing eyes shone with humor. "Have you ever known anyone to be run over by their own cart?"

"Well, no, but that doesn't mean it couldn't happen. Where's the manservant?"

"Inside, apparently inconsolable."

Ela asked Deschamps to fetch him. A master's death was devastating to servants, especially older ones who could find themselves suddenly without a job or a home and with few prospects for the future.

"Do you think the cart wheel killed him or was he already dead when it ran him over?" She peered at Pinchbeck's face.

It looked strangely placid, like he lay there asleep on the damp ground.

"I'll need to strip him and examine him for other marks once we get him back to the mortuary. There are hoofprints in the lane and in the courtyard, but it hasn't rained properly for a couple of days so they might not be from this morning."

Deschamps emerged from the house with a much younger man than Ela had expected, maybe five-and-twenty. He wiped at his eyes as he approached but any tears had dried. "I c-can't believe he's gone," he stammered.

"How long have you worked here?" asked Ela softly.

"Eleven years. Since I was a lad. He hired me to scrub pots in the kitchen and I've w-worked my way up—" He sniffled and rubbed at his eyes.

"Do you think it could have been an accident?" asked Ela.

"Never! He traveled in the cart by himself all the time. The horse is an old faithful companion that never put a foot wrong. Someone must have shoved him under the wheels." The servant's lip quivered. His distress seemed genuine. "That's why I raised the hue and cry."

"You saw him leave this morning, but he came back. Do you have any idea why?"

The lad shook his head. "None. He was headed to Exeter to collect some goods he ordered that docked on a ship in Exmouth last week. He was going to stay there overnight, then come back tomorrow."

"Do you know who he was meeting? Or the name of the ship?"

"I don't. He didn't talk business with me. Kept it all to himself."

"Do you have any idea what the goods were?"

He shook his head again. "They're all kept in the warehouse."

"Where's that?"

"I don't know."

Odd. Why would his own manservant not know where he stored his goods?

"Did he hire a champion for the wager of battle?"

"For the what?"

Ela stared at him. Was he simple? Or had his employer deliberately kept him in the dark? Or both? If Pinchbeck traded in goods that were illicit or illegal in some way he might prefer an employee who lacked penetration. She decided to change direction. "Did you hear anyone else outside this morning?"

"No, but we all went back to bed after he left since there was no work that needed to be done urgently with him away."

Convenient. "Was anyone else here? The stable boy? Where is he?"

"He went to put the horse away, but he won't have heard anything. He's partly deaf. Doesn't hear anything unless you're bellowing in his ears."

Again, Pinchbeck might have chosen staff who would hear no evil. She looked at Giles Haughton. He'd been kneeling by the body this whole time, but now he rose to his feet and turned to the servant. "Did your master have any enemies that you know of?"

The young man's mouth twitched. "He wasn't well liked." He seemed reluctant to admit it, which was admirable in a loyal servant. "He drove a hard bargain in business and had gotten on the wrong side of some folks."

"Do you know any names?" Again the lad shook his head like a simpleton. "Thank you. We'll call you if we need you."

Once he was out of earshot, Haughton looked her in the eyes. "Our obvious suspect is Drogo Blount."

"But he's under guard at the castle. It couldn't be him."

She felt his suggestion as a slight to her management of both her household and the castle garrison.

"Perhaps he paid someone to do it."

"Someone from inside the castle?" Much as she hated the idea, it wasn't impossible. The soldiers were a motley crew from all over the country and even abroad. Their loyalty was bought with coin and could probably be sold just as easily.

"Or maybe he arranged it before he was caught poaching. He could even have orchestrated his own arrest so he'd be safely under guard when the murder happened."

Ela frowned. "But we have no evidence whatsoever that it was him."

"Who else stands to gain from Pinchbeck's murder? Does he have sons or daughters waiting to inherit his wealth? They might have grown impatient. Or perhaps it was a business deal gone sour. There are several avenues to investigate." Haughton looked down at the body. "The jurors can ask around locally, and we should send a messenger to notify his next of kin. The terms of his will should be interesting."

"I'd like to know what's in that warehouse of his. How can his own manservant not even know where it is? That in itself is odd to the point of being suspicious. Is there anything left to investigate here or should he be removed to the mortuary?"

"He can go. I want to look around more for signs of a struggle or of another horse or vehicle. Pinchbeck's horse had wide, round feet, so if another horse was here since it last rained I'll know."

Ela wanted to watch him work. She knew she had a lot to learn from him about the pursuit of justice. If she had to wait until she'd sufficiently cajoled and bribed the king, so be it, but she would be high sheriff of Wiltshire one day or she wasn't her father's daughter.

"What do you think of Blount?" She asked the question with no little trepidation.

Giles Haughton sighed. "I don't know what to think of him. You know him to be a hero from your own husband's lips, but he was caught poaching on another man's land."

"A knight's career only lasts as long as his fighting prowess."

"Yet apparently he was willing to fight for life and property on Monday." Haughton's voice revealed his doubts.

"You think he never intended to fight? That it was just a cover?"

Haughton shrugged. "His arrest had the effect of uncovering Pinchbeck's dubious claim to the property and his own more ancient and sturdy claim. If Drogo Blount is found innocent he almost couldn't have planned it better."

"I had the same thought. I intend to inquire into how he's spent every minute of his time since yesterday." She was burning to get back to the castle and quiz all involved. He'd made himself a little too at home in their midst.

"You should arrest him."

She didn't like the idea of chaining him to a wall in the damp, cold dungeon. He could sicken and even die down there. "He's already under guard."

Haughton lifted a brow. "You seem oddly resistant to holding suspects in your jail."

"Depriving a man of his liberty is a serious business. I was criticized last month for letting Morse remain free for too long. When I did finally relent and jail him he was deprived of his herd during calving time—then found innocent at the trial."

"True, but sometimes wisdom is the better part of valor. It's safer for you—and for everyone else—to keep an innocent man locked up than to let a guilty man roam free and sharpen his sword for another kill."

She sighed. "Drogo Blount saved my husband's life on the battlefield. Surely that means something?"

"It does indeed, my lady. I'm sure your conscience will be your guide."

Ela felt the tiny sting of censure. Was he asking her to mind her emotions and proceed with more calculation? Blount was already under arrest if not actually chained to the wall.

And something else was bothering her. "Why would Pinchbeck go on a journey only days before something as important as a wager of battle for his home?"

"Perhaps he was fetching his champion? Did he announce who it would be?"

"I never heard a word. He could bring who he likes, but he's still required to be there in person. Why would he make the long journey to Exeter when he had to be back for the contest?"

Haughton paced about the courtyard in front of the house. The ground was packed bare dirt, much trampled. "Here's a footprint I haven't seen before." He pointed at a long, narrow print, somewhat smeared. "That's a bigger foot than Pinchbeck's. His feet are small for a man his size."

"What about the stable boy?"

"Barefoot and also much too small to have made these. The manservant is slightly pigeon-toed and leaves a smear with his toes at every step."

"Well observed." She hadn't thought to watch him walk. "Perhaps the housekeeper has big feet?"

"I'm afraid I didn't ask to look under her skirt and see them." He shot her a wry look.

"A job for a woman," she retorted. "Let me ask her." It was unlikely that a woman would have great clodhoppers like this, but she approached the house and called through the open doorway. The housekeeper appeared. A harried-looking older woman with gray hairs poking from her head-wrap, she muttered as she approached. "A bad business. I never liked the master leaving in the dark. Always told him he'd come to some harm."

"Why did he leave before dawn?"

"Habit, he said. The early bird catches the worm or some such nonsense. Nothing good happens outside under cover of darkness. You're safer home in front of your own fire. That's what my mother always said."

"Wise words. Did he say when he'd be back?"

"He didn't, but he's rarely gone more than one night. He doesn't like to sleep abroad."

So he had intended to be present for the contest. "May I see your feet?"

The housekeeper stared at her for a moment like she'd lost her wits, then frowned and lifted her skirt. Her bare, bony, red-hued feet chastened Ela. They were as small as her own and certainly not responsible for the prints outside.

"I don't usually wear shoes around the house. It wears them out for no good reason."

"Quite." Ela couldn't imagine how cold the clay tile floors must be, but it wasn't her business. "Thank you for your help."

"What help?" The housekeeper screwed up her face. "Who are you?"

"I am Ela of Salisbury," she replied, wondering that she didn't know her. Of course these country people wouldn't know King Henry if he rode to their door without his colors. "And I commiserate with you on the loss of your master."

"Who's going to find the killer?" The housekeeper demanded. "Or will he come back to finish us all off?"

"Who goes there!" A man's voice rent the air. One of the soldiers. "There's someone in the bushes over there. Charge him!"

CHAPTER 3

The horses all scrambled into action. Ela rushed across the courtyard and peered down the lane after them.

"Come out now or I'll set the dogs on you!" called Haughton.

Since they didn't have dogs with them, Ela thought this an idle threat. Apparently their quarry did, too. One of the men dismounted and went beating into a small knot of woods. Another pushed his horse into the thicket and nosed around. After a few minutes they rode back.

"I swear I saw a flash of white."

"Could have been a deer."

"Or a face."

Ela sighed. That would have been too easy. She walked back to the house and called for the housekeeper. The woman came shuffling out again, looking none too pleased at the interruption. "Where is your master's warehouse that he uses to store the goods for his business?"

"I don't know. Why would I need to know?"

"Where are his written accounts, then?"

"In a chest."

"May I see it?" The woman was obtuse to the point of rudeness.

The housekeeper looked at her like she was mad, then turned and walked down the hallway. The red clay tiles were none too clean. Ela followed her, peering into the dark sitting room where a single high-backed chair faced the fire.

The housekeeper led her into a back room with a single window covered with an oiled hide where she suspected there had once been a glass window. The house seemed run-down and poorly maintained. Possibly because Pinchbeck saw no point in sinking money into a property he couldn't sell or pass on to his heirs.

She pointed at a dark wood chest. It was old, with crude carvings, and looked as though it had seen some travels in its time. She tried the lid, but it was locked. "Do you have the key?"

"The master always carried the key."

Ela hurried back outside and asked Haughton if they could check Pinchbeck's robes for the key. Under his cloak they found a small cloth scrip with a few pieces of silver. Haughton also discovered a well-hidden compartment deep inside his cloak, where they found a much-folded scrap of parchment with something written on it in a crabbed hand.

No key.

"What does this say?" She peered at the parchment. There were some numbers and two words.

"Vitus Morees?" He didn't sound sure.

"Is that Latin?" She read Latin as well as French but didn't know every word.

"Not that I'm aware. Perhaps it's a name?"

She scrutinized the letters. Vicus Moseef? The letters didn't gather together to make meaning no matter what she did. They checked the rest of his body for keys, which felt rather rude with him lying there on the damp ground in his own yard. They found five valuable coins secreted in the bottom of one of his shoes, but no key of any description.

The red-faced housekeeper stood in the doorway, watching with an expression somewhere between distaste and disgust.

"He doesn't seem to have the key on him. Who else would have one?" She was now burning to see the inside of the chest, as well as the mysterious warehouse and its contents.

"His son, Osbert. He lives in London. We've sent a messenger for him."

"What messenger?" Pinchbeck's household mystified her. The staff were by turns incompetent and surly and seemed barely adequate even to the maintenance of one cantankerous old man, yet they'd already dispatched someone to London?

"Jim, the lad from next door. He's a handy rider and knows the way. He's delivered messages for the master before."

"Do you expect him back tomorrow?"

"Only if he's grown wings."

Ela realized she was used to royal messengers who would risk their health—and their horse's—to deliver an urgent message. This boy might take days to get there and back on an ordinary nag.

She glanced at Haughton. At that moment a cart rolled into the yard pulled by a shaggy chestnut pony. Haughton nodded to the man riding on the back of the cart, and he and the driver jumped down, picked up Pinchbeck's body with little ceremony, and heaved it into the cart like a sack of turnips. Ela winced as his head thunked on the wood slats.

Back at the mortuary, Haughton had stripped the body before Ela arrived. She startled at the sight of the man's pale fleshless body and his exposed male member, and averted her eyes, then became embarrassed by her timidity and strode forward.

"Rigor mortis has set in."

"Indeed."

"And bruising has appeared around his neck. It appears that he was strangled."

Ela looked at Jacobus Pinchbeck's rather wrinkled, turkey-like neck and could see some faint purplish marks. "So someone strangled him by force, shoved him to the ground and then ran over him with his own cart."

"That's what it looks like."

"Why run over him at all if he's already dead?"

"To make it look like an accident and delay or avoid any investigation."

"Except that no one who knows him believed it was an accident."

"Perhaps the person who killed him didn't know him well."

"It might have been a business associate who knew he'd be leaving for Exeter early this morning?"

"Might it?" Haughton asked the question casually.

Ela frowned. "Well, I don't know. Who else would know he'd be leaving at that hour? And why would they make him turn back around when he'd already left home?"

"Perhaps they didn't. He could have been strangled elsewhere, half a mile down the road, say, then driven back here and dumped in his own yard."

"Why not leave him on the road where they killed him?"

Haughton shrugged again. "The London road has some traffic even before dawn. Perhaps the killer wanted time to get away before the death was discovered. We have more questions than answers, and all we can do is try to uncover the facts as we find them."

"Soldiers are waiting at the house for Pinchbeck's son, Osbert, to arrive from London. It will be a day or more, given the length of the journey. They have orders to fetch me so I can be there when he opens the chest and for him to take me to the warehouse."

"Your diligence is to be commended, my lady. Are you not tempted to leave the grunt work to Simon de Hal?"

"Let it not be said that a murderer escaped punishment on my watch. I'm simply doing de Hal's work for him in the meantime. He shall know all our findings."

"Perhaps you're also trying to keep your mind off the tiresome exigencies of your move." He lifted a salt-and-pepper brow.

"You're starting to know me too well."

"I can't help but wonder if a certain justiciar is behind your sudden displacement from the castle." He spoke in a very low voice.

"I've wondered the same." She'd told Haughton of her suspicion that Hubert de Burgh, the king's justiciar, had deliberately poisoned her husband. "He removed my husband from the path of his ambition, and now he plans to dispose of me. I won't be so easy to kill, however, not being of a trusting nature."

To publicly accuse the king's justiciar of murder would be to sign her own death warrant. Haughton had pledged to share the information carefully and quietly, in the hope that seeds of de Burgh's misdeeds might grow and the resulting thorns of gossip entangle and take down the arrogant justiciar one day.

That was all the revenge she could hope for.

That and finding justice for others.

Unfortunately, it was the lot of the sheriff to seek justice for the unlikable and undeserving as often as the wronged innocent. Still, odious as he was, Pinchbeck didn't deserve to be murdered in cold blood.

"They didn't take his money," she mused. "So it wasn't a common thief."

"No. There's a different motive here."

"Perhaps we'll find it in the contents of the warehouse."

"Or not. If his key was stolen from his person, then the thief and killer could have emptied the warehouse in the meantime."

Ela nodded. "Perhaps Pinchbeck's secrecy was his own undoing."

BACK IN THE CASTLE HALL, Ela's children watched and helped as their goods were packed into wooden chests, rolled into bales, stuffed into sacks, and otherwise carried out to the carts waiting in the yard. Ela was no stranger to moving—she'd followed her husband on many of his jaunts around the kingdom at the behest of his brother King John—but she hated to remove her father's old candlesticks and plates and tapestries from the place he and they had always called home.

She didn't dare leave them in case—for some unknowable reason—she might never return.

Perish the thought.

"Mother, can Drogo come hunting with Bill Talbot and me?" Will's voice had a hint of begging in it. He'd already grown attached to the battle-worn knight.

"No, my love, I'm sorry. He can't leave the castle."

"But he'd be right with us the whole time."

"Perhaps you didn't hear my answer the first time?" She hoped for an edge of steel in her voice. It didn't do for the children, even her firstborn son, to bicker with her in front of the soldiers and the staff.

Will pouted but stumped off. Drogo Blount sauntered over, his leathered face creased in a smile. "Your son's energy is to be envied."

"If only we could bottle the surplus," she sighed. "Perhaps I've done you a favor by keeping you in from the hunt."

"My days of galloping for sport are behind me," he agreed. "And I wish to speak with you about Fernlees Manor." His jovial expression vanished as he said the name.

Ela's stomach tightened. "What about it?"

"Since Pinchbeck has met an untimely death, the contract that existed between him and my father has now expired. The manor should return to me."

"Unfortunately, the ownership of the estate remains unclear since the change of ownership was never officially recorded. The fate of Fernlees was to be determined by wager of battle. Now that one combatant has died, the contest must be postponed until Pinchbeck's heir arrives and a clerk of the law is consulted."

She watched his face as he digested the news. His smile evaporated, and a hardness came over his features. "So I'm to be cheated of my chance to reclaim my ancestral home?"

Ela felt the sting of his rebuke. She stung back. "Some might think it very convenient that your opponent should die just as he was preparing to hire an expensive champion to defend his property from your claim. Don't think that you aren't a suspect in his death."

"Me?" His eyes widened and his lips parted. "I've been a prisoner in this castle the whole time."

"You might be accused of sending a proxy to do the deed. You have friends in this castle, and I've counted myself among them, but don't push your luck too far or it may run out."

Blount stared at her and she could almost see the stream of thoughts flashing behind his faded green eyes. "Pinchbeck's heir should be aware of how the property was entailed back to the Blount family."

"We shall find out when he arrives. Perhaps he'll put up no argument and you'll be back living there by next week." She thought it unlikely, given human nature and fact that Osbert Pinchbeck was apparently a London businessman, but it wasn't impossible.

"And if he claims it I can fight him for it?"

"As long as the claim remains in dispute, yes, but that may not be necessary. I'm sure you've learned not to rush into a fight that could be averted."

"Ah, if only I had." The smile had returned to his eyes, and one corner of his mouth hitched higher. "It would have saved me a lot of trouble."

His disarming honesty was endearing, and Ela felt herself soften toward him again. "Speaking of saving yourself trouble, do mind yourself until the murderer is discovered. I don't like tongues wagging."

Ela suddenly wondered why he was out here jawing with her and not cleaning weapons in the armory. As if he'd read her thoughts he excused himself and headed back in that direction.

"Do you have time to sort through the linens, my lady?" Sibel interrupted her thoughts.

"Good idea. And we must decide which gowns and cloaks will come with us to Gomeldon and which can be passed on to someone else. No sense packing and moving more than we need."

~

WILL and Bill Talbot crashed back into the hall shortly before dusk, ruddy and damp with rain and expounding over the abundance of deer in the woods. Ela listened half-heartedly, while wondering how best to pack her vellum and inks to minimize damage, until Bill Talbot asked if he could have a quiet word with her.

She looked around. Her children were teasing each other and pushing the last of the food around their plates. The soldiers laughed and supped their ale. "What about?"

"A private matter," he said softly.

Ela would trust Bill Talbot with her life, and she rose and beckoned for him to attend her in her solar. They climbed the stairs together and found Sibel busy folding up the bed curtains. Ela wondered whether he expected her to dismiss Sibel too, but he gestured for her to continue. "Sibel is family," he said. "And I trust her with a confidence." His voice was barely above a whisper.

Ela felt a tiny prick of fear. "What confidence?"

"It's Drogo Blount." Bill frowned. His pale blue eyes rarely showed concern, but now they positively radiated it. "There's something…odd about him. I've been thinking back and I think I met him before, some years ago, while marching to Lincoln with William. It was a long time ago, of course, and a man changes over time, but—"

He paused and Ela felt her breathing grow shallow. "You think he's an impostor?"

Bill Talbot drew in a deep breath. "I can't be sure, but I remember him being a taller man, more willowy, and with a wispy beard that clung around the edges of his jaw, much like your husband had at the time."

"He has quite a thick beard that covers his cheeks."

"His hair is salted with gray now, as is mine." He ran a hand through his own thick hair. "But I remember him as fairer, with eyes more brown than green."

"Have you spoken to anyone else about this?"

"No. I wanted to tell you first. It took me a while to realize I'd met him. Or at least I think I did. It was at least ten years ago."

"Who else would have known him back then? Or served with him and William?"

"That's the problem. Everyone I can think of is dead. William Marshall, for example, or Peter de Campo. I've been racking my brain to think of someone who was there, but there may only be common soldiers left among us who witnessed him."

Unease seeped through Ela. Had she let a perfect stranger into her castle all because he told fine stories about her husband and flattered her children? "So if the man handling weapons in our armory is not Drogo Blount—or Thomas Blount as he was supposedly christened—then who is he?"

Bill Talbot shrugged his big, broad shoulders. "I can't be sure it isn't him. Time can shrink and wizen a man like the sun shrivels a grape. I just wanted to warn you to be wary."

"Do you think he killed Pinchbeck?" The question now burned at the front of her mind.

"It's not impossible. The castle has a large number of people coming and going. Even under guard he could have exchanged words with someone he knew and commissioned a murder on the promise of payment once he regained the estate."

"But wasn't he confident of winning it in the contest?"

Bill Talbot laughed. "He's a middle-aged man. Broken and tired. He'd have beaten Pinchbeck himself handily, for sure. But a hired champion? He'd have been lucky to leave the fight with his life, let alone his dignity."

Talbot had a point. Still— "He's not much older than me. Not nearly as ancient as you," she quipped.

The air felt heavy and oppressive. She could almost see Sibel's ears burning as she folded the heavy curtains.

"Not everyone ages as well as me. I have young William to keep me on my toes."

"I'm surprised he hasn't worn you to a nub by now."

"His youth and vigor are a tonic to me."

"He needs your steady guidance more than ever now his father is gone." The familiar sadness bloomed in her chest. "I hope to get him safely married to Idonea de Camville by this summer. Before he gets any wild ideas."

"I'll be sure to promote the joys of marriage at every opportunity."

"But you've never been married."

"That makes it easier for me to wax rhapsodic about it," he replied with a wink.

Ela had to laugh. Bill Talbot had never shown any interest in marriage, even when she'd paraded kind and pretty young girls under his nose with that intent. As a knight with a solid position in her household he was a respectable catch in the eyes of many girls' parents, but he'd repulsed them all.

She'd long suspected he preferred the company of men. If he had relations with any in the style of the ancient Greeks, he was discreet about it.

"I appreciate your warning and shall perhaps perform a few small tests on Drogo Blount. So far he's been convincing, but perhaps I've been too quick to believe in him."

AT NIGHT the pale moonbeams streamed through the high window and painted a hard-edged blade of light across her bed. Her bed curtains had been packed and carted off to her new home. Without the familiar cocoon of warmth they created, she felt like a turtle without its shell. No doubt the feeling would only intensify when she left the familiar halls of her forefathers to repair to Gomeldon. It was one of many manors that she'd held for years but knew only as a means of producing income and not as a home for her family.

And this was the first time in her life she'd live in a new place without her husband as a source of comfort. Since her early marriage, she'd never traveled except to be by his side.

She laid her hand on the empty side of the mattress. She still kept to her side of the bed as if William might materialize beside her, place his hand on her hip and lay a soft, familiar kiss on her neck. At night she nursed her grief and even wallowed in it, so she could pack it safely away during the daytime, when duty called her to be solid and steady for her children and everyone else.

Was it blasphemy to hope that William's spirit watched over her and provided some unseen layer of protection? Ela said a decade of her rosary just in case the wish was sinful. The familiar prayers soothed her, but sleep remained elusive. Tomorrow would be their last full day before the move and was bound to be fraught and stressful.

Ela did her morning rounds at dawn, surveying the castle and its enclosed garden, pigstys and storerooms, in the company of a soldier. When she found Deschamps giving orders to soldiers at the west gate, she asked him to attend her in her solar.

Her room was now bare as a monk's cell, the tapestries rolled up and removed and even her desk and prie dieu taken to be loaded onto a cart.

Her back stiffened as she heard Deschamps feet on the stairs, and she wondered if she should confide her fears in him. No doubt he already thought her a fool for welcoming a mysterious poacher into her home, and he might soon be gossiping about her with Simon de Hal.

But the safety of the castle and its residents must come before her own ego.

Her private solar was unfamiliar territory to the old soldier, and she saw he couldn't resist a quick look around as he reached the top of the stairs.

"God be with you, Sir Gerald. I have a question for you. Have you heard any gossip among the men about Drogo Blount not being who he says he is?"

If he had heard such gossip it was his duty to warn her immediately, so in effect she was accusing him of...something.

He hesitated. "I can't say I've heard anything specific. Most of the soldiers garrisoned here are men too young to have campaigned with Blount, but—now that you raise the subject—I admit I do have my own concerns about him."

"Oh?" She didn't want to ask any leading questions.

"I wish I could recall the events more clearly in my mind, but I feel almost sure that Blount was with us during the campaign to Normandy under King John's command. I recall him being taller and more well-built and having a different inflection to his voice."

"And why did you not bring this up sooner?" Was he hoping to see her make a mistake and fail? She berated herself for the selfish train of her thoughts.

"I wasn't sure. I'm still not sure." He looked genuinely contrite. "He certainly knows his way around arms and armor, and I've heard him sharing details of his exploits with the men. He's very convincing, but still...something doesn't quite feel right about him."

"Do you believe we have grounds to imprison him?"

"For poaching? Yes, if the property is indeed Pinchbeck's and not his."

"Except that Pinchbeck is dead so it appears the property may be legally Blount's now."

"If he wasn't poaching we'd have no other grounds to hold him. He's committed no other crime. He's a good worker."

Ela sighed. She'd almost hoped that he would give her grounds to lock him up. It would make her life easier. But she could hardly imprison the man who saved her husband's life without just cause. "So he can remain here in the castle, under guard but not in the dungeon, after my departure tomorrow?"

"Yes, my lady. I'll fill Simon de Hal in on all the particulars of the situation."

A sudden trumpet blast made her jump. "Someone's arrived." Her ears pricked to hear the sound of hoofbeats on the stones over the drawbridge. "With a retinue."

"Perhaps de Hal is here a day early?"

CHAPTER 4

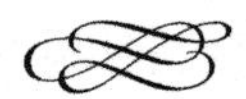

Ela hurried down from her solar, followed by Deschamps. Sibel exclaimed from the bottom of the stairs. "I was looking for you! Your mother has arrived."

"How wonderful." Ela's heart sank. She'd told her mother she was moving tomorrow. Why would she arrive for a visit now, when they'd packed everything and most of it had already been carried to Gomeldon? She hoped her mother wasn't going to encourage her to barricade them all in the castle and force Simon de Hal to besiege it.

Her mother was already in the great hall, handing her cloak to a maid. "Darling, you must be rushed off your feet."

"Exactly, so I'm afraid I don't have time to entertain you." Alianore's maid entered leading both of her mother's pampered black poodles on embroidered leads.

"I didn't come to be entertained! I came to help you pack and move."

Ela blinked. Her mother would use a servant—maybe even two—to lift her own cup to her mouth if she could get away with it. "We're nearly done. In fact all the spare bedding has been rolled and taken away so there's nowhere for you to sleep."

"Never mind that! I can share your bed for the night. I left dear Jean at home. He's no use in a crisis."

"What's the crisis?"

"The move, of course!" She leaned in. "It's disgraceful that the king is making you shift your whole household when your beloved husband is barely cold in his tomb." Ela was grateful for her low tones. She didn't need the garrison soldiers to hear her mother scolding their monarch. "And from the halls of your dear father."

"It is inconvenient, but I plan to return."

Her mother's eyes widened. "How?"

"Have you broken your fast?" She wasn't about to go into her plan to bribe the king in front of every soul in the hall. Deschamps or any one of the garrison soldiers might work—silently or otherwise—to keep a woman from taking the role of sheriff and wielding command over them.

"I ate a bite or two before I left. You know how travel upsets my stomach. How are my darlings!" The children, who had been politely holding back, ran to greet her.

Ela slipped away, anxious for a few words with Drogo Blount. It was time to put him to the test.

Ela found Blount in the armory, sat at the long scarred table honing the blade of a great broadsword. He looked up as she entered and sprang to his feet. "My lady." He bowed slightly. Everything about his words and actions suggested respect—even submission—but she sensed coiled tension in every muscle of his body. He must be burning to know if Pinchbeck's son had arrived.

She decided to keep the question alive as a distraction

while she probed him on other matters. "I do so enjoy talking to you about my husband. It almost feels as if he were here again when his deeds are on our lips."

"He was a great hero."

"What year did you first meet him, and where?"

"It was before his marriage to you, my lady. When he was but a lad of twenty-two or twenty-three. We met at a tournament near Ely, and he almost thrust me from my horse during the jousting."

This information meant nothing. Her husband loved tournaments and had competed at fifty or more. Blount would know that. Anyone would.

"Did he have a beard back then? I'm trying to picture it." She tried to act the nostalgic wife. Though in truth the thought of her husband's golden stubble did cause a surge of feeling in her heart.

"Yes, he had a fine growth of hair around the outside of his jaw, blonde like his hair, and a light mustache."

"And yourself?" Her question was an odd one, and he frowned.

"I scarcely remember. My hair wasn't a thick and grizzled as now, for sure." He smiled, but it didn't reach his eyes.

She smiled back and hers surely didn't either. "Where did you first fight together?"

"Was it in Burgundy during the fight for Dijon? Or in Egypt when we tried to take Acre?" He gazed skyward as if the answer might be written on the wood of the ceiling. "When a man has spent his life marching from one fight to the next, it's hard to remember things clearly."

Ela's chest tightened. It was not *at all* hard for a soldier to remember the order of events where he'd risked his life. She'd spent her life surrounded by fighting men, and most could recall even the tiniest details of the battles they'd survived. Blount wasn't old enough to be losing his wits due to age.

He'd failed that test.

What might only a close friend know about her husband? She searched her mind for something that couldn't be gleaned from gossip and secondhand stories. "I love to hear details about his life when he was away from me. Men can be so different among other men than they are when home with their wives." She tried to look cheerful and ready to be delighted. "Tell me something you know about him that might surprise me."

Blount made a show of looking puzzled. His gnarled, tanned hands fussed with the whetstone, tapping it gently on the table. "I do remember how he loved to sing. We all did when we'd drunk enough, but he had the deepest, richest voice of all the king's men."

"What was his favorite song?" Her heart leapt. Anyone could know that her husband sang. His big voice boomed out in a cathedral and could be heard above the crowd at a feast. But he did have a particular favorite song.

"Ah, what was it?" He pressed a knobby finger to his mustache, as if that might open the vaults of his memory. "A very old song from the land of his forefathers. Something about a lark and a fair maiden in a wood."

"The damsel in the dell." Ela knew it well and he was right. The breath rushed from her lungs. It was such a specific fact that it reassured her that Drogo really did know her husband and the knowledge warmed her heart.

"He would start to sing while the others among us were eating the candied fruits or honeyed pies or other sticky delicacies. I do remember that he never had a taste for sweet things."

"True." Ela felt a flush of pleasure rise over her. "He didn't like them at all, even fruit, unless it was spiced or pickled."

Her smile was genuine now, and his finally reached those jade eyes. "An odd quirk in anyone when such treats are prized by most."

He'd passed her test with flying colors. Perhaps a man could confuse the events of battles, especially if he'd taken a blow to the head or fallen from his horse one time too many. And a man's appearance could alter sharply over time, especially if his life experiences weighed heavily on his limbs and features.

Drogo Blount wasn't an imposter. He was the man who'd served with and saved her husband. Her heart filled with renewed affection for him.

"It gives me pleasure to recall those old times when we were young and brave enough to take on any foe without a moment's pause."

"Apparently you still are. You have no idea who Pinchbeck planned to hire as his champion," she teased him. "It could have been a six-foot-tall knight who's won every tournament in England in the past six months.

"Aye." He looked rueful. "As a fighting man I have to take my chances."

Unless you swing chance in your favor and avoid the contest by killing your opponent. The dark thought crept into Ela's consciousness. Drogo certainly had good motivation for wanting Pinchbeck dead. Knowing and even loving her husband didn't change his motivation to regain his family estate without shedding his own blood.

"WILL and I have decided we must ride to Lincoln to serenade his bride." Her mother was all smiles when Ela emerged from the armory with her fears only partly assuaged.

"I never said anything about serenading her." Will looked embarrassed.

"You shall charm her with your height and youthful beauty. Many a young girl has been swept off her feet by less."

"It's not like I haven't met Idonea before. She's been Papa's ward for years."

"You haven't seen her since either of you reached the age of—" Ela's mother paused. "Since you've both blossomed from childhood into full awareness of the other sex."

"Mother!" Ela didn't want her mother to launch into a detailed account of how to conduct a flirtation. Especially not in front of the younger children. It would scare the girls, for one thing.

"Will must know how to woo his bride!" Her mother exclaimed. "A young girl's heart can't be bought with money alone, though I won't deny that it helps."

"Will doesn't need to worry about winning her heart. That will come with time." She patted her son's arm. She didn't want him to get skittish when negotiations were coming along so well between the families. For all she knew his meeting with Idonea might upset all their careful plans. Far better that they should be legally wed first and work out their differences later. "Your father and I were strangers when we married. We grew to appreciate and love each other in the natural course of married life."

Ela's mother tutted. "I've been married four times, my dear. Trust me that the wedding night is more enjoyable when the couples have had a chance to anticipate it during the course of several meetings."

"Mother!"

Will smirked.

"It's not my fault I keep outliving my husbands," she sighed. "But with each marriage I bring more wisdom and experience more joy. As you will, too, when you're finally ready to remarry."

"I'll never remarry." Ela was firm on that point.

"Your grief is still fresh." Her mother's face showed sympathy. "It'll grow less keen in time. You're still young enough to bear more children."

"I have eight, Mama. Is that not enough?" Why should women's only role in life be the bearing of children? Could her hard-won wisdom not be useful in areas outside of marriage and family?

"Your new husband might want an heir."

"All the more reason not to marry a new husband. What if he wanted his own son to take Will's place as Earl of Salisbury?"

Her mother didn't have a good answer for that.

"See? I have good reason to remain a widow and to nurture my children to fill the roles history has prepared them for."

"What of Isabella's marriage to William de Vesci?" Her mother was adept at changing the subject when it didn't suit her.

"Negotiations are underway, and I hope for a summer wedding."

"What a shame that it won't be at this dear castle."

"The boy's grandfather was King William of Scotland. I'm sure his family can produce a suitable castle for the festivities." She lifted a brow.

"Ugh, Scotland is so far away and so dreary and treeless. Do let's hope we don't all have to trek up into the highlands for dear Isabella's wedding." Her mother feigned a shiver. Her eyes were smiling though. She must have forgotten about her future grandson-in-law's royal roots, and now the memory was sure to warm her during any arduous journey to their nuptials.

"Anyway, back to my plans to visit Lincoln. We can descend on Nicola de la Haye and charm her into forgetting how your husband seized control of Lincoln and usurped the role of sheriff there for years despite barely visiting the place."

"Thanks for reminding me." Nicola herself had not mentioned the matter in the letter Ela had lately received and which had warmly encouraged relations between her granddaughter and Will. "I think she might see the marriage as her final victory over us, and I'm not looking to disabuse her of that notion."

"She's older than I am," said her mother with toss of her head that caused her veil to flutter. "I'm sure she'd prefer to retire to the country and hand the keys of the castle to someone younger and more vigorous."

"Unlikely, but you never know. I'm not making any journey farther than London until we can see how things sit with Simon de Hal. I want to make him aware that I have every intention of presiding as sheriff myself in the not too distant future and that I will be watching every move he makes."

"So he'd better not start collecting bribes and seizing property to line his own coffers."

"Exactly."

ELA'S MOTHER spent the rest of the day convincing her to pack and remove almost everything that wasn't literally nailed to the walls or floors. "You don't want to come back one day and find it gone!"

At dinner that night Drogo Blount joined the family, as was his habit since arriving, so he could regale the children with exploits from their father's past. The children hung on his every word and begged him to sing one marching song after another, which he did with impressive gusto.

After dinner, her mother tugged her sleeve and drew her to a quiet corner. "Who is that frightful fellow? He reminds me of a player King John had at his elbow all one summer. Always talking and singing and regaling everyone with nonsense."

"He saved William's life in battle some years ago. While they were in the Holy Land."

"I don't believe a word of it. Did you invite him to visit?"

Ela hesitated. Was she really about to tell her mother that she'd invited a poacher to her table? She had told her own children to always tell the truth even if it was uncomfortable. "Actually, it's a complicated situation..." She explained it as briefly as possible.

Her mother stared, blinking. "And now the man who caught him poaching is *dead*?"

"We suspect it's completely unrelated and the result of some business dealings Pinchbeck was involved in."

"Oh, my innocent daughter." Her mother peered down the length of her aristocratic nose. "You always were too trusting for your own good."

"I try to take people as I find them until I see reason to do otherwise."

"So now you have a murderous poacher playing the lute to your children at your own fireside."

Ela glanced past her mother to where Drogo Blount was doing just that. "Tomorrow he'll be Simon de Hal's problem."

"And a very good thing if you ask me. Women are too softhearted to manage matters of justice."

Ela was wondering if she could muster enough energy to argue with her mother when the hall doors swung open and the porter shuffled over, face red and breath quickened with urgency. "It's him, my lady. The dead man's son."

CHAPTER 5

Ela peered past him to the door. She could hear hooves clattering and raised voices in the courtyard outside. "Osbert Pinchbeck? He's here, right now?"

"The soldiers intercepted him as he rode up to Fernlees, and they brought him here."

"Show him in. And please summon Giles Haughton. He must interview him."

"Heaven help us." Ela's mother crossed herself. "You're moving your entire household in the morning, and now you have another houseguest?"

"I need him here. I don't want him going through his father's effects or traveling to his warehouse until I've seen them, too."

"Why do you care?" hissed her mother. "As you said, he'll be Simon de Hal's problem in the morning."

"I care about justice, Mama," Ela protested. "I care that the dead man's killer be caught. I care that the right man shall inherit Fernlees manor and pass it along to his heirs. I care that Salisbury isn't beset with squabbles and lawsuits and bad feeling that could set the stage for another murder down the road."

"You are your father's daughter."

"If I had a silver penny for each time you said that—"

"You could buy this castle back from the king with a nice fat bribe," whispered her mother drily.

Ela wanted to laugh, but now was not the time. "You know me too well. It's just a matter of gathering the right resources. So, as you see, I must stay on top of local matters."

"Well, it's all far too agitating for me, so I'm going to bed." She kissed Ela on the cheek.

"Perhaps I'll see you up there before dawn." Ela heaved a sigh of relief as her mother kissed her children, gathered her poodles and swept from the hall. The last thing she needed was Alianore sitting in judgment when she interviewed the new arrival.

Osbert Pinchbeck was a tall man like his father. Lanky, windblown and visibly annoyed, his cloak heavy with rain, he looked around the hall in confusion. Ela approached him. "God go with you, Master Pinchbeck. I am Ela of Salisbury."

"What is the meaning of this? I arrive at my father's house after long hours of fast travel and am told I cannot stay there but must report immediately to the castle."

"You are aware that your father was murdered?"

"Run over by cartwheels, the neighbor said."

"The body showed signs of strangulation so we suspect he was killed." She watched his face.

He frowned but didn't show much sign of surprise. "Have you made an arrest?"

"We have not. We're investigating the circumstances of his death and the motives of any possible suspects. Are you aware that you were not to inherit Fernlees Manor on his death?"

"What?" Now his surprise looked genuine. "Why wouldn't I? I'm his sole heir. My older brother, Wilfred, died of the pox when we were boys."

Sibel took Osbert's wet cloak and he looked like he wanted to protest, but he didn't. His eyes followed her as she took it and hung it on a hook near the fire. Ela glanced at his boots and observed with interest that that his feet were long and narrow.

"Your father acquired the property under rather unusual circumstances—which do not seem to have been legal or official—but even so they gave him ownership only for the term of his own life."

"Utterly untrue. I have the contract myself." He patted his scrip. "Everything signed, sealed and legal as the assizes. But that doesn't make me a suspect. I have a profitable business in London. I'd hardly kill my father for a crumbling old manor out in the sticks."

"No one is accusing you of murdering him."

"Then why do I feel like I'm under arrest?" His beady eyes darted around the hall.

"Do you have the key to your father's chest, where he kept his accounts?"

"Yes. I brought it with me, for obvious reasons."

"And the keys to his warehouse?"

He hesitated and she could almost see lies hatching in his brain. "What warehouse?"

Ela tilted her head. "Come now, Master Pinchbeck. We both know your father traded in goods. He stored those goods in a warehouse, and we have good reason to believe there's a connection between his business and his death."

"How so?"

"Whoever killed him knew that he would leave the house before dawn and waylaid him on the road. According to his staff he was on his way to pick up a shipment of goods and take them to his warehouse."

"Anyone in the vicinity could have watched his house from a hedgerow, waiting for him to leave." Although he must be younger than her, his pale skin had the texture of parchment and creased when he frowned.

"Did he have enemies that you know of?"

"I know nothing about any enemies. As I said, I live in London."

"Did your father visit you in London?"

Another pause. "From time to time. He handled the purchasing of goods. I handled the selling."

"What do you trade in?"

"Flutes." He blinked rapidly.

"The musical instrument?"

"The very same." He pulled one from his worn leather scrip. It was a carved wooden thing, rather insubstantial. The kind of instrument a boy might make himself from a reed to while away a summer afternoon.

"You have an entire business selling flutes?"

"Music feeds the soul, my lady," he said with a simpering fake smile that sent a nasty shiver down her spine. His father had said he traded in decorative objects. Someone was lying —probably both of them.

"May I have the key to your father's chest? We'll travel there to open it at daylight."

He stared at her. "No. Why should I give it to you?"

Ela wanted to protest that she was high sheriff of Wiltshire and that he was currently under her jurisdiction. But that was painfully untrue. "As castellan of Salisbury Castle I command you to hand me the keys and the documents immediately or spend the night in the dungeon." Instead of raising her voice, she lowered it. The tactic worked with her children and the servants.

"You'd put me in the dungeon for what crime?"

"Obstructing the course of justice," she said coldly. She was pretty sure Osbert Pinchbeck had obstructed the course of justice in one way or other and intended to do so again. "The contract and the keys, if you please." She held out her hand. It looked small and thin hovering in the air, but she held it steady.

Osbert's face grew hard and his eyes smaller as they swept around the room. Then he reached into his scrip and pulled out a folded piece of parchment with an unbroken, crudely stamped seal, and a big, rather rusted, iron key. She took them. Since the document was still sealed she'd need to set up an occasion with witnesses to break the seal so it would have to wait. "I shall safeguard them until morning. You'll sleep here in the hall under the protection of my guards. Tomorrow we'll ride to Fernlees."

At least now she knew where he stood. He claimed the manor. Drogo Blount claimed the manor. And it was essential that they not meet and discuss the matter—or fight it out —under her roof.

She pointed Pinchbeck to a table of soldiers and told him to take a seat and food would be brought to him. She sent young Ellie to the kitchen to ask a scullery maid to prepare food and drink for him. Then she asked a soldier to fetch Gerald Deschamps. Deschamps must have been hovering nearby for he appeared like a sprite.

"Blount and Pinchbeck must not meet or talk." She kept her voice low.

"Blount can sleep in the armory tonight."

"But there's no fire in there."

"He's a soldier and used to privation. He can warm himself with ale."

Ela sighed. "I don't have a better plan for tonight. And

keep Osbert Pinchbeck under close observation as well. There's something...slippery about him."

"Like father, like son, eh?"

"I suspect so."

Ela spent some quiet time with her children and her dogs, while keeping half an eye on Pinchbeck. He was not a garrulous sort and looked uncomfortable in the boisterous company of the soldiers.

Hopefully, he wouldn't be found dead in the morning. She never knew what would happen lately. Even her own stronghold felt unsettled and unsafe right now, and tomorrow she must turn over the keys to a man she'd never even met.

After a restless night listening to her mother's elegant little snorts, Ela rose in the dark and dressed herself. She didn't want to call Sibel and wake her mother. She hurried downstairs—observed Pinchbeck sleeping on a cot near the fire—and quickly made her rounds. By the time her children straggled to the table to break their fast she was fully awake and had a smile plastered on her face. "Are you all ready for the move?"

"We're not children, Mother," muttered Richard, over a mouthful of porridge.

"Oh, really? Then what are you?"

"Don't worry, Mama." Petronella bit into a bread roll. "We're all a bit anxious but it'll go fine."

"I know. I'm supposed to be telling you that." Her children really were more mature than she gave them credit for. "I have to ride out this morning to see to some business, but you'll all travel by cart with Sibel and Bill Talbot. I'll meet you at Gomeldon later."

"Is someone dead, Mama?" asked Stephen.

"Why would you ask that?"

"Because when you won't tell us where you're going someone is usually dead."

"What nonsense." She sighed. "But it is an investigation into a murder. I must make sure nothing falls between the cracks before the new sheriff takes over. He's bound to have his hands full just learning about the household so it might be some time before he follows up on this…death."

"It sounds very exciting, Mama." Stephen's big dark eyes peered at her. "If I wasn't going to be a bishop I might want to be the sheriff."

She laughed. "You could be both, you know. Some men join the church later in life."

"After they've had a wife and children?" He looked scandalized.

"Sometimes. Their wife would have to die before they join the church, though."

"Oh, I wouldn't like that. I don't want to kill my wife. I think I'll just be a bishop."

The older children fell about laughing, and Stephen looked both confused and pleased that he'd produced such hilarity.

Ela saw Pinchbeck stirring and excused herself from the table.

"Good morrow, Master Pinchbeck. I hope you slept well enough despite the commotion of a castle hall."

He shot her a dark look. "I'm ready to read my contract, then ride to Fernlees."

"The contract will have to wait until legal witnesses are in place. But we shall ride to Fernlees after you've broken your fast."

"I'm not hungry. Where's my horse?"

"He'll be brought out front saddled and ready." She'd

arranged for Haughton to ride with them, and a group of four soldiers in case they needed to split up.

The weather was dry and fine, with spring wildflowers blooming in every patch of grass. Ela half listened to Pinchbeck discuss funeral plans with Giles Haughton while enjoying the sweet song of the nesting birds.

Fernlees Manor looked picturesque in the sunlight despite areas of visibly rotting thatch and flaking wattle. The old house needed a caring owner to lavish it with love and money. Blount had the former but none of the latter. Pinchbeck was the reverse. She doubted that poor Fernlees would be restored to its former glory in the near future.

The housekeeper hurried out to greet them and the stable boy offered to take their horses, though Ela said the soldiers would hold them.

"He can take my horse. I'm staying," retorted Pinchbeck.

"I'm afraid not. We need legal review of the documents you brought with you and of any we find today. The ownership of the manor is in dispute—consider it in probate—but you can stay at the castle in the meantime. The new sheriff arrives today."

Ela wondered if de Hal's horses were already clattering through the arch. Unlikely, since he was coming a fair distance and probably wouldn't arrive until the afternoon.

Osbert Pinchbeck harrumphed and grumbled but led them into the house. He clearly knew the place, passing easily down the hall and into the rear sitting room, where his father's carved oak chest, a full yard long and blackened with age, sat.

Ela pulled the key from inside her cloak. For a second she wondered if she should hand it to him. The chest was surely his father's possession, and now his, even if the house wasn't. But something made her keep it in her hand. She slid the key into the lock and turned it. The mechanism was smooth, and she heard the bolt slide. She tried to open the lid but it was surprisingly heavy, or tight, and wouldn't budge.

Osbert Pinchbeck stepped forward and, using the heel of his hand, pried the lid upward. Ela's heart sank at the sight of the contents. The entire chest was filled with stacks of parchment. Some folded, some with their ink-scratched messages staring skyward. There must be a hundred—nay, three hundred—documents in the chest, and she could see the entire day slipping away into its gloomy depths.

"Mostly business contracts and receipts. Bills of sale and the like. Nothing of interest," said Pinchbeck quickly. He snatched one off the top of the pile. "This one is for irons. Three dozen of them."

"Irons?" Ela pictured the cuffs and chains in the castle dungeon. "I thought you sold flutes."

"For ironing clothes. The kind you put in the fire then—"

"I see. You sell flutes and irons. What else?"

He pulled up more accounts listing numbers of frivolous items like ribbons, polished metal mirrors, brass candlesticks. Cheap trinkets produced overseas and shipped to England for sale. The kind of things a traveling peddlar might hawk as he passed through town.

Ela grew exasperated as they sifted through the endless documents. "There must be something in this box that reveals the location of his warehouse."

"Where is my contract concerning the ownership of Fernlees?"

"Under lock and key at the castle. The matter of your father's murder is more pressing than the matter of who owns the manor. I don't want the one to interfere with the other."

"I fail to see how the two matters are related." Pinchbeck was growing visibly agitated. "My father is dead. Therefore, as his only son, I must take possession of his estate."

"Be careful," said Ela coolly. "Or you'll find yourself a murder suspect."

"I was a hundred miles away!"

She held his gaze. "You could have hired a killer if you were so anxious to inherit."

"It wouldn't be the first time I've seen such a motive," interjected Giles Haughton, crossing his arms over his chest. "There's a reason greed is one of the seven deadly sins."

Pinchbeck's mouth opened and closed. "This is outrageous. My dear father is dead and you're rifling through his records to—to—"

"Find out who killed him," said Ela. "Don't you want to know?" His lack of emotion was extraordinary. He didn't seem like a bereaved son at all.

"Of course, but—" He blew out an angry snort, then bent over the chest and stuck his hands in among its contents. "There must be something in here with the location of the warehouse. I know he rented it, and he was a stickler for keeping records." Ela glanced at Haughton, and—as usual—his eyes shone with amusement.

After some time spent pulling rumpled sheets of parchment and scuffed leather-bound account books out of the chest and piling them haphazardly on the floor, Osbert Pinchbeck paused, holding an unfolded sheet in his hands. "It's a lease. For a property off the London road near Crackmore."

"Crackmore? That's in the middle of nowhere." Surely a warehouse would at least be in a town. Ela took the sheet from him. The lease was for ten years and included a small plot of land with a timber frame barn.

"It is on the way from Exeter to London and that seems to have been his route, if you will," said Haughton. "It's probably an old barn that he uses to store goods. Quite sensible, if you ask me. No one would think to break into an old cow barn."

It was far enough away that it would take most of a day to ride there and back, and Ela couldn't spare the time. Not when she had to move her entire household and welcome—if that was the right word—the new sheriff. And it might turn out to be a wild-goose chase. It would have to wait.

She flipped through the account books, which seemed quite fastidious and consistent in their method of recording purchases and sales, though there was no easy way to tell which goods each figure referred to. There were no goods listed. Jacobus Pinchbeck had used some kind of numbered code to identify the items. His son unsurprisingly claimed to have no knowledge of its meaning.

The housekeeper and scullery maid hovered anxiously nearby, as if awaiting their fate. "We'll return to the castle and review your document," she said to Pinchbeck. "This chest must remain here locked and unmoved, and I shall give the key to the new sheriff for safekeeping."

She hoped de Hal wouldn't lose it or just give it back to Pinchbeck before they'd even finished the investigation. But that was out of her hands. The chest and its contents would belong to Pinchbeck's heirs whether the house did or not.

She locked up the chest and tucked the key back into her cloak, and they headed outside. She was about to remount her horse with assistance from one of the soldiers when they heard another horse trotting down the lane. The hoofbeats slowed, and she heard the rider turn into the courtyard. Hesitating, with both feet still on the ground, she watched a man ride up on a sweaty bay horse.

The newcomer wore a fine-looking cloak and boots of new leather. He looked at the soldiers and at Ela and Haughton and Pinchbeck as if surprised to come upon such a party of strangers in the courtyard of his own home. He had clear blue eyes and a flaxen beard that accentuated the hard-angled features of a man about her own age. A sheathed sword peeked from beneath the fur-trimmed hem of his cloak. Everything about him radiated confidence that Ela found unnerving under the circumstances. He doffed his hat and nodded to her. "Good morrow, my lady, gentlemen. Thomas Blount at your service."

CHAPTER 6

"Thomas Blount?" Ela repeated the name aloud. Was this a dream? It had the surreal quality of one. On the other hand, her life had lately been tipped and shaken upside down like a plundered purse so why not have another Thomas Blount appear out of the morning mist?

"The very same. This is my childhood home. My father sold his interest in it to Jacobus Pinchbeck for his lifetime, and since I hear he's now deceased I've come to claim my inheritance."

Giles Haughton looked at Ela as if he was trying to suppress a guffaw of laughter.

"Jacobus Pinchbeck was my father, and I have a contract stating that he bought the freehold. Which means the house must remain in the Pinchbeck family after his death." Osbert Pinchbeck visibly puffed himself up. Though he was tall, the new Thomas Blount was taller. Pinchbeck looked confused. As well he might, since there were now two Thomas Blounts, one nicknamed Drogo, trying to wrest the house from his grasp.

"There is a man at Salisbury Castle who claims to be Thomas Blount." Ela could see no reason to prevaricate.

"An impostor." He didn't even look surprised. "No doubt he emerged when he heard the house's owner died."

"Actually he appeared before Pinchbeck was killed."

"He just turned up at the castle and announced himself?"

"No, he was arrested for poaching on the grounds." Doubts about Drogo snuck up on her again.

But was this Thomas Blount the man who knew her husband well and saved his life?

"You knew my husband?" Ela peered at him. His face didn't look familiar, either from her own hall or from the court of King John, where she'd spent much time as a young bride.

"You know my name, my lady, but I don't have the pleasure of knowing yours."

Ela felt affronted, then scolded herself for the sin of pride.

"This lady is Ela of Salisbury," intoned Haughton gruffly.

"I thought as much but didn't want to presume." He bowed to her. "It's an honor to finally meet you."

He hadn't answered her question. This Thomas Blount struck an uneasy note with her. His manners were certainly more elegant than the rougher Drogo, but had a foppish, almost flirtatious quality that suggested a simpering courtier rather than a fighting man hardened by many battles.

"You were a friend of William Longespée?" Giles Haughton repeated the question for her. He was turning out to truly be a friend of hers.

"Oh, yes." She waited for him to elaborate, but he didn't.

Ela frowned. "Then how have I not met you?"

"No doubt we have, and you've just forgotten me."

"And you me, apparently." She stared at him. "There are now three men claiming ownership of Fernlees Manor before its owner's body is even interred. And frankly I view you all as suspects in his murder."

Pinchbeck and Blount both emitted blustering sounds of protest while Ela frantically contemplated locking them all up, at least until she could finish moving her household and turn the case over to her unfortunate successor.

"How would I kill him when I was in London?" yelled Pinchbeck.

"Or I, when I was in the same place?" said the new Thomas Blount more coolly.

"If you were in London, how did you hear of his death? You're not his son so messengers would hardly come looking for you."

"News of a murder travels fast."

"Not that fast." One more reason to mistrust this slick new pretender to the throne of Fernlees. "Where is the document you spoke of?"

He turned and opened his saddle bag, then pulled out a worn and folded piece of parchment. Ela walked forward and extended her arm to take it.

"Why should I give it to you?"

"Because at this moment I am the acting sheriff of Wiltshire and I'll have you arrested if you don't."

He dangled it just above the reach of her fingers. Tossing this Thomas Blount down in the dungeon was starting to appeal to her. Then he lowered the document enough for her to take it.

She turned it over. "The seal is broken."

"How would I know what it said if I hadn't broken the seal?" He spoke slowly, as if she might be slow to comprehend him.

"The seal is our only assurance that the document hasn't been tampered with." Ela resisted the urge to speak just as slowly to him. "However, tampering is often easy to spot and as I work with quill and ink myself I have a practiced eye for it." She peered right in his eyes—bright blue as a summer sky—as she said it. He blinked once.

She opened the document and scanned it. The hand was crabbed and oddly slanted, as if written by someone elderly or infirm. Unlike most legal documents it was in French, not Latin. "I, Radulf Blount, being of sound mind and body, do freely give the Manor of Fernlees and all its appurtenances to Jacobus Pincheck in payment of my debts. He shall hold the manor for the full term of his life, however long that shall be. On his death the property shall revert to my family, either to myself if still alive, or to my heirs and assigns, notably my son Thomas Blount. Witnessed this day of—"

It left the property to Thomas Blount...but which man was the real Thomas Blount?

Ela looked at Pinchbeck. "This is how your father described the transaction before he was killed. He knew he only held the property for his own lifetime."

She was burning to know what the sealed document Pinchbeck had given her actually said. She could have secretly peeled off the seal, read it, then stuck it back by gently heating the wax seal—she had plenty of experience unsealing her own letters after remembering something she wanted to add—but subterfuge didn't sit well with her, even if it was for a good cause.

"Unlike this one, the document my father gave me was sealed, so I haven't read it." Pinchbeck fidgeted and fumed, shifting from foot to foot. "But he assured me it permanently secures the property for our family."

"Did your father tell you that you'd inherit?" she asked Pinchbeck.

"Always." He hissed the word.

"He had no other children?"

"Two daughters, long married off."

Ela lifted a brow. "They're to inherit nothing?"

"I'm the only male heir."

Each person in this intrigue was more odious than the last. Of the three, Drogo Blount was the one she found least offensive—in fact, she rather liked him—but possibly he was the most suspicious of all. She folded the letter and tucked it into the lining of her cloak. "I'll give this to the sheriff when he arrives today. It's evidence in a murder investigation."

Thomas Blount—or whoever he was—protested loudly. His horse grew agitated and started to stamp and paw at the ground, causing Ela to take a few steps back. She looked at the guards, who stood nearby, one still holding her horse's reins. "Bring Master Blount back to the castle with us."

THEY RODE BACK to the castle at a trot, with both Pinchbeck and the new Thomas Blount flanked by guards.

It galled Ela that she might never get to see Jacobus Pinchbeck's warehouse. She was curious to see if his goods actually were the fripperies each Pinchbeck spoke of or something more sinister.

Carts headed for Gomeldon rolled past them as they returned to the castle, carrying the last of the beds and bedding and other necessities that couldn't be moved earlier.

Ela sent Haughton to fetch two jurors to attend while they opened Pinchbeck's sealed letter. Might as well get that over with before de Hal arrived or she might never know what was in it and the person with the most generous bribe for the new sheriff would end up owning Fernlees. At least if she saw the contents she could form her own opinion.

A deep sadness clung to her as she walked through the great arch into the castle. There were no guarantees in life. Once she left today, she might never live there again. She'd repeatedly reassured herself that she could buy her rights back from the king, but de Burgh might somehow prevent it. She might never even be allowed inside the castle walls again if Simon de Hal proved a nervous or vindictive sort.

Her gloomy mood didn't seem to affect anyone else, though. The soldiers—everywhere, as always—seemed more ebullient than usual, perhaps anxious about the new sheriff or anticipating lavish feasts as he settled into his new quarters.

The servants bustled about like hens chasing their chicks, and the cook—who unfortunately for Ela and her family was staying at the castle—had the kitchen humming with preparations for a grand welcome dinner for de Hal and his party.

And now she had to tell Deschamps there were two Thomas Blounts. Where was he? He'd probably already forgotten she existed in his anxiety to get everything ready for his new master.

Ela asked a servant to find Deschamps and went to retrieve the letter from her solar. The sight of the empty room made her gasp and curse her own foolishness. All her furniture, including her desk and the small box where she locked her private effects, was packed and now rolling down the road toward Gomeldon. She'd have to send someone after it to fetch it and bring it back. Her room looked grim without its furniture or hangings. Somehow it seemed darker and smaller.

She turned and hurried back down the stairs with instructions to bring back the entire box. At least she had the key with her. She kept it on a cord around her neck.

Deschamps appeared and Ela did her best to explain the appearance of the new Thomas Blount. Deschamps looked like he wanted to laugh. "Two of them? One alone was enough trouble." He glanced toward the armory. "I'm having to keep my wits about me to closet him in there. Keeps wanting to come out and rub elbows with the soldiers."

"Both Thomas Blounts—and Osbert Pinchbeck—are suspects in Jacobus Pinchbeck's murder and must be kept under close watch. None of them should leave the castle."

"Best way to ensure that is to put them all down in the dungeon and chain them to the wall." Deschamps's expression showed he wasn't kidding.

"Only one of them can be guilty." And she still wasn't even sure it was one of them. "Do you really want to imprison two innocent men? The next assizes will be many weeks hence. The Lord bids us to do unto others as we'd have them do unto us. Surely you can keep them occupied—"

"And separated? It's not so easy, my lady. At least if they're all in the dungeon, no one will wind up dead."

Ela sighed. "But how will we know which Thomas Blount is the real one? Surely letting them mingle with the soldiers and the new sheriff will allow them to reveal some telling trait or story that identifies each as the true Thomas Blount or the impostor?"

Deschamps looked annoyed. "The thumbscrews might help."

Ela bristled. "You know my husband didn't approve of torture. It brings a false answer quicker than a true one." Deschamps looked like he was about to make a pro-torture counterargument, so she quickly changed the subject. "I've called for jurors to witness the reading of Pinchbeck's sealed document. We'll see where that leads us. Is there news of de Hal's arrival?"

"He's expected before Vespers, my lady, weather permitting."

She nodded. She hoped to greet him and make her way to Gomeldon before dark, but she'd wait here until midnight if she had to. If she turned the keys of the castle over to him herself, he could less easily ignore her in the future.

Ela supped alone on some pheasant and a cup of wine while she waited for Haughton to return with the jurors and the dispatched soldier to return with her box. Her dogs were removed as well as her children, and it seemed like the hall had already been turned over to strangers. She even wished her mother were here to keep her company right now, though in the next breath she sighed with relief that Alianore was safely at Gomeldon. Ela had half expected her to insist on staying to give Simon de Hal a lecture about the role of the great earls of Salisbury and how Ela's father would turn in his grave if he could see his beloved daughter being driven from her ancestral home.

HAUGHTON and the jurors arrived back before the letter, which gave them time and reason to commiserate with her on the chaos of moving. Haughton hadn't moved house since his marriage many years earlier, and the two jurors, Peter Howard the baker and Stephen Hale the cordwainer still lived and worked in the same places they'd grown up, within the castle's outer walls.

Ela couldn't help wondering how long they'd be able to stay in their childhood homes. The old cathedral within the castle walls was almost completely dismantled, creating an unsettling vista of ruination. One by one, businesses were removing to New Salisbury and it wasn't impossible to imagine the great castle mound, built in ancient times, deserted again with nothing left but the great castle towers jutting up into the sky. Or even those might one day be looted for their stones like her beloved cathedral.

She kept these maudlin thoughts to herself.

At last the soldier returned with her box, and she unlocked it and retrieved the letter. She, Haughton, the jurors and Osbert Pinchbeck sat at the table. Thomas Blount alias Drogo Blount was in the armory sharpening blades under the keen eyes of a senior guard, and the newest Thomas Blount sat sulkily in a far corner of the hall, shooting loaded glances her way.

"Whose seal is this?" asked Ela, peering at the dark red wax.

"My father's." Pinchbeck fidgeted with anticipation.

Ela carefully broke the seal and unfolded the parchment. The contract was written in the same hand as the earlier one —Radulph Blount's—and did indeed transfer the freehold ownership of the property to Jacobus Pinchbeck "and his heirs and assigns for all eternity for the sum of twelve pounds." She read it aloud, and watched a smug expression spread across Osbert Pinchbeck's face.

"See? I told you. They made a second bargain for silver. Now, if you don't mind I shall go take up residence at my property." He made to rise.

"Not so fast," said Ela. "The original contract, providing for a lifetime transfer of the property, was never recorded and made legal. Nor was this one. As far as the law is concerned the sale never happened."

"Even so, it's a gentleman's agreement. You can see their signatures right here." He pointed to the two inked scrawls.

This was true. And a gentleman's agreement had legal standing. Once again they were back in wager of battle territory. "Your father understood that his ownership was challenged."

"By a poacher!"

"By a man who claims to be the true owner of the property."

"As you can see, his father relinquished all his rights some fifteen years ago." Pinchbeck's staring eyes bored a hole in her. "The property is mine."

Ela suddenly felt very tired. This was not her battle to fight. Let the new sheriff preside over this dispute while she minded her own more pressing business of resettling her household. At least now they all knew what the contract said. Not that it helped much.

"If I can't take ownership of the property today, I'm heading back to London." Pinchbeck stood.

Ela glanced at Haughton. Pinchbeck was still a murder suspect. Even more so now that he stood to inherit the manor. He could have killed his father and had time to ride back to London before the neighbor came to find him. Or he could have hired someone—even the neighbor—to kill him.

Her brain ran to suspicion rather than trust these days. Even murder could be bought for the right coin.

Haughton stood. "I'm afraid we can't let you leave. There's a murder investigation underway, and you're a suspect."

Pinchbeck stared at him, uncomprehending for a moment, then it sank in and his eyes grew wider. "I'm to be imprisoned for my father's murder?"

"Calm yourself, Master Pinchbeck," said Haughton firmly. "These two men here are jurors who will be present at the murder trial. Please take this time to convince them—to convince all of us—that you didn't kill your father."

Pinchbeck stared from Haughton to the two jurors. "I didn't kill him. I was at my house in London. It's near Billingsgate."

"Was anyone with you?" asked Peter Howard, a stolid and steady character who'd long proven himself a valuable member of any jury.

"Nay. I have no wife, as I said. And no children. Who would be with me?"

"You don't have a servant?" asked Ela.

His face creased into a grimace as if he wanted to laugh or scream but couldn't decide which. "No, I don't have a servant. There's an old man who minds my shop, but he's gone at night and is more than half blind even in daylight. I hire a lad to help me unload the cart sometimes, but he wasn't with me any day this week."

Haughton sighed. "The neighbor who was sent to fetch you, he found you at your house near Billingsgate?"

"Yes."

"How did he know it? Had he been there before?"

"Yes. My father used him as a messenger for his business. Sometimes he even drove a load of goods into London for him."

"What's this neighbor's name?"

"Jim Cheswick," Pinchbeck said quickly. "He's not important. Just someone who helped my father from time to time."

"Did your father have a shop in London as well?"

"No, he sold goods at my shop," Osbert was starting to look nervous. "I paid him for them and sold them."

Ela's ears pricked. "Your father imported them and you sold them?"

Osbert looked around. "Yes."

"So he profited from selling the goods to you, and you profited from selling them on to someone else."

"When they sold, I did. Sometimes he'd buy a whole load of stuff no one wanted and I'd end up having to store it or find somewhere to dump it."

Ela blinked. "So basically, you were in business together, with Jim Cheswick carrying loads between his warehouse and London."

Pinchbeck hesitated. He didn't look at all happy to have these details of their relationship coming out.

"But you have absolutely no idea where his warehouse is?" Ela asked. None of this made sense.

"He would never tell me where the warehouse is, nor whom he bought the goods from. He didn't want me to be able to take over the business and cut him out so he kept me in the dark." Pinchbeck plucked at the frayed end of his sleeve.

"I want to think that this gives you motive to kill him, but now that he's gone and you have no idea who he bought from, how will you buy goods for your business?" Ela was intrigued.

"I don't know," said Pinchbeck lamely.

Possibly he'd been hoping to take up residence at Fernlees and live off the fat of the land, which an industrious farmer could very well do. The land looked like good grazing and had likely produced fine wool in the past. Even Jacobus Pinchbeck had run a decent flock on it. Still, Ela doubted whether this Pinchbeck would know one end of a lamb from the other. Fernlees was on the London road, however, which gave it potential for trade or a profitable sale.

The sound of trumpets made her startle.

Simon de Hal.

Her gut clenched and she rose to her feet.

Haughton told Pinchbeck to sit down and stay seated until told to move. Ela's entire body tensed as the door to the hall opened and a crowd of men marched in like an invading army.

CHAPTER 7

Simon de Hal was a man of slightly above average height, his black hair streaked with silver and blandly handsome features set in an expression of easy confidence. Ela felt herself shrink before his hubris, but gathered her courage and moved toward him with a smile on her mouth.

"Welcome to Salisbury Castle."

De Hal bowed low. "It's an honor and a pleasure to meet you again, my lady."

They'd never met before and she knew almost nothing about him. Even if they had met she'd certainly never have imagined herself placing the keys to her castle in his uncallused palm. She could hardly declare this meeting a pleasure. "I trust you had a good journey. The weather is fair."

They exchanged a few more tiresomely banal phrases while he snuck glances around his grand new quarters.

"This is Giles Haughton, the coroner. We've been investigating the murder of a local merchant." She gestured for Osbert Pinchbeck to rise, and he did and bowed. "This man's father, Jacobus Pinchbeck, was killed, and now in addition to the killer being at large, there is a dispute over the property he left behind."

"Oh."

She introduced the jurors and was about to elaborate when Simon de Hal interrupted her. "Would you do me the honor of showing me to my chambers? I'm fatigued after the journey and would like to rest a while."

Ela gaped. She'd just been dismissed like a servant and now he intended to command her as his porter.

Nearly all her servants had removed to Gomeldon, so she beckoned to a young boy who cleared the plates and replaced the rushes. "Please show Sir Simon to the solar at the top of the stairs."

"But I've—" No doubt the boy was about to explain that he'd never been allowed up there.

"You'll do fine. Good day to you, sir. I'll call on you tomorrow to see if you need anything."

She swept away before he could protest. Not that he would. Having exited the hall in a flurry, she now stood at a loose end in the courtyard while de Hal's servants carried in rolls of bedding and chests and crates of his goods.

Her carriage stood ready but their leaving was delayed by Sibel fussing over the last few things she wanted to bring, including the children's terrier who'd refused to be caught earlier. Ela finally caught the little white rascal herself and held him tight in her arms as she climbed in and pulled the door behind her.

Ela's head pounded as they rolled down the hill and out the gate. De Hal was thrilled to have reached the giddy heights of castellan—for the king's garrison, no less. He'd seen her as a tiresome social call he was quick to excuse himself from.

Again she chastened herself for the sin of pride. Did she expect the new sheriff to fall at her feet and kiss them? His head was full with settling his household into the castle and finding his way around. No wonder he didn't have the heart to hear every confusing detail of the Pinchbeck case right now.

She settled back against the hard seat cushion and tried to let the rhythmic trotting of the horse lull her into quiescence. She couldn't shake the feeling that she'd been conquered and routed and was being driven from her home in defeat.

She'd been born in Salisbury Castle and walked her first steps there. She'd given birth to her children in the familiar solar. It was the home she'd shared with her husband, who now lay dead and cold in the strange new cathedral he'd bitterly opposed building.

Was her planned fight to come back simply a show of pride or greed? Perhaps she should settle into a quiet life at Gomeldon with her family and devote her days to overseeing the creation of the perfect row of espaliered pear trees or the Christmas banquet of the century. Perhaps she could even learn to make lace or weave a tapestry with unicorns on it.

"Why are you laughing, my lady?" Sibel looked amused.

Ela kissed little Snowflake, the terrier, on her pink nose. "I honestly have no idea."

For all Gomeldon's rustic beauty, Ela saw only its faults as they rumbled into the courtyard. The courtyard still had weeds and the thatch was unevenly colored from where it had recently been repaired. Chickens pecked willy-nilly around the foundations and the freshly dug garden beds to the right of the front door looked like fresh wounds in the landscape.

She chided herself for her lack of gratitude. She could be like Drogo Blount with nowhere to call home. She hoped

Simon de Hal would deal kindly with Drogo. She knew she'd miss his company, and so would her children, even if there was something of the scoundrel about him.

"Ela darling, we thought they were holding you hostage over there!" Her mother appeared in the doorway.

"Or maybe I had a hard time bringing myself to step over the threshold."

Her mother sighed. "I know how you feel. Moving is always hard, but as a noble lady you don't get to choose your home. Fate—in the form of your father or your husband—chooses it for you."

Ela suspected there was some truth in this not just for the wives and widows of nobles but for all women. Easily buffeted by circumstance, they learned to build their hearth wherever they found themselves. It irked her. "I no longer have a father or husband. Am I not mistress of my own destiny?"

She walked to the door and her mother stood aside to let her in.

"Your spirit is both refreshing and tiring, my dear."

"I know. I feel the same way." She sighed. "Are the children settled in?" She couldn't hear them.

"They're all outside exploring the woods with Bill Talbot. He's told them there might be an ancient Saxon burial ground deep in the forest."

"Is there?"

Her mother shrugged. "What do I care about ancient Saxons? Come see the kitchens. The cook is struggling to get the fire to draw properly."

Ela noticed the air was smoky. Since the excellent and capable castle cook had to stay behind, they'd been forced to hire a new cook in a hurry. She was an older woman who supposedly had cooked for a monastery in Kent. "Was the chimney swept?"

Her mother shrugged again. Ela sighed again. Settling into her new home would take a while.

~

THAT NIGHT no one wanted to go to bed. They sat around the big fireplace, talking and singing. Her mother told the story of their hasty move to Normandy after Ela's father died. Bill Talbot sang the song he'd performed as a pretend troubadour. Ela's mother lamented over how she missed French cooking.

"Shh!" said Ela, half joking. "The new cook will hear you. It's not like the castle where there's a six-foot stone wall between us."

"I like a wood house," said Alianore. "They don't hold on to the cold and damp the way a chilly old castle does."

"I miss the castle," said Stephen with a sigh.

"We all do," said Ela. "Maybe we'll move back there one day."

"So Will can be sheriff?" asked little Ellie.

Ela froze. "Quite possibly, yes." She didn't like the idea of being a dowager in her son's home. She preferred to be mistress of her own domain. Her mother was the same—maintaining her own household and marrying for the fourth time rather than living quietly under Ela and William's roof. "In the meantime we must enjoy this lovely home. Listen to the quiet!"

There were no soldiers drinking and laughing and shoving each other, or calling to each other across the battlements at the change of guard. This house didn't have a village crawling right up to its walls, with all the attendant talking and shouting and clucking of a hundred people's chickens.

They listened. Beyond the crackling of the fire there was an eerie silence. Not even the branches of the forest stirred.

"I think I hear the man in the moon singing," whispered Nicholas.

"There's no man in the moon!" retorted Ellie, blonde curls bobbing.

"How do you know? Have you been there?" asked Stephen.

"There isn't. There's only God and Heaven in the sky," said Ellie.

"And angels," said Petronella.

"Oh, yes. Angels too," agreed Ellie. "I forgot about them."

"Well, we don't want to keep the angels up past their bedtime," said Ela. "With all our singing and chattering."

"I don't think they'd mind, Mama," said Ellie. "I suspect they like it when humans are happy. They'd rather us be singing and laughing than crying over Papa."

Ela's heart clenched at the reminder of their terrible loss. "You're right, my love. And Papa would feel the same."

"Do you think he's looking down at us from Heaven?" asked Stephen.

"I don't know," said Ela. "I think he would, though, if he could."

"He might be busy playing a trumpet with the angels," said Ellie seriously.

"Do you think he can hear our prayers?" asked Richard, who'd been very quiet all night.

"I hope so," said Ela. "Say a prayer for him tonight." She got up, suddenly anxious to get moving. She did worry about her husband's soul. The commandment said, thou shalt not kill, but did God hold it against you if you killed people during a holy war for Jerusalem? William had loved to drink and make merry. And there was the adultery. His brother John's quarrel with the pope. And the times he'd coveted his neighbors' goods—Lincoln Castle for example.

She hurried up the stairs, taper in hand, wanting to say a prayer for William. He was a good man for all his faults.

Her bedroom furniture from Salisbury had been put back together, not much the worse for its travels. Her bed curtains were creased from being folded but at least her bed was a cozy cocoon again, and Sibel had built a small fire to keep the room toasty overnight.

Sibel helped her undress and put on her nightgown. Then she undid Ela's long hair and brushed it out. "Thanks for helping the children settle in while I was busy today. You're a very important member of the family. You know that, don't you?"

"Of course, my lady." She gently worked a knot from the ends of Ela's hair with her fingers. "I love the children as if they were my own." She hesitated and seemed to draw in a long breath. "I have a question."

"What's that?" Her tone made Ela turn to look at her, almost pulling her hair from Sibel's fingers.

"I was wondering if you might have a place for a niece of mine. She's a young girl just turned eighteen and ready to work. It might be good to have some help in case my fingers get too old and crooked to braid your hair."

"Sibel, you're my age! Your fingers are perfectly fine."

"I know but it's good to look ahead into the future. My brother says I can come live with him and his family when I'm too old to work and—"

"You're not planning to leave!" The idea struck panic into her heart even as her own selfishness shamed her.

"No." Sibel let her hair fall. "I'm really not. I just—" She looked like she regretted her request.

"You just want some help? By all means! If doing so will keep you here I'd be happy to employ your niece. What's her name?"

"Her name is Hilda Biggs. She's the daughter of my sister

Ann, married to Roy Biggs who works a small farm not far from the old stone henge. She's used to taking care of children and babies as she's the oldest of eight."

"Ah, you're thinking ahead to Will's and Isabella's weddings and what will follow." The thought brightened her rather somber mood. It would be wonderful to have a baby to cherish. Her eldest daughter, Ida, was married and lived in Bedfordshire with her husband but they had not yet been blessed with children.

"Indeed I am. And I'm sure she'd be a great help with the older children, too."

"Hilda sounds like a very sensible name." Ela pictured a nice, solid, plain girl with rosy cheeks and rough red hands. Hopefully young Will wouldn't be tempted. He was in that foolish stage where a young man could find himself swooning over a doorpost if the sun caught it right. The sooner he was married the better.

"She's certainly a sensible girl," said Sibel. She'd started brushing Ela's hair again, with long, smooth strokes. "And not afraid of hard work, either."

Ela could tell that Sibel was happy about her niece coming and that warmed her. Sometimes she felt like she'd stolen Sibel's life from her—keeping her locked up in a tower like St. Barbara while her chance at marriage and children slipped away. She was glad to give something back for once.

THAT NIGHT ELA dreamed she was walking through a wood at night. She was alone and could hear every whisper of sound from the trees, the mice, even the tiny worms moving beneath the soil. She had to get somewhere before dawn, but she didn't know where and wasn't sure she was on the right path.

Only thin wisps of moonlight, filtering down through great branches, lit her way through the unfamiliar forest. Over and over again, she lost her way and found herself wondering which way to go. Still, she forged ahead, knowing that it was better to keep going than to try to find her way back along the dark paths.

She knew she couldn't stop and rest. Something would get her. She didn't know what but she had to keep moving.

She awoke with a start, heart pounding, her nightgown damp with sweat.

"Mama, I can't sleep." Little Nicholas peered through a gap in the curtains. "It smells strange here."

She patted the bed, offering for him to climb up. "It is strange here. It's new and different and will take some getting used to." She helped him under her quilted coverlet, glad of the company after wandering alone in the forest of her mind half the night. "You'll settle in soon. Don't worry."

She realized her words were for herself as much as him.

"I liked living in a castle with the soldiers there to protect us."

Ela stroked his hair. She'd debated whether to move to their fortified manor house halfway across Wiltshire, but she didn't want to be too far from Salisbury and de Hal. They didn't need the protection of stone walls. This wasn't the Anarchy, or even the troubled times of King John. "We're very safe here. And we have guards to protect us in addition to Bill and your brother Will." She'd chosen the guards from the castle staff.

"I miss my papa."

"I miss him, too." He'd been gone so much they should be used to his absence, but there was a cruel difference between knowing a loved one was sleeping abroad and knowing he'd never come back. "He'd want you to get some sleep so you can learn your lessons in the morning."

"Latin is so boring."

"But so important. How else will you read God's word?"

"Why does God only speak in Latin? Why can't he speak French like us?"

Ela wanted to laugh. "He speaks all languages, but his word is written in Latin. I'm not really sure why. Tradition I suppose. If it were up to me it would also be written in French and English and every other language so the people can understand it."

"Why don't we speak English since we're in England?"

"English is the language of…the common people. We're nobles. We brought our language with us when we came from France eight score years ago."

"But we're English now. We should speak English."

"You're probably right." She was starting to miss the eerie solitude of her dream forest. "But for now we speak French and we read Latin. Now go to sleep!"

She laid a kiss on his cheek. He still had soft, round cheeks like a little boy, and one day they'd harden into ridges with rough stubble on them. She should cherish this moment with her baby who was no longer a baby. But she had a lot to do tomorrow and didn't want to be unrested and testy in an already unsettled household. "I love you, my pet. Sweet dreams."

"You too, Mama." He nestled his head deeper into the crook of her arm and almost immediately she heard his breathing deepen. She lay awake, her mind running down tunnels. Who had killed Jacobus Pinchbeck? Was Drogo the rightful owner of Fernlees? Who was the strange new Thomas Blount? What was stored in the warehouse on the London road?

Would Simon de Hal be a good and fair sheriff for Wiltshire? She realized she dreaded this almost as much as she hoped for it. If he proved to be honest and hardworking and well respected she'd be selfish to seek the post for herself.

Sleep was elusive, and the first rays of sunlight peeking through her curtains dragged her from her bed and her baby. Today she must oversee the planting of the new kitchen gardens. She must make sure their stock of wood for heating and cooking was good and dry, and that the cook knew how and when to order supplies for their meals.

And when her duties at home were done she intended to ride to the castle and offer her services to Simon de Hal.

APPROACHING THE CASTLE ON HORSEBACK, with one of her guards at her side, Ela half wondered if the soldiers would now have orders to turn her away. They greeted her as usual and didn't even look surprised to see her.

Albert the porter did look surprised and made a cheery fuss, wanting to blow his trumpet to announce her arrival. She begged him to just quietly announce her, as she had business with the sheriff.

De Hal and his cronies were sat around the table near the fire with Deschamps, enjoying their midday meal and a good amount of wine from the looks of it. Their talk was loud and raucous and reminded Ela of the soldiers when they got in their cups. She wondered if Mistress de Hal would be joining him in Salisbury or if she'd remain sequestered in some distant rural retreat so he could enjoy the life of a bachelor here at Salisbury.

After Albert announced her, de Hal looked distinctly annoyed for a split second before looking up at her and rising—unsteadily—from the table.

"Mistress Ela, what brings you back so soon? Miss the bracing gusts on this high mound?"

"No, indeed," she lied. "But I did want to wrap up our unfinished business from yesterday. It was wrong of me to try to tell you every detail of a case when you'd barely walked through the door."

"'Tis no matter. Will you join us for a cup?" He gestured for a servant to pour her some wine. Another servant brought a chair for her.

Ela let the servant take her cloak and lowered herself into the chair, knowing that de Hal was impatiently waiting for her to sit so he could retake his own seat without being rude.

She fingered her cup of wine. "It's the matter of Fernlees." She hadn't seen Drogo or Thomas or Pinchbeck as she entered. "The question of ownership—"

"Has been resolved," said Simon cheerily.

"Oh? How?"

"I decided it myself."

CHAPTER 8

Simon de Hal paused to take a gulp from his cup of wine. “Osbert Pinchbeck shall keep Fernlees as his father intended. Of the two men claiming to be Thomas Blount, one or both of them is a miscreant and I suspect the latter. Either way the elder Blount was a degenerate who relinquished control of the property and they're likely no better and don't deserve it. Fernlees now belongs to Pinchbeck and the deed will be recorded to reflect that.”

Ela was speechless for a moment. As sheriff, of course he had the right to decide matters of property—

“Where are they?” She looked around.

“Who? Pinchbeck has gone to his manor.”

“Drogo…and Thomas Blount.” Or whoever he really was. She only really cared about Drogo.

“The tall fair one has been put outside the castle walls, and the shorter one is in the dungeons where he belongs, up on a charge of poaching. The man who accused him is dead, but his son wished to press the charges.”

Ela felt her breath grow unsteady. “Drogo Blount was a

close friend of my husband, William Longespée. He saved his life in the Holy Land."

De Hal looked astonished. "But he's just a...he's a—"

"A good and brave knight who's fallen on hard times since grave injuries ended his career as a warrior."

"But poaching?"

"On the land that was his ancestral home." She felt awkward defending him, but someone had to. She knew William would want it. "He's been maintaining weapons in the armory. Can he not remain here to work?"

"A criminal inside the castle walls?" He looked both amused and appalled. "With his hands upon instruments of death? I think not. He's a poacher. Caught red-handed from all accounts."

It was true. Even Drogo hadn't tried to deny it.

"What will be his punishment for poaching?"

"I'm not one to hang a man for poaching unless it's his third offence. But perhaps the loss of a hand would remind him to keep his hands off other people's property."

Ela's stomach lurched. The loss of a hand would make it impossible for Drogo to support himself. Yes, the poaching was misguided but like most poaching was done out of desperation. Despite his cocky attitude Ela truly believed Drogo was a good man at heart. "Would you spare him the punishment if I offer him a role in my household?"

De Hal stared at her as if she'd lost her wits completely. "But why?"

"To repay my husband's debt to him for saving his life."

"I suppose this is why a woman can't be a sheriff!" De Hal slapped the back of the man next to him. "So tenderhearted they can't bear to inflict punishment on even a low criminal."

Ela smarted. "I simply feel that a momentary mistake does not of necessity have to end a man's useful life. Have you never made an error of judgment?"

"Not one that breaks a law. I'd hardly be sheriff of Wiltshire if I was prone to lawbreaking."

She stood rigid. So he wanted to wave the "I'm sheriff and you're not" flag in her face. He had captured that flag. She didn't know how, but he was indeed sheriff and she wasn't. "He would repay Osbert Pinchbeck for the poached pheasants. I'll guarantee it."

De Hal tipped his head sideways and stared at her. "Are you not worried he's a murderer?"

"No more than anyone else who's killed in the name of the king. How will you proceed to seek the man who killed Jacobus Pinchbeck?"

"Oh, that." He waved his hand dismissively. "Giles Haughton explained the facts of the case to me, and it's clearly an accident. The man got knocked down by his own horse and run over by his own cart in the dark." He turned to summon a servant to bring more wine for his cup.

Ela could hardly believe this. Haughton had told her he didn't think it was an accident. "But he had bruises around his neck. His manservant says he left home already—"

"It was dark. No one knows exactly what happened. He could have bruises anywhere on his body from his horse or cart. I've heard the details and declared it an accident. Pinchbeck's son inherits Fernlees, and we can attend to more pressing matters."

"But he had a warehouse and no one seems to know where it was or what was in it. He could have been killed by a business associate or—"

"Or by a stray bolt of lightning. Giles Haughton admits there were no traces of a killer to be found. To your good health, my lady!" He raised his cup, clearly ready to toast the end of his participation in the case more than her well-being.

Ela's sense of justice was affronted by his lack of interest. Surely Haughton had mentioned the footprints at the scene?

What of the neighbor who'd carried the news to his son? No doubt de Hal didn't like that the events had happened before he'd arrived and under her jurisdiction. But she could see a small silver lining. She lifted her cup half-heartedly. "So Drogo Blount doesn't stand accused of murder, just poaching?"

"Just poaching, if you can put it so lightly. I don't think the king would look so kindly on a man pilfering pheasants from his forests. But if you're so determined to save him from his fate, then so be it. He must pay back the value of the pilfered pheasants to Osbert Pinchbeck, but now he's yours to command."

He turned to another man and asked him to fetch Drogo Blount up from the dungeon.

"I thank you. To your health," she raised her cup and took the tiniest sip she could manage. Not that she truly feared being poisoned, but—

Ela had planned to offer de Hal her expertise and counsel on any matters pertaining to the shire, but since he'd already rejected them soundly on the one case where he'd be sure to need them, she held her tongue.

The murder of Jacobus Pinchbeck had happened on her watch. She didn't believe his death was an accident. And she intended to find out who killed him and bring them to justice.

Ela called on Giles Haughton at his home. In the castle she'd simply asked someone to summon him, so this was new. She had to inquire where he lived and make her way—in the company of her guard—to a neat house on a back street near the outer walls. She dismounted, handed her horse to the guard, and knocked on the door herself.

He opened it looking more rumpled than usual and surprised to see her.

"May I come in?"

"Please do. My wife has gone out shopping or I'm sure she'd have welcomed you more competently than I."

Ela stepped into the front room and he offered her a seat on a hard wooden chair. The fire had gone out. "I'm sorry to bother you at home," she began, feeling suddenly anxious about pushing her way in. "But Simon de Hal told me he's decided that Jacobus Pinchbeck's death was an accident. What do you think of his decision?"

"That it was one of expediency. He sees the case as uninteresting and doesn't want to waste his time on it." He leaned back slightly. "I also suspect that Pinchbeck offered him a good sum of money."

Ela loved his bluntness. "That's what I suspected. I, however, feel duty bound to investigate further, and I'm hoping you'll help me."

"As coroner it's my job to find the killer. But if the sheriff has told me the matter is decided, I'd be going behind his back." His expression was unreadable.

Ela paused. "And how do you feel about that?"

"My allegiance is to the truth."

"And you don't think it was an accident?"

"Circumstances suggest otherwise. I believe he was strangled, then run over to deflect suspicion."

"I want to know who Pinchbeck was traveling to meet with. And I want to see the contents of his warehouse. I don't believe that he was able to make such a substantial living just selling flutes and other fripperies."

"You may have a point."

"Will you ride to the warehouse with me?"

He stared at her for a moment. "Now?"

"There's no time like the present, as they say."

He blinked and ran a hand through his uncombed hair. "Allow me a few moments to dress myself."

~

BEFORE LONG HAUGHTON was mounted on his bay palfrey and they left the castle through the north gate, heading out toward Crackmore. The guard remained behind to rest his horse and wait for her return. It was a good long way, but they covered the roads at a steady pace and the soft ground was easy on the horses' legs.

They had ridden almost right through Crackmore before they even realized they'd arrived, because there was no sign or milepost.

"How will we know the building?" asked Haughton, looking around. Fields of sheep seemed to be the only inhabitants. "If we can even find a building."

"The lease didn't describe it, but it was signed by a John Hope. We can ask for his barn."

"If we can find a living soul."

They rode up on a cluster of mean cottages not far off the London road and approached to find a young woman in a stained green dress feeding chickens in a weedy garden. Ela asked about the barn, and the woman pointed to a knot of woods to their left. "It's in there. You can't miss it. You're the third person to ask this week."

Ela glanced at Haughton. She wanted to ask what they looked like, but his look stilled her tongue. Perhaps it was better not to draw attention to their investigation. They could always ask her later. She thanked the woman, and they rode around a freshly tilled field toward the woods. "Who else would have come? Could it be Simon de Hal's men?"

"Since yesterday? Hardly." Haughton snorted. "Too busy drinking to his newfound glory."

"The murderer?" Ela looked around at the quiet scenery. "We didn't find the key on Jacobus Pinchbeck's body. Yet he was headed to the warehouse because we know he was picking up a load of goods. The murderer must have removed the key."

"True. For all we know that's why they killed him."

"What could he be storing that was so valuable as to cost his life?"

They entered the woods on a narrow lane and found the barn in the middle of the trees. It was very ancient, covered with moss and mold, and probably predated the trees, which might have been grown to either shelter or hide it.

They dismounted and tied up their horses. Ela felt her ears pricking and straining for sounds in the wood. A thick layer of dead leaves covered the ground. The trampled leaf litter told of human traffic, but there was no sign of whom or when.

The door had a heavy iron lock of great age on it. Ela tried the door—unsurprisingly it was locked. But the door moved.

"Someone's forced the door off its hinges." Giles Haughton pulled out his knife and slid it into the hinge side, then wiggled it back and forth. The door jostled looser in its frame, then popped out, so it was just hanging from the lock. It was easy to see where the frame holding the hinges was rotten, allowing the door to be pulled out, then slid back in.

"So now we don't know if anyone has the key at all." Ela hesitated. The space inside the door was pitch-black in the windowless barn. "And we have no light."

"I always have light." Haughton went back and rummaged in his saddlebag. "Murders are nearly always committed in the dark so I find myself in need of it often."

He pulled out a rush for a rushlight, held it between his teeth and lit it with one deft stroke of a flint. Cupping the tiny flame in his hands he walked slowly back. Ela stepped aside as he walked through the unhinged door and led the way into the cavernous barn.

The smell hit her first, before her eyes had a chance to adjust to the dark. A heavy, musky smell like old, damp... something. She pulled her hand to cover her mouth.

Giles Haughton had forged ahead into the space. She could make out some crude crates, of the kind hastily nailed together from rough-sawn boards to hold goods for a sea voyage. They'd been forced open, and the goods removed, leaving an empty space inside the splintered wood. "Whatever notions he stored here, someone wanted them."

"Hold this." Haughton handed her the rushlight. Then he got down on his hands and knees and started feeling around on the floor among the empty crates. He stood up, with a few creaks of his knees, holding something long.

"Is that a flute?" Ela remembered Osbert Pinchbeck and his talk of flutes.

"Appears it is. And it seems to be filled with something." He held it under his nose, then wrinkled his brow as he sniffed. "Can't say for sure but it might be opium."

"What's that?"

"It's the oil of a poppy that grows in faraway deserts. It's cooked into a resin and provides powerful pain relief. I've known old soldiers who swore by it for their ailments."

"Then the Pinchbecks are importing more than notions. But why hide this...opium in a flute?"

"Because it's one of the most valuable substances there is. Worth more per ounce than gold to the right people."

"I don't believe you."

"People will do anything to get their hands on this substance once they've learned to crave it."

"Why do they crave it?"

"Sweet relief from pain. From the harshness of life, even."

Ela frowned, still skeptical. "They'd kill for it?"

"It's been known to happen if a man is desperate enough for its succor. And the quantity that was stored here would be worth more than several men's lives. Hence the need to disguise the resin as something no one would care much about."

"But why store it here at all? Why not just take it straight from the port to the shop in London, where Osbert Pinchbeck could sell it?" The Pinchbeck's true business was now clear to her. "They're not hiding the goods to avoid import duties because those haven't been levied for years."

"No doubt their product is worth more if they dole it out in small quantities. Scarcity drives value. If they stored it in London it wouldn't be a secret for long and might attract robbers. I'm sure you've observed that it has a distinctive aroma. Also, by not revealing the true profits of their trade they can avoid a full tax on their holdings."

Ela felt a sudden chill at the thought of this clandestine trade happening right under her husband's nose for years. "So who are the two other people who knew about the warehouse and came before us?"

"I'm certain one of them was Osbert Pinchbeck. If his father dangled him on a tight rein as a kind of shopkeeper while keeping most of the profits for himself, it gives him more of a motive for murder."

Ela struggled to breathe. The close atmosphere of the barn, with its musty smell, gagged her. But she didn't want to reveal weakness by running for the door. "Do you think Osbert Pinchbeck capable of murder?"

"Everyone is capable of killing, my lady." The rushlight flickered as he moved closer. "Even yourself."

His words cut to the quick. "I killed to save my own life. A planned murder is quite different."

"The planning would be the easy part for a businessman

like Osbert Pinchbeck. The execution is where nerves fail. But if the stakes are high enough…"

"I did observe that he has feet similar to the print we saw at the scene. It would be interesting to visit his business in London and see what he's selling. Or we might discover that he's run out of goods because of his father's death. I can send Bill Talbot to London to investigate."

"Didn't Pinchbeck meet Talbot during his time at the castle?" asked Haughton.

"I don't think they spoke. Besides, Talbot is a master at playing a part. He could affect a stoop from an old wound and pretend to be one of these used-up knights who craves opium."

"It could be a dangerous business. London is nothing like Salisbury. It attracts swindlers and cutthroats from every nation."

"Bill Talbot can handle a sword."

"Bill Talbot can win at tournament, which is not at all the same thing as defending yourself from a ruthless criminal."

"I shall advise him to be cautious." She didn't much like him casting aspersions on the most gallant knight she knew after her husband. "Is there anything else here?" She was almost getting used to the smell. It had a vinegary undertone.

Haughton walked further into the gloom, holding the rushlight with its tiny flame ahead of him, though it gave little illumination. The daylight streaming through the unhinged door behind them was brighter. He kicked at something. "Nothing but empty sacks and opened crates. Anything stored here has been taken elsewhere."

"I suppose Osbert Pinchbeck could hardly be blamed for wanting to claim the goods before they were stolen."

"If it was indeed him that took them." Haughton walked back to her. "And not a greedy rival."

"Which is why we need to see the contents of Osbert's

shop. If the shop is well stocked, then he could have killed his father to keep the profits for himself. If the shop is empty, then most likely he's innocent of murder and someone else has seized the goods."

"One can't draw conclusions that easily," Haughton said slowly. "He could have sold the goods wholesale to another merchant to avoid detection."

"I see you've learned to be suspicious of almost any person and action."

"A hazard of my trade."

"That I wish to learn. I appreciate your sharing your wisdom."

"I hope we'll see you back in the castle as sheriff." He said it with sincerity, and the rushlight illuminated his face enough for her to see him looking right at her. "I know you see the quest for justice as something almost sacred."

"It is sacred. If I can't avenge my husband's murder, at least I can seek justice for others."

Haughton stilled. He blew out the rushlight, so she couldn't see his face.

Ela's heart started to pump harder. Had she said the wrong thing? She'd confided in Haughton that she thought the king's justiciar had killed her husband. He'd said he would quietly spread the rumor in the hope that one day it would catch up with him.

"I'd like to see you avenge your husband's murder," he said softly. "And seek redress for de Hal being placed as sheriff in your stead. That, too, could be de Burgh's work."

The king was young and impressionable, and if Hubert de Burgh was seen as his right hand, it was just as likely that he acted as his head in some things.

It was also possible that the king wanted to teach her a lesson about who was in charge. And kings were always looking for inventive ways to raise income from their nobles. Making her buy the role of sheriff was just typical.

The decision to deny her the role of sheriff could have come from either or both of them. "Hubert de Burgh is a very powerful man," said Ela quietly.

"And a proud one. And pride comes before a fall."

"I can but hope. In the meantime I'll seek solace in pursuing Jacobus Pinchbeck's killer, since Simon de Hal doesn't care to bother."

She took one more look around. Her eyes had adjusted to the gloom, and she could now see all four walls in the light from the doorway. The walls were dark with mildew and the floor slimy with moss and mold. An unpleasant environment to stand in. "Is there anything else we should look at?" She deferred to his years of experience.

"Nothing that I can see. I looked for cart tracks outside and sure enough they were there." They headed to the door. "But that's to be expected if this barn was used to store goods. I couldn't tell if they were fresh or not."

"Because of all the leaf litter. I noticed the same."

"It is an ideal location to store troublesome goods. Convenient yet obscure and well hidden."

"If I were sheriff I'd post a soldier to keep an eye on it," she said ruefully.

"As coroner I could ask for the same, but it's empty now so there'd be little to gain. We need to know who the two people were who came and asked directions before us."

On their way back through the village they stopped and spoke to the same woman. Her description of the two men made them sound like half the men in England and made her sound like a half-wit. Perhaps she'd been paid to be vague.

"Jacobus Pinchbeck seems to have surrounded himself with an army of simpletons. Did you ever speak to the neighbor, Jim Cheswick?"

"Aye. I wouldn't call him a simpleton, but he's hard of hearing and his hands are palsied so much that I'm surprised he can ride. I don't think him capable of killing a rabbit, let alone a large man like Jacobus Pinchbeck."

"His feet?"

"Long and narrow. He did pass messages regularly between the two Pinchbecks but claimed to know nothing of their business. He said it could well be his prints outside the house that morning as he rushed over to see the body before setting out for London."

Ela sighed. "So the footprints tell us nothing."

"Such is often the case."

They rode for home, returning to Salisbury barely before dark, and Ela had to ride the last miles to Gomeldon by moonlight with her guard.

She arrived back at the manor to find the place in chaos.

CHAPTER 9

"My lady, where are they supposed to sleep?" The cook had worked herself into a lather over the two new additions to the household. Drogo Blount sat at the table in the kitchen, finishing off a piece of pie. The new girl—Hilda, Sibel's niece—stood in a doorway anxiously plucking at her clothes.

Ela's heart sank at how pretty Hilda was. Long lashed, golden haired, neat featured and with a figure that showed even through her shapeless gown, she would be a temptation to any man who wasn't a monk.

"They can sleep in the kitchen."

"Then where shall I sleep?"

Ela looked around. She wasn't used to this. At the castle any number of men of all ranks might sleep in the great hall on any given night. The kitchen and its attendant rooms could accommodate an array of servants. This house was on a far smaller scale. There were several bedrooms on the upper floor, but between her, the children, her mother, Sibel, Bill Talbot and various other members of the household, every corner was accounted for.

"As cook you must sleep in the kitchen. Surely there's room for another pallet for Hilda?" She smiled at the girl. "Welcome to our household."

The cook looked doubtful, then scowled at Drogo. He looked up from his pie at Ela. "I'm quite happy to sleep outdoors. Wouldn't be the first time."

"That won't be necessary." The whole reason she'd brought him here was to prevent him sleeping outdoors. "You can sleep either in the back hallway next to the storeroom or in the cow barn. I'll leave it up to you."

Neither was a particularly pleasant option, but they'd keep him out of the spring rains, at least.

"What exactly is he doing here?" asked the cook, looking down her nose at Drogo. "What is his job?"

"Whatever I decide it shall be," said Ela coolly. "And I'll thank you to manage the kitchen and leave the rest of the household to me." She wondered if gossip had already started. Drogo did have the air of a rascal about him. "Master Blount, please attend me in the parlor once I've had a chance to remove my cloak."

Where was Sibel? Ela felt herself overheating in the oppressive atmosphere of the kitchen. Usually Sibel would have whisked her cloak away by now, but everything was topsy-turvy here at Gomeldon.

She left the kitchen and headed into the sitting room, where another fire blazed. She was struggling with the neck of her cloak, trying to undo the clasp, when Sibel came running in. "I'm so sorry, my lady! No one told me you were home."

"Well, there's no trumpeter here to announce my arrival," she sighed. "This new arrangement will take some getting used to. Is Hilda settling in? I told the cook she could sleep in the kitchen, unless you'd prefer her to sleep upstairs with you." Sibel was already sharing a room with two other female servants.

"Anywhere you choose is fine." Sibel removed her cloak and folded it over her arm. "Thank you for giving her the opportunity."

"You're most welcome."

"Let me fetch you supper. The children and your mother have eaten already. They're upstairs reading and playing games." She settled Ela into a chair near the window.

The dogs gathered at her feet and nudged at her hands until Ela stroked and petted them. "I see you're all settled in, aren't you, little ones?"

Drogo came in and bowed deeply. "I don't know how to thank you for raising me from the castle dungeon. I'm not sure they had any purpose for me down there but to feed the rats."

"There was a risk that de Hal and his men would be so busy feasting and celebrating their new abode that they'd forget you were down there altogether," she said wryly. "You'll be far more useful here, and safe from harm." He couldn't stay there forever, of course, but then she didn't plan to be there that long, either. "We have no armory here for you to attend to, so your duties may be light."

"As a tired old soldier you won't hear me complain of that." His crooked grin always warmed her heart. "I'm glad of a place to rest and happy to do any work you need done." His humble heart impressed her. Would that she held such humility in her own.

"Could you perhaps see to the management of the livestock and the garden? There are two boys to attend to the day-to-day tasks, but an eye to oversight never goes amiss." She was quite capable of overseeing the management of the stys, chicken pens, bee skeps and beds herself, but it would give him a sense of purpose.

She hadn't given up entirely on the idea that Drogo might

have a claim to Fernlees that could be proven in time. Now was not the time to press a suit, with all of Salisbury being in upheaval over the arrival of the new sheriff.

"I'd be most pleased. Perhaps one day I'll be able to tend to my own farm and gardens. I relish the chance to hone my hand at skills that are, after all, far more practical and useful than wielding a sword." Clearly he still had hopes for Fernlees, as well.

"In the heat of battle there is no skill more useful than wielding a sword," Ela reminded him. "I don't take the skill and sacrifice of warriors for granted, even in time of peace. My sons will all train as knights, whether they are destined for the church or the king's court. We are only free and safe if we can defend ourselves from those who'd make us slaves."

"Well said, my lady." He bowed again. Ela was tempted to ask him to join her at the table. She did enjoy his company and easy conversation, but perhaps it was best if she kept a certain distance between them in this narrow new world where every word and deed was observed by each member of the household. She bade him good night and listened with satisfaction as he walked back into the kitchen and told the cook that he'd be managing the farm and would prefer to sleep in the barn loft.

Sibel brought Ela's food to the table, along with a cup of wine. Supper was a slice of the ham pie she'd seen Drogo enjoying, with carrots and parsnips browned in herbs. The new cook showed promise for all her rather difficult attitude. Ela had noticed that the best cooks—and those who could rise to the challenge of feeding a large household well—were often somewhat abrasive.

As she no doubt was herself sometimes. Ballads and romances might be filled with simpering maidens, but the day-to-day world bustled forward under the critical eyes of stern housewives and cooks and dairymaids.

Ela hoped she could stay awake long enough to kneel at her prie-dieu and say a few decades of her rosary. She missed the chapel at the castle terribly. She'd appreciated the opportunity to attend every mass, even though she only went once or twice per day.

Perhaps she'd start haunting the new Salisbury Cathedral —built from the rummaged stones of the cathedral raised and loved by her ancestors—by appearing for every service, even the ones in the middle of the night. Would Bishop Poore praise her piety or question her sanity?

"Why are you laughing, Mama?" Richard's voice made her spin in her chair.

"Was I? I'm almost too tired to think straight. How do you like our new home?"

"It's all right. I like not having a fortress all around us. I can come and go as I please without having to explain myself to anyone."

"So independent! Soon all of my children will be married and settled in their own manors." She cupped his cheek. "You'll make a fine husband to the right young girl."

"I'd be a fine bishop," he retorted. "Even Papa said so."

"That would be a terrible waste!" Alianore's voice boomed across the room. Ela jumped. She'd half forgotten that her mother was still here. "The king needs you to defend the realm. And I need you to provide me with great-grandchildren to fuss over."

Richard managed not to roll his eyes, but Ela could tell he wanted to. Boys his age had little sense of humor. Alianore swept toward them and settled into a chair. She wore her nightgown with an embroidered robe over it. Ela was always either up and fully dressed or disrobed and in bed, but her mother had a variety of in-between garments for when she was resting in the house.

Sibel brought her a cup of warm spiced wine that she

accepted gracefully. "This manor is lovely. You should be quite comfortable here. The house is commodious enough and with half your children ready for marriage you'll soon have more space than you need."

"I'm not ready for marriage," protested Richard.

"No one's talking about you," scolded Alianore. "Why do boys—and men—always think you're talking about them? Will and Isabella first, to secure their inheritances before someone else can claim the wards they're marrying."

Ela shot her mother a glance. She didn't need Richard to know exactly how mercenary these arrangements could be.

"Whose inheritance am I supposed to marry? I suspect you have it figured out, Grandmamma," he said.

"A crowned head of Europe would be ideal, my dear." She sipped her wine.

He looked skeptical. "I think that might be aiming a bit high."

"For a Longespée? Never. Your father was a king's son, and don't you forget it."

"How could I? I hear it every day from someone or another."

Alianore looked at Ela. "You should ask the king whom he'd like Richard to marry. Have you asked him yet for permission for Will's and Isabella's marriages?"

"It would be a formality only, since he arranged the wardships. I'm sure he'd be surprised if we didn't at least try to plan the marriages."

"I know that, my dear, but you should call on him to formally request permission." Alianore tilted her chin. "And while you're there you could discuss any other pressing matters that might come to mind."

Like my wish to be sheriff.

Or my strong suspicion that his justiciar poisoned my husband.

Ela wasn't even sure she could look the king in the eye so

soon after her husband's death. Surely he must have suspicions too. Anyone at court must wonder why one minute William was raging with fury at Hubert de Burgh and a few days later he lay dead after dining at de Burgh's table.

Ela realized her mother was still talking. "—you can stay at my London house. It's closed up, but we can get it ready in a day or two."

Ela wanted to protest that one move was enough for now, but she realized that the two proposed marriages gave her a perfect no-pressure excuse for an audience with the king. She could soften his heart with gifts, then press her request to be sheriff.

And, while in London, perhaps she could pay a call to Osbert Pinchbeck's shop.

IT WAS a full three weeks before Ela began the journey to London. Her mother finally went back to her own home and husband, and sent servants to get her London house ready for Ela. The journey was long enough to require careful planning and packing, and Ela needed time to commission an impressive gift for the king.

Will came along to renew his acquaintance with his royal cousin. Bill Talbot traveled with them as protector and friend, and Sibel came to attend to Ela.

They set out in the newest carriage with well-padded seats, room for baggage, and large wheels that traveled fast over the roads. Four sturdy palfreys would pull it and give them reliable riding horses to use once they arrived. Will and Bill preferred to ride the whole way—but they could take refuge under the roof if rain clouds opened hard.

They stopped once to eat and rest the horses and once to stay overnight. The inn was the best she knew of, but Ela still brought her own linens from home as she didn't trust them to wash theirs between customers. Ela shared the bed with Sibel and Will and Bill shared a bed in the next chamber. She strongly disliked sleeping abroad and strange beds made her itch.

The next day, they rumbled along at a steady clip, enjoying the spring vistas of new grass, budding trees and wildflowers. Outside the window, Will declared that he wished someone would try to rob them because he knew exactly how he'd handle it. Ela wanted to call out that one should never wish for violence, but Bill Talbot immediately quizzed him on strategy. Together they mentally fought their way through several alarming scenarios that gave each horseman passing them on the road a distinct air of menace.

It was past nightfall when they finally arrived in the city, but luckily the coachman knew Alianore's house and its stables well so they were able to find it in the dark. Ela felt stiff and cramped from the long day's confinement and could barely wait to get out of the carriage.

Will wrinkled up his nose after he dismounted and handed his horse to the ostler. "I don't know how people live here in London all the time. I can barely breathe for the smoke." He extended a hand to help her climb down.

"I want to scold you for complaining, but I feel the same," said Ela, stepping onto the cobbles. She hadn't much enjoyed spending extended periods of time here so William could be near his late brother King John while he attended to business at Westminster. "People whine about the gusting winds of the castle mound, but the breezes disperse the smoke of all the fires. Here it seems to hang in the air and settle on everything in a layer of black grime."

They walked into Alianore's house, which always had an odd smell, possibly from the many hangings that stayed locked up in a damp, unaired and unheated house for much of the year. Servants had come ahead of them to light the fires and knock down the cobwebs, but they couldn't chase away the musty odor of disuse.

The beds felt damp, even with fresh linens, and Ela struggled to keep her complaints in her head and not air them to Sibel, who was likely none too happy to be here either. She spent a restless night, wondering if she'd be able to greet Hubert de Burgh with the required politeness or if she'd be unable to stop herself spitting in his eye or hurling accusations of murder.

IN THE MORNING, Sibel dressed Ela with even more care than usual. Ela's mother had tried to convince her to wear her most elaborately embroidered gown with a rich belt and a gold and jeweled brooch at her neck, but she pointed out that she was still in deep mourning and did not want to put on a show of extravagance even for the king.

They broke their fast with pastries Sibel purchased from a local bakery, then set out for the palace. At home Ela always rode astride and controlled her own horse, but this time she rode in her mother's highly ornamented sidesaddle, with Bill leading her. They could easily have walked the short distance to the palace, but that wouldn't have made for the right sort of entrance.

Ela had written to the king asking for an audience. He'd replied that he was at home in Westminster and she must call on him at her leisure. She wasn't sure if his casual approach was an insult or a warm family gesture, but she hoped he wouldn't be in the middle of pressing business when they rode up.

"How should I greet him, Mama?" asked Will, riding alongside her. He was nervous and excited to the point of his handsome face being flushed. "Should I bow to him like a king or hug him like a cousin?"

"Definitely the bow. Let him initiate anything that follows, including conversation."

"But he's a boy my own age."

"With a crown on his head. He's been king for ten years. He has wisdom beyond his years, or so I hear." It was odd that she didn't know him better since her husband had been such a close companion of his father, but the influence of de Burgh—who had long been at odds with her husband over one matter or another—had cooled the relationship between the Longespées and the crown.

Will frowned. "I wonder if he likes to hunt."

"I don't doubt it."

"Can he fight?"

"I'd be shocked if he couldn't. It's his duty to defend his nation."

"And my duty to serve him," said Will thoughtfully. "I hope I like him."

Bill Talbot—who'd been silent until now—convulsed into laughter. Will looked confused.

"Will, you're so straightforward that you can be very funny without realizing it," said Ela. Sometimes her son's lack of guile worried her. "I love your honesty, but sometimes speaking your mind isn't the best approach."

"Don't worry, Mother. I won't insult him with bluntness the way I do my brothers and sisters."

Ela pressed damp palms into the lap of her gown. So much of her future—and her children's futures—rested in this king's slim, young hands. And, unfortunately, in the hands of his justiciar.

"You should be yourself," she reassured him. "You have nothing to hide." She congratulated herself for keeping her suspicions about his father's death to herself. "The king will be glad to have a bold, brave young man like you at his side."

"Is he a knight yet?"

Ela looked at Bill Talbot, who shrugged. "I don't know if kings have to attain knighthood. I think the coronation might suffice to shower them with glory."

"Don't worry, Will," said Bill. "You'll be a knight soon enough. First let's get you married and then worry about the rest."

Once through the gates, they handed over their horses and shook out their cloaks before following a herald in through the entrance arch. Ela had brought a gift of a very expensive enameled gold drinking cup in a carved oak box, which was handed to a page.

They were welcomed by two ladies-in-waiting about the same age as Ela's oldest daughters, and their cloaks were spirited away by young pages. Then they were led into a room with a bright, painted pattern on the walls and invited to take a seat until the king was ready to greet them.

More pages brought wine and fruit and Will made conversation with the ladies-in-waiting, to the point where Ela was getting ready to scold him and remind him they were here to secure his marriage arrangements.

She assumed they'd be summoned into another room, perhaps even the formal throne room, to meet the king. She almost dropped her cup of wine when the young king walked right up to her, took her right hand and kissed her fingers. "Countess Ela. What a pleasure."

"Your majesty." Ela bowed her head. "Thank you for meeting with us." She introduced Will, who did a reasonable facsimile of a polite bow, and Bill Talbot, whose manners were unfailingly perfect to the occasion. "As you know we're here to formally request permission—"

"I read your letters and I see no objection to either

marriage. The crown is delighted for the association between these noble families to continue." Ela felt a tiny weight lift in her heart. "May I speak to you privately?"

Ela blinked. "Of course." She fought the urge to glance at Bill Talbot and followed the king out of that room into another brightly decorated chamber. They walked through that room and into another, which contained carved wooden chairs, a table with two grand silver candlesticks on it—and Hubert de Burgh.

Ela felt the blood drain from her face…and her heart.

De Burgh was a tall man with a long, angular face that some thought handsome. In middle age he still had the muscular body of a younger man and his dark hair had gray only at the temples. He regarded her with a cool ease that was distinctly unnerving.

"I believe you know my justiciar?" asked Henry.

"Yes." said Ela as calmly as she could. The king already knew the answer. He'd tried to broker the truce between de Burgh and her husband after his role in the outrageous marriage proposal. Ela could still hardly believe that the king had granted permission for de Burgh's young nephew to ask for her hand when William was missing overseas. It was all de Burgh's doing, of course. "Most recently he attended the assizes at Salisbury."

"Ela was bravely filling the role of sheriff in her husband's absence," said de Burgh.

An absence created by his untimely death at your hands.

"The trials went smoothly and justice was served," she said quickly. "I look forward to serving the king as sheriff of Wiltshire in the future."

Ela hated how fast everything was moving. Her entire pretext for being here was dismissed in just a few words. And now this? She'd hoped for time to lay a soft mattress of pleasantries and familial remembrances to drop her hard requests on.

"It's not customary for a woman to serve as sheriff," said Henry. "Women cannot serve as jurors."

"Perhaps women should serve as jurors," she replied, already hating the direction of this conversation. She didn't want her fate lumped in with that of all women. "We often have insight into local matters and access to a network of conversations that's outside the reach of men."

The young king seemed to consider her words. She could see the family resemblance to her husband in his height and clear, thoughtful gaze. He had brown hair, though, not blond. He also had a serious, almost monkish air that distinguished him from men of action like her husband and her son Will.

"Women have the important duties of their household to occupy them," said the king. "Few can spare the time to participate in public matters."

Ela was very tired of this argument. "Young women with babies are busy, certainly, but the elders among us—and I include myself in this group—have both the time and hard-earned wisdom to serve effectively as jurors and in many other capacities."

Henry paused for a moment, and the hint of a frown creased his wide brow. "Yourself excepted, my lady, it's an accepted fact that women do not have the penetration of men in serious matters."

Ela felt a surge of frustration, and she worked hard to keep her expression neutral. "Many ordinary men lack the capacity to understand complicated matters relating to justice, and some women possess a keen intelligence that few could rival." She didn't intend to populate the hundred with every dairymaid in Wiltshire, nor suggest that any empty-headed noblewoman could be a sheriff. "Do you not think that the best minds of the country should be put into the service of your majesty and his subjects?"

She wondered if she was becoming forthright to the point of insolence. No doubt she sounded arrogant and self-aggrandizing including herself among the best minds. Henry's face revealed nothing of his true thoughts.

De Burgh started laughing. "I'm just imagining the hundred, filled with pastry cooks and serving maids and housewives, all gossiping and carrying on and tittering over the details."

"Are you picturing me among their number?" said Ela quietly, her fury barely controlled. "In this humorous scene?"

"Of course not, my lady. You are distinguished from the mass of women by your birth, your education and your upbringing."

"I believe I have all the qualities required to be sheriff of Wiltshire. I have sat at my husband's right hand these many years while he's executed the business of the county so I have considerable experience in the matters at hand. More than anyone else in Wiltshire, I dare say."

"The countess makes a compelling argument," said Henry. "I'm inclined to agree with her."

"You think we should put women on juries?" De Burgh looked astonished to the point of mockery. "That any woman could be a sheriff?"

"Not ordinary women. No." Henry's youth and insecurity flashed in his eyes. "But educated, noble women such as Ela are an entirely different matter."

Ela debated mentioning Nicola de la Haye's role in Lincoln but decided against it. The situation was complicated by Ela's own husband's repeated effort to curtail Nicola's powers, and now Will's impending marriage to her granddaughter. She knew she and Nicola would have a lot to talk about if they found a few quiet moments together.

"I thank you for your consideration. It was thoughtful of you to install a new sheriff while I'm in mourning and recovering from my husband's shocking and untimely death—" She couldn't resist a cold glance at de Burgh.

He didn't flinch.

"—But I look forward to serving the people of Salisbury in the near future."

"Let us raise a toast to the future. And to the excellent marriages of two of your children," said Henry. His confidence was back. An elegantly dressed young page poured them all a cup of spiced wine. Ela drank, hoping it wasn't poisoned. Henry III was young and had time to become a great king, God willing.

The conversation turned to pleasantries at last, and Ela chattered easily about people they both knew and Will's love of tournaments and hunting. She brought up her other children who were approaching marriageable age, inviting suggestions of good matches for them.

They parted with affection, and she was returned to Will and Bill Talbot. Then they were all ushered into the great dining hall to enjoy the king's hospitality.

Ela made conversation with the other nobles there, accepting their condolences on her great loss. Will was introduced as a worthy opponent on the tournament grounds—much to his delight—and he quickly made himself a favorite with the ladies-in-waiting.

The king was in and out of the room, conducting business and entertaining his guests as if the two were the same thing—which they mostly were.

~

Ela excused them in time to get back to her mother's house before dusk. She didn't like being abroad in London after dark. There were too many cut-purses and vagabonds.

Back outside the palace gates, Will let out a large sigh. "That went well! I half expected the king to challenge me to a joust at Winchester."

"It went well because the king approved your marriage to Idonea."

"That too," said Will. "Tomorrow will we all visit Osbert Pinchbeck's shop?"

"You and I will call there," interjected Bill. "While your mother rests safely at home."

Ela shifted in her uncomfortable sidesaddle. That was the sensible approach, of course. But then a sensible woman would hardly want to be sheriff of Wiltshire, now, would she?

CHAPTER 10

After lengthy negotiations it was decided that Bill Talbot would enter the shop alone. Depending on what he found they'd plan a return foray. Ela didn't much like this, but all three of them going at once was too cumbersome and Will, ever looking for some action to run headlong into, refused to be left outside by himself.

The shop itself was in a seedy neighborhood close to the river. The river here was wide and deep enough for a large ship to bring any goods right into the center of the city. Pinchbeck docking his goods many miles away at Exmouth and driving them over the roads into London would have seemed madness if she and Haughton hadn't learned that the goods weren't what they seemed.

They left the house on foot and walked the mile or so along increasingly smoky and crowded lanes, until they came near. Then Ela and Will peeled off to waste time in the open-air market while Bill Talbot called in at Pinchbeck's shop.

Ela had deliberately worn a plain-looking cloak that wouldn't draw attention to her as a woman of rank. Will unfortunately stood head and shoulders above the crowd and with his bright gold curls, flashing blue eyes and long sword, drew attention from all quarters. She managed to keep him busy at the spice stalls, where she bought small quantities of spices for the kitchen at Gomeldon. She was just purchasing a few lengths of embroidered ribbon for her daughters, when Bill Talbot appeared at her shoulder.

She paid quickly and moved away from the stall. "What news?" Curiosity burned her.

Talbot's expression was odd. "The shop was near empty. Just a few odds and ends. Some of those cheap flutes and a few flimsy birdcages, some low-quality cooking pots. The shelves were almost bare."

"Were there people in the shop?"

"Only an old man sitting on a stool in the corner. He seemed to be half blind or half deaf or both. I couldn't get any sense out of him."

"So the shop was near empty and lacking customers, which means Osbert Pinchbeck didn't kill his father." She was leaping to the imagined conclusion she'd discussed with Haughton. "Because if he had he'd be doing a brisk trade in his secret goods."

Bill's normally cheerful face creased into the closest approximation of a frown that he could make. "I think that is the intended impression..." He paused, looking over her shoulder as two young boys ran past them, shouting. "I couldn't help feeling that the shop is a facade."

"A facade?" She couldn't catch his meaning.

"A false front designed to deflect the interest of the general public and the law. The shop is in a building of three stories. I didn't see another entrance to the upper floors from the inside or the outside. The building was too large to be a likely home for one man living alone. I suspect that if I could have got past the hoary guard, hunched on his stool, that I would have found myself in the bowels of Pinchbeck's true business."

"Ah." The same two boys came running back, jostling her hard as they ran past.

"Have a care!" yelled Will after them. "Did they cut your purse?"

Ela checked her bag, which now bulged with spices and ribbon. "No. But we shouldn't stand around here on the street waiting for someone to try. Let's deposit my purchases at home and formulate a plan to gain entry to Pinchbeck's lair."

THEY SAT in the front parlor of her mother's house, eating just-bought hot meat pies and trading ideas. Bill had convinced them there might be a room upstairs for customers to enjoy a trance induced by the poppy resin. "The opium deprives a man of his senses as well as his pain. They'd need somewhere quiet to enjoy it, where they're not at risk of being robbed or otherwise disturbed." He'd heard of such places—not in England but in port cities overseas—from soldiers he'd known.

"I can go," protested Will. "I'll pretend to be a knight with a painful injury to my—" He frowned, no doubt struggling to imagine a part of his body in anything but perfect condition.

"To your pride," scolded Ela. "No one would believe for one second that you aren't at the peak of fitness. You positively glow with health and high spirits." Bill Talbot laughed and agreed.

She sighed with frustration. "And even I can see that I can't go. Pinchbeck's secret society of opium eaters is not likely a place for women. At least not women of my age and station." It was entirely possible that unfortunate women were also there to be served—along with the blissful resin—for additional profit. "Bill Talbot will have to revert to his career as a master of disguise."

"Which will be challenging since the old man—who probably isn't blind or deaf in the slightest—had ample opportunity to examine me and find me unsuitable."

"Perhaps I could pretend to be a man." She could see Talbot was ready to protest, so she held up her hand. "I'm not suggesting that I go alone. And Will sticks out too much to attempt a disguise. But if I were, say, a small, wizened man, and you were my companion, he'd be less likely to peg you as the same person who came in earlier."

Bill Talbot still looked like he wanted to crush the idea under his foot. "These places attract unsavory people. It would be dangerous."

"Childbirth is dangerous, and I've survived it eight times. I won't speak, so he won't hear my female voice. You can tell him I'm mute or foreign."

Bill looked skeptical. "Where would we obtain our disguises? We could hardly go in the fine clothes we brought to meet the king."

"I'm sure Will could procure us some dismal rags for a few pennies. What do you think, Will?" She didn't want to leave him out altogether. She knew his youthful pride would smart at that.

He brightened. "Certainly. I've heard Londoners will sell the clothes right off their backs for the right coin."

"Then we can pretend to be a pair of old sailors who've fallen into the arms of this sweet escape and crave it like the devil craves sin." Ela hated to admit she was getting unreasonably excited at the prospect of this plan. "We can say we heard of the place from a fellow shipmate."

"And if they ask his name we'll call him—" Bill Talbot frowned.

"Will, or Bill or Liam—" said Ela quite seriously. "The inhabitants of this room alone can agree that half the men of our time are christened William." She giggled. She felt almost like an opium eater already in her craving to gain entrance to their private lair.

Will laughed. "Why did you call me William, then?"

"So you could walk in your father's shoes."

"My mother did the same," agreed Bill with a chuckle. "And it is a fine name." Then his chuckle faded. "Still, this is a terrible idea. I consider it my duty to keep you safe, so I must advise you against—"

"Silence!" said Ela. "Do you dare to contradict your countess? Would you not march into battle at my command?"

He looked at her, probably trying to decide if she was serious. She was and she wasn't. "We're not going to actually eat the resin. We're going to purchase some and gain the knowledge of what's behind the doors of Pinchbeck's establishment."

"But how does that serve the people of Salisbury?" Talbot looked sheepish for asking. "We still won't know if Osbert Pinchbeck killed his father."

"A murder investigation is not like a tournament where you win or lose with one thrust of the lance. It's a delicate, multilayered operation like the baking of a pie."

"It's not fair that I can't come." Sometimes Will acted like a three-year-old.

"You already have an important role." She reached into her purse. "Make sure the clothes are close enough to the right size that they'll look convincing." She handed him the money, and he tucked it into the purse on his belt. "And don't get robbed."

Ela finished the meal and wrote a letter to the king thanking him for his time and flattering him for his wisdom and insight into the nation's affairs. He hadn't mentioned the fine enameled gold cup she'd brought, so she said she hoped he'd enjoy it. At least then he might inquire about it and actually see it. Otherwise the cup might disappear into a courtier's household. She'd send him another expensive present once she returned home and thought of the right one. She was dripping wax on the letter when Will returned, ebullient, with an armful of grimy clothing.

Bill Talbot took the garments from him and spread them out on the table.

"I got two different costumes. The larger blue one is for Bill, and this brown one with the hood is for Mama."

"Goodness, it does reek," said Ela. The mud-colored linen was stained with perspiration and had a smell that could wake the dead.

"It looks like something an old sailor would wear," said Will proudly.

"True indeed," agreed Bill.

Both robes had sleeves frayed from wear and ragged hems. "I bought them off two urchins," said Will. "Both about my age. I would have bought their hose and shoes if they had any. I had to buy those separately at the market, but I found old, well-worn ones."

Ela tried the scuffed baggy leather shoes on over her own well-fitted ones. "These will do."

They dressed, then obscured their features with a light dusting of soot from the fireplace, which also served to make Ela's lack of facial hair less obvious. Sibel—who had stood by silently wringing her hands over every aspect of this plan—helped coil and pin Ela's long hair under a greasy brown linen cap, then pulled the hood over it.

"I hope you don't catch fleas from this garb. I shan't take a breath until you get back safely," said Sibel as she surveyed her handiwork. "But I trust Master Talbot to take care of you."

The stockings were loose enough to hide the outline of her legs, but Ela still felt strangely naked with her calves exposed beneath her knee-length tunic. But who looked at a man's legs? And today, she was a man. "I shall wear a knife at my belt as well," she replied. "It'll make me look more convincingly male."

"You've proved you know how to use a knife," said Bill. Then he reddened. "I'm sorry. You probably don't want to be reminded—"

"It's fine and a true fact. Show me how to attach Will's knife to my belt."

Sibel crossed herself and muttered a short prayer for their safety.

OUTSIDE ELA FELT EXPOSED by the bright daylight. "How do I look?" she whispered. Bill shot a sideways glance at her. "Disreputable." He winked.

"Excellent." She'd applied the soot looking in the mirror. Just enough to settle into the fine lines around her eyes and mouth and obscure the feminine smoothness of her skin. It made her look ten years older and ten times uglier. "I don't feel like myself at all."

"You certainly don't look like yourself."

"You don't either." Bill was usually a fine dresser, choosing clothes that draped elegantly over his well-toned body. He rarely covered his crown of thick, lightly-silvered gold-brown hair, which was now hidden under a grubby linen cap. "If I didn't know you, I'd worry you might cut my throat."

"Perfect."

They walked slowly up the grim, sunless street to Pinchbeck's shop, with its crudely painted sign and the scarred door with three different locks on it. The front door opened readily and they walked into the dim interior, which was just as Bill described it, with a few odds and ends and the old man apparently dozing on his stool.

"We'd like to buy some," said Bill brusquely, in the language and accent of Somerset.

The old man's gaze snapped up at him. "Some what? Some flutes? Some birdcages?" His voice was a crusty snarl.

"We heard about this place from an old shipmate. We're lately from the port of Venice. We seek the sweet relief of the poppy juice." He whispered the last bit with a plaintive tone that would have touched her heart if she didn't know he was lying.

"Wait here." The old man rose slowly from his stool—he did appear to be old—and shuffled toward the door. He rapped on it and muttered something unintelligible. Someone must have been on the far side, because the door immediately opened even though he wasn't touching it.

Ela's curiosity burned hard as the door creaked open—and revealed Osbert Pinchbeck.

Her breath caught in her throat. *It's his shop. Of course he's here.* Had she not expected to see him?

Pinchbeck stepped into the doorway and surveyed them both with his hooded eyes. "You look familiar."

Ela held her breath.

"Ay," said Bill. "That we might be. Been here there and everywhere over the years." Ela wondered where he learned to do the Somerset dialect so well. "We have silver." Ela hoped that was the password for entry. It usually was.

Pinchbeck turned and walked from the doorway. Bill followed and Ela stepped through after him, heart pounding.

She heard the door close behind them, and Pinchbeck led them up a steep, narrow flight of wooden stairs.

Ela steadied herself with a hand on the wall as she climbed. The interior of the building was so dark she could barely see. And the smell! The air reeked of unwashed feet, greasy rags and the malodorous cooked resin.

As Ela's eyes adjusted to the gloomy interior of the second floor, she startled at the sight of two men half sitting and half lying on a pallet in the corner, eyes closed like they were asleep…or dead. The only light in the room came from what appeared to be a fist-sized hole in the wall up near the low ceiling. There was no fire.

"You want to take it here, or buy it to go with you?"

"Here," said Bill. Ela's gut clenched. She wanted to stay and observe, but her flesh crawled with discomfort in this dark, mean place. The men who frequented this place were likely sailors or traveling mercenaries or the like who'd picked the habit up overseas. With no permanent home in London, they'd need a quiet place where they'd be free from molestation while they slipped into a poppy-induced trance.

Pinchbeck walked to a ladder in the back of the room. "Climb up. It's more comfortable upstairs."

Bill waited for Ela to go first. His knightly manners wouldn't allow anything else. She gripped the ladder, silently praying she wouldn't reveal her gender. It didn't help that she had the fine, pale hands of a lady, though she'd wisely smudged them with soot to conceal their contours. She climbed as quickly and confidently as she could, considering that she hadn't climbed five ladders in her whole life.

Bill wisely followed close behind her, shielding her from Pinchbeck's gaze. She emerged through the floor of the room above, which was far brighter, since it had a glass window, dingy with soot, and a small fire that took the edge off the cold air. A flimsy table and two mismatched wood chairs sat in the middle of the room. A man lay slumped in one corner, apparently fast asleep like the ones below.

"You can sit at the table or over there on the bed." He gestured to an empty pallet covered with a frayed blanket. Ela headed for the table. That would at least harbor fewer fleas. Pinchbeck named the price per ounce. It was enough to buy a meal for two with good wine at the best inn on the London road.

"We'll take half an ounce," said Bill. Ela struggled to keep her eyes focused on Bill or the table. She longed to peer around and take in the details.

"Your friend a mute?" said Pinchbeck drily, as he turned to unlock a small door in the wall near the fireplace.

"Doesn't speak English," muttered Bill. They both watched Pinchbeck go through the door and close it behind him. He returned a moment later with a tiny lump of the black resin sitting in his none-too-clean palm.

Ela's gut recoiled. She hoped she could manage to pretend to eat the substance and not actually ingest it.

Bill, ever confident, handed the required coins and broke off a small piece of the resin. Pinchbeck brought a malodorous and half-used unlit tallow candle to the table and mumbled that he could soften the resin with a flame if he wanted. He produced a flint and a dented spoon and offered them, but withdrew them when neither of them moved to take them.

"You do look familiar." Pinchbeck's voice grated on her already pricked nerves. "I could swear I know you from somewhere."

Ela tried to gaze vacantly at something, hoping he'd think her an imbecile or damaged by war. Bill just shrugged. He used his thumbnail to peel off a small section of the resin. He looked at it for a moment, sniffed it, then put it in his mouth.

Pinchbeck watched intently. Ela could feel herself

growing dizzy as if she'd already eaten the potent substance. She reminded herself to breathe.

Bill stayed motionless for a moment as if he was transfixed by the experience, then he nodded slowly. "'Tis fine for sure."

Pinchbeck's face creased into an oily smile. "It's the best. From the poppy fields of Ghandhara. You won't find anything like it in England."

Ela knew it was her turn. She avoided looking at Bill in case his expression might cause her to lose her composure. She picked off a bit of the resin with her fingernail, as Bill had done. As she raised her thumb to her mouth, she weighed the risks versus the benefits of trying this strange new substance.

She decided to somehow hide it in her hand. Her fatherless children needed their mother without her brain addled. But with Pinchbeck's cold, beady eyes staring right at her—already filled with suspicion—she knew she must at least appear to eat it.

She stuck it under her tongue, hoping it would have less effect down there, then sat back in the chair as Bill had done.

"Sweet dreaming!" said Pinchbeck, like a creepy court jester. "I'll leave you to it." He took the candle, flint and spoon back into the other room. Ela wondered what you were supposed to do with them. Maybe inhale the foul vapors as it melted? The air was already heavy with the scent.

Pinchbeck locked up that room and headed back down the ladder with only a surreptitious glance at them.

Ela heaved a silent sigh of relief that he was gone. She snuck a peek at the man in the corner. His eyes were closed, but he might still be a spy. She executed a small fake cough and tried to remove the resin from her mouth. It had already half dissolved but a small black speck emerged and she shoved it into her sleeve.

Bill's eyes had a strange shine to them, and his cheeks looked flushed as if he'd been running.

"Are you all right?" she whispered. She glanced again at the stranger in the room with them. His chest rose and fell beneath his rough brown tunic in the slow, steady rhythm of a sleeper.

"Yes." He looked at her as if seeing her for the first time.

Ela did not find his answer convincing. *Do I feel all right?* The light from the window seemed brighter, to the point where she found herself squinting at it. She couldn't say the room was spinning, but it wasn't exactly rock still either. She gripped the table with one hand to steady herself.

"Maybe we should go," he whispered, looking through her rather than at her.

"Won't that seem odd?" she whispered back.

"What else will we learn?" He blinked slowly a few times. "I do feel a bit strange. Like everything is…melting."

Ela wasn't sure what they might learn, but they would learn it only by staying and they'd come this far. She didn't want to leave yet. But she didn't want Bill to become incapacitated and reveal himself or her to anyone. "We can go if you need to."

He put both hands on the table—which revealed its flimsiness by tipping as he tried to stand. Ela, stopped it falling to the floor. At that moment she heard footsteps on the ladder. She shot a meaningful look at Bill, and he half collapsed back in his chair.

A man's head appeared where the ladder entered through the floor. He had dark, oily curls and dark eyes with thick lashes. He climbed out, standing quite tall, and Ela half expected him to offer words of polite greeting to them, but he didn't. He simply looked at them as if they were sheep in a field.

More footsteps on the ladder brought the long narrow

head of Osbert Pinchbeck back into view. Pinchbeck crossed the room without acknowledging them and unlocked the door again with a key from his belt. Then both went in and the door closed.

The light from the window seemed to have stretched and to be reaching toward her like a long finger of accusation. She shifted her chair to avoid its bright touch. She was still gripping the table, knuckles white beneath the thin layer of soot. She tried to let go of the table but found the floor unsteady beneath her.

The oddness of it all made her chest tighten, and she found her breath coming in shallower and shallower gasps. Bill was now slumped forward with his head in his hands. Did he still want to leave? Now might be a good time, with Pinchbeck engaged in conversation. She could hear voices through the door but couldn't make out the words.

Until one.

Fernlees.

CHAPTER 11

The word seared into her mind. Had she really heard it or just thought it? She pricked her ears. Their words were muffled by the wall—or the opium scrambling her brain—and she couldn't tell one from another. The floor seemed to be tilting like the deck of a ship and Ela pressed one foot into it to steady herself. Why would anyone take this poppy resin willingly? It wasn't a pleasant sensation.

Bill still held his head in his hands and suddenly started to rock back and forth in his chair. It was a sturdy chair but no match for Bill's height and weight as they thrust against it. It tipped back and fell to the floor with a hideous thud, and Bill with it.

Ela leapt to her feet. "Are you hurt?" She quite forgot to hide her voice, then froze in regret at the sound of it aloud.

The door creaked open, and Pinchbeck's head thrust out. He stared at Bill—with no sign of care or concern—then at her. "Don't break the furniture or you'll pay for it."

Ela nodded, praying he hadn't heard her speak. He closed the door again. Ela knelt over Bill, who was now writhing on the dusty wood floor, rolling from side to side, his head in his hands. If he was badly hurt he seemed unable to tell her.

What had she been thinking to bring him to such a sinister hovel and actually eat opium? She'd been enticed by the adventure without thought for the consequences. What if his brain was permanently addled, or if he'd broken himself in the fall?

The sleeping man in the corner had stirred when the chair crashed back. Now he was muttering something unintelligible to himself while staring at Ela. Ela strained to hear the conversation on the other side of the door over his ramblings.

Thomas Blount.

The sound of those two words jolted her, and her eyes swiveled to the door. Did she hear the name or just imagine it? She'd half forgotten about Thomas Blount. Or that there were two Thomas Blounts, one sometimes called Drogo. Who was the other one and why did he call himself the same name? Her brain couldn't seem to follow one thought properly into another.

The ceiling was getting lower all the time. Any minute it might touch the top of her head, and then it would start to crush her. She crouched to avoid it pressing down upon her.

Bill's chest rose and fell unsteadily and he too was now muttering to himself—something about fine new ale for the king's men.

Ela's heart pounded. This was rapidly turning into a disaster. Any minute Bill was going to reveal himself as a knight or call her by her real name. Then Pinchbeck would know they were there to spy on him and—

The door opened again, and Pinchbeck and the curly-haired man emerged. Pinchbeck's face looked drawn and she saw his hand tremble as he locked the door. The darker man crossed the room with a disdainful glance at poor Bill, who lay squirming on the floor murmuring about casks of salted meat. Pinchbeck followed with small, agitated steps.

Ela averted her eyes and pretended to be preoccupied by visions as they descended the ladder. Once they reached the bottom she strained to hear their conversation. "—A twelvemonth at most. By then it will all be forgotten." The second man's voice was deep and had an unsettling tone that set Ela's teeth on edge. "Then you can take up as lord of the manor."

She heard a door open downstairs. Likely the one to the shop where the old man sat on his stool.

Bill had stopped muttering and now lay on the filthy plank floor with his mouth open and a trickle of spittle falling from his mouth. Ela felt deep regret at putting him in this position. Clearly the potent resin was having a far greater effect on him because he hadn't managed to spit it out.

She hoped he wouldn't now become a slave to its power and crave it tomorrow and the next day as well. She still couldn't fathom how someone could want to be felled by this strange substance. She shot a glance at the other man and was appalled to see that he now stared at her with wide open eyes.

She stared back for a moment, unsure if he was deliberately watching her or if she just happened to be in front of his blank, thoughtless stare. *I've had enough.* Mild desperation gripped her. But how could she rouse Bill off the floor, especially without speaking? Her voice would betray her as a woman.

She knelt over him, tugging at his shoulder. He started to babble again, something about the art of the swordsman. Again, Ela stole a glance at their companion and met his ghoulish stare.

Maybe she could run home and fetch Will and a servant

to carry Bill out of here? But it was unlikely she could do that without betraying their identity at least on their return, and Bill was too vulnerable to leave alone. He might say anything and get himself killed before she could come back.

After weighing the good and bad she decided it was safest to wait there for the resin to work its way through his body. But how long would that take?

IT WAS full dark when the other man slowly rose and left. He'd tried to ask Ela for money, but she pretended not to hear and he eventually climbed shakily down the ladder. She relaxed for a moment, glad to be released from his unyielding gaze.

Bill still lay sprawled on the floor. She could barely see him as clouds obscured the moon, the fire had burned out, and there was no other source of light. "Bill!" She knelt on the floor and shook him. "Wake up! We have to get out of here."

She wondered if Pinchbeck was still below. She'd heard voices from time to time as a customer came and went. She was about to peer down through the hole in the floor, into the grim, windowless space below, when she heard a door open, footsteps on the stairs, and several voices emerged into the space below.

"Bill!" she hissed, right in his ear. "Can you hear me?"

His eyes flickered open, and he looked at her. Her heart surged with hope, which ebbed somewhat as he stared at her, uncomprehending.

The ladder creaked under the weight of feet. Ela crept back to her chair and hung her head in her hands so they couldn't get a good look at her if they brought tapers. Her confidence in her male disguise had waned as she sat here hour after hour able to reflect on how different she looked from Bill and the other opium eater.

She avoided glancing up as heavy feet clumped across the floor. "One down I see," exclaimed one of them in crude London speech. She winced when he kicked Bill with his toe as he walked past.

The men talked loud, as if they were already drunk, and seemed familiar with the place. They went and flopped down on a pallet in one corner, and Pinchbeck followed them up. He passed through the room and unlocked the door again—this must be where he kept his stash of opium—and emerged in a few moments with another wrapped lump.

They must have discussed quantities and costs as there was no discussion or exchange of money; they simply each broke off a piece and ate it, still talking in such crude slang-laden speech that she could barely catch the gist of it.

Ela watched surreptitiously, waiting for them to fall into the drugged stupor she now expected. They didn't, though. They continued to talk rapidly in an incomprehensible mix of dialects. Pinchbeck tried to leave to go downstairs, but they called him back with shouts and rough taunts, and he came—white faced and clearly unsettled—back into the room, where he stood awkwardly watching them.

Ela wondered why he hovered at their beck and call. Were they simply good customers or did they have some hold over him? She wanted to sneak a better look at them, which was hard since they were seated almost behind her. She went around the table and crouched on the floor, trying again to wake Bill. She looked up at the men—and was horrified to see all four of them staring straight at her.

"Who the feck are these eejets?" asked a man with stringy pale hair. The other two at the table laughed.

"Sailors," said Pinchbeck sheepishly. "New customers."

"Mewling newborn babes from the looks of it," said a man

with straggly reddish hair and a missing front tooth. "What ship are you on?" His question had a taunting leer to it, as if he knew there was no ship and never had been.

Ela decided to remain mute. Bill stirred and stared at her, then—at last!—struggled to his elbows and eased himself up off the floor.

"What vessel are you on, sailor?" called the third man, older, with a weathered brown face.

Bill Talbot half crawled back into the chair with a look of great concentration on his face and slowly said the name of a ship that Ela recognized as one of the late King John's personal vessels. She wished she could close her eyes and disappear.

"That one's been sunk nigh on ten years. Went down in the straits of Gibraltar in a storm. Try again landlubber!" called the red-haired one. "Why are you lying?" He glanced back at Pinchbeck. "Did you know your customer's a liar?"

Pinchbeck blinked and looked hard at Ela and Bill. Ela felt the blood draining from her skin as his eyes raked over her face and down her ill-fitting garments. "I could swear on my life I've seen you somewhere else."

"We must go," managed Bill, rising unsteadily to his feet. His chair scraped noisily on the floor.

"What? Just when we're all becoming friends?" said the fair man. "Join us for another morsel of the devil's sweetmeats." He held up the dark lump that lay on a cloth in front of them. The others laughed.

Ela was on her feet and ready to take a step toward the ladder.

"Sir William Talbot," said Pinchbeck suddenly. He stared at Bill, transfixed. "I didn't know you at first in those rough clothes and with that layer of grime, but now I recognize you. We're neighbors in Salisbury. I have a manor nearby."

Ela's heart clenched. Now she did take a step toward the ladder.

"I have a manor nearby!" The first man mocked Pinchbeck's tone and accent. "Wish I had a bloody manor."

"You deserve a manor, mate," said the redhead.

"I do and all."

Ela looked from one to the other.

"What are you doing here?" asked Pinchbeck, who looked as confused as she felt.

"I must go," murmured Bill, still drugged and drowsy. Gripping the back of the chair he took a lumbering step toward the hole in the floor.

"Not so fast, mate." The leathery-skinned man was soon up on his feet. "*Sir* William Talbot? Are you a knight?"

"He looks like a bloody knight," exclaimed the redhead. "Tall as a bloody oak."

The oldest man now had his fingers pressing into Talbot's chest—which Ela thought was bold in the extreme since Talbot was a head taller than him and they'd already established that he was a trained fighter. The man had a wiry energy, a sense of coiled menace, that further chilled and alarmed her.

"If you're a knight, then where's your sword?" taunted the man. Before Bill had time to react, he'd pulled Bill's dagger from his sheath and held it in his hand, examining it.

Bill's eyes grew wide. He was clearly still struggling to stand and focus, and wasn't able to react appropriately. Ela had a horrible feeling in the pit of her stomach. If he could just laugh and tell them that he couldn't be a perfect knight every day. But his brain was addled and his reflexes gone. Frustration welled inside her that she couldn't even try to talk their way out of this.

"And what of you, little sailor?" mocked the leather-skinned man. "You aren't a knight. You don't look like you could lift a sword or hoist a yardarm." He peered at her.

Ela tried to take a step toward the ladder, but he grabbed her tunic and held it roughly, then spun her around to face him. "Don't you know it's rude to leave when someone's talking to you?" he asked as if deadly serious. Crude amusement shone in his eyes.

He looked down at her chest. His fist clutching her tunic had pulled it tight, revealing the outline of her small breasts.

"Well, well, well. What have we here?" He put a hand over her left breast, cupping it.

"Unhand me!" She heard the high-pitched sound of her voice echo off the smoke-stained walls as she elbowed him hard in the chest.

"A woman!" He yelled it. "Well, there's only kind of woman you'll find in a place like this, and this here is a feisty one! How many kisses for a penny? Will that buy me the whole night?"

Her nerves jangled. What the hell was Bill doing, or rather not doing? Had he lost his wits altogether?

"Won't answer me, eh? Sir Knight, how much for your woman?" he mocked. "She's not a pretty one. Older and looks unclean."

Ela wasn't sure what happened next but the result was that the wizened man lay writhing on the floor, clutching his mouth, and Ela felt Bill's arm firm around her waist, carrying her toward the ladder.

"You're Ela of Salisbury!" Pinchbeck's voice penetrated the fog of confusion and terror that clouded her brain. "Jesus save us. It's Ela of Salisbury."

Bill now had her slung over his shoulder like a sack of flour as he climbed onto the flimsy ladder. Ela gripped him tight, trying not to bang her head on the floor-ceiling as they headed down below.

The men above were yelling, the injured one wanting revenge and Pinchbeck pleading with him that these were not people to be trifled with, he had a business to run, etc.

Ela clung to Bill as he plunged down the flight of stairs. He kicked down the door out into the shop, knocking over the old man on his stool, plowed through the dusty, near-empty shop and out into the street. "Hold tight," he hissed. And then he ran.

~

BACK IN THE sanctuary of her mother's house, Ela steadied her nerves with wine while Sibel washed the grime from her hands and face. She'd never been so glad to dress again in her own fine clothes.

It took a while before she felt brave enough to face Bill and Will again. She'd roped them into this fool scheme. She walked into the parlor feeling more than apologetic. "Well, that was a truly terrible idea."

Neither of them spoke. Which made her feel worse.

"Are you recovered, my lady?" said Bill at last.

"I'm fine," she lied. "It's you I'm worried about. I regret exposing you to that evil substance."

"It certainly had a more powerful effect than I anticipated. I don't really remember what happened until I found myself hitting the man who insulted you."

"They all know who I am." Ela felt hollow. "Pinchbeck said my name aloud. I wonder how long it will be until all Salisbury knows I was dressed as a man and lounging in a den of addled sailors."

"You should have let me go instead," said Will.

"There was no need to go at all," said Ela more sharply than she intended. "What did we learn? We already knew or at least strongly suspected that Pinchbeck sold the poppy resin there. As far as I know, there's nothing overtly illegal about that."

"It's certainly illegal for him to pretend he's running a shop selling cheap flutes when he's raking in coin for selling a powerful drug. He must owe the king a great sum in unpaid taxes."

"True enough." She bit her lip. "I wonder if that's enough to keep him quiet about what he saw?"

"Perhaps I should visit again and remind him of that," said Bill.

"Don't be ridiculous. No one I care about is going near that evil place again. Those men probably cut throats for sport. Even Pinchbeck seemed wary of them. If the truth comes out it shall be punishment for my own foolishness."

"I wouldn't say it was foolish—" offered Bill, always chivalrous.

"Reckless, then. I do get so frustrated that as a woman I am doomed to only see the outside of things. I have to watch history unfold from a safe distance and instead of being a force to create it I have to be satisfied with other people's accounts of it. Why can't a woman lead an army?"

"Going into battle is overrated," said Bill. "The armor is hot, the fighting is exhausting, and you're soon hungry and thirsty and unable to relieve yourself and people keep trying to hack your limbs off. Then if you survive it you're stinking and exhausted and still several days march or even a sea voyage away from home and your bed."

Bill spoke so earnestly that she had to laugh. "I know I should celebrate the luxury of peace and safety. Still, I can't help but wonder if the sunlight looks different as it falls across the Holy Land."

"You could make a pilgrimage," said Will. "I'd be happy to attend you. We could visit Jerusalem and—"

"I'm sure the king would find it a nuisance. There's too

much conflict in those parts for his nobles to venture there for their own purposes. I don't wish to let my pride and willfulness lead me into mischief again."

"Perhaps to Rome? It's a holy land in its own right," offered Bill.

"My duties lie here." Ela resisted sighing. "Venturing overseas would be an expensive indulgence that serves no purpose but the sating of my own idle curiosity. Perhaps when all my children are grown the Lord may call me to make a pilgrimage. In the meantime, please talk me out of any more stupid ideas that pass my lips." She took a bracing sip of her wine. "We missed Compline."

"Matins isn't far off. We could all go and thank God for our deliverance." Bill looked ready to leap into action.

Ela's stomach clenched at the thought of heading out into the public streets again. "Not tonight. And you must rest. There may be lingering aftereffects of the resin. I'd like to attend Prime tomorrow if you're up to it."

"I'll make it my business to be up to it," said Bill warmly. "And Will shall be there as well."

Will didn't looked so thrilled at the prospect of leaving his bed before dawn.

"We must pray for the success of your marriage," she chided. "That's why we came to London, after all."

"I'd still like to meet Idonea beforehand. What if we hate each other?"

"What nonsense. You've met before already. Surely you remember?"

"I don't. She was probably a gangly eight-year-old and me a snot-nosed lout. I bet I pinched her or pulled her plaits or something."

"You'd never have done that," protested Bill. "I trained you to be a gentleman from when you were knee-high."

"If I did those things the blame would rest squarely with me. But surely she must want to meet me as well?"

"Not if she's a sensible girl who heeds her elders. I've heard nothing but good reports of her. Her grandmother informs me that she's as intelligent and well educated as she is beautiful."

"Her own grandma would say that, wouldn't she? Why don't we know her better if she's been Papa's ward for years?"

"It's a long story, my love." She sighed.

"Are you afraid Idonea won't like me?" Will's brow crinkled. "That she'll meet me and reject me?"

Ela's gut clenched a little. The thought had crossed her mind. For all his golden good looks and impressive physique her son did not have the keenest mind in the kingdom. Of course, he was still young and had much time to acquire gravity and wisdom. "How could she be anything but thrilled to marry the future Earl of Salisbury? And for the heir to great wealth and property to be such a tall, fine, handsome man to boot—she'll be pinching herself to see if she's dreaming."

Bill cheerfully agreed. Will looked doubtful.

"You remind me of your father at that age. She'll be as pleased and proud to be William Longespée's bride as I was. Now let's sup and get some sleep so we can attend Prime and leave for Salisbury at dawn."

Ela couldn't wait to get away from the crowded and filthy city. She missed the familiar clamor of the castle and its garrison and felt a pang of loss that they weren't heading back there.

Gomeldon was a little too quiet—rather like being buried alive—but at least she wouldn't be tempted to dress as a man or thrust herself among criminals. Or at least she hoped not.

CHAPTER 12

Back at Gomeldon, Ela found the cook in a mood. They'd arrived late at night but starving and thirsty. Cook had huffed and bustled her way through a late supper without meeting Ela's gaze, which was unsettling. Did she feel herself too important to work outside daylight hours?

The next morning Cook had banged and clattered her way angrily through preparing breakfast, and Ela had barely finished her eggs when the cook approached her at the table, wringing her hands. "May I have a private word with you, my lady?" She shot a glance at Sibel. "When you've finished dining."

Ela felt a tiny buzz of alarm. What could she have to say that Sibel shouldn't hear? Was there already dissent in her new household? "Yes. Give me a few moments, then attend me outside in the herb garden. We can discuss your needs for the kitchen."

She could see that Sibel was also alarmed by the exchange. "I can't think what I've done to cause offense, my lady."

"I'm sure you've done nothing of the sort. Perhaps it's a personal matter that she wants to keep private."

Sibel nodded and took her plate away to the kitchen.

Ela headed out to the herb garden with a sense of foreboding. She braced herself for a long list of complaints and wondered how hard it would be to find another cook capable of feeding a large household on short notice.

Newly started sprigs poked from the damp earth—mint, sage, parsley, rosemary and more—promising fragrant meals for the months to come. She breathed deep of the blossom-scented spring air and enjoyed it for a few moments before the cook came hustling toward her across the flagstone path.

"My apologies for interrupting you, my lady." She turned and glanced over her shoulder toward the kitchen door.

"What's troubling you, Mistress Hart?"

"It's that Drogo character, my lady." She rubbed her hands on her apron. "And the new girl." She pursed her lips as if she couldn't bring herself to say the next part.

Ela's heart clutched. "Is he...interfering with her?"

"Exactly! And worse yet, she's encouraging him." She shook her head so hard her wrap almost came undone. "You can imagine why I didn't want him sleeping in my kitchen."

"Surely he wouldn't try anything under your watchful eyes?"

"That may be, but even my watchful eyes need to close from time to time." Her mouth settled into a wry line.

"Of course. I'm sorry. I didn't mean to make light of the situation. I'll have words with him."

"She's a fine girl and reasonably hardworking, but looks like hers are a liability." Ela couldn't help but agree. She was rather relieved the girl was entranced by Drogo and not Will. "And he'd make no decent husband for a young girl."

"Indeed not." Drogo's prospects—without the inheritance

of Fernlees—were limited at best, dismal at worst. "And he's far too old for her."

"Old enough to be her father!" The cook shook her head again. "I still don't entirely understand what he's doing here."

"He saved my husband's life," explained Ela for what seemed like the hundredth time. She seemed to expend a lot of energy making excuses for Drogo. "In the Holy Land. I owe him a huge debt of gratitude."

"I see," said the cook, in a tone that suggested she didn't see at all. "I don't wish to be impudent, but he has the air of...of...."

"A scoundrel," said Ela softly. "And worse yet, he's a lovable scoundrel." She smiled ruefully. "Which is the most dangerous kind. Perhaps I can find him another situation, but that will take some time. In the meantime, I'll speak to him and tell him to keep his hands to himself."

"In my experience with that sort of man, your words will have as much effect as telling a fly not to bother you." The cook raised a grizzled brow.

"True enough, but my husband took his debts to his friends very seriously. I'd be doing dishonor to his memory if I turned his old comrade out on the street."

The cook said nothing.

"My husband's only been dead a few weeks," said Ela, feeling the need to explain why she might put her dead husband's wishes before those of her living household. "He died in March. I can still scarcely believe he's gone."

Her voice quavered on the last few words, and she realized that she hadn't come far in processing her grief.

"I'm so sorry, my lady. Losing a husband is a hard thing to bear. Mine's been gone nigh on fifteen year, and I still turn over at night thinking I can lay an arm on him." The cook's hazel eyes got a strange look in them that touched Ela's heart.

"My condolences on your own loss." Ela's heart suddenly felt like it had been scooped out. But life went on, and she still had to deal with all its irritating little details. "Please don't hesitate to come to me with any concerns about this situation or any other. I'll speak to Hilda as well."

~

Ela summoned Hilda into her bedchamber so they could have a heart to heart. The poor girl was trembling with fright.

"Have I caused offense, my lady? If I have I'm ever so sorry and—"

Ela hushed her. "First, you must learn not to speak to your master or mistress until you are spoken to." That was rule number one for working in a great household, but perhaps Sibel had failed to instruct her properly.

"I'm very sorry, my lady, I—"

Ela hushed her again. "I summoned you here because it's me that has something to say, not you." She smiled a little to show the girl she wasn't angry. The girl looked like she was about to start babbling again, but this time Ela held up her hand, and Hilda pressed her rosebud lips together. "The cook is concerned that you and Sir Drogo"—he was a knight after all, even if he was also a poacher—"are developing too close a relationship."

The girl colored violently, which only made her more dazzlingly beautiful. She hung her lovely head, and a thick lock of gold hair tumbled from her knotted veil.

"I can quite understand his appeal. In addition to being a brave knight, he's a charming man with a quick wit."

The girl's blush deepened, and she looked ready to effusively agree but managed to stop herself.

"He's not a husband for you, Hilda," she said firmly. "Even

if there weren't great differences in your social standing"—he was sleeping in a barn after all—"he's twice your age and has battle injuries that will affect his ability to support himself in the coming years, let alone a family. You have far better prospects than him available to you."

The girl's lips twitched.

Ela felt like congratulating her on her silence. "Do you have anything to say?"

"Well, it's just that—" She twisted her fingers together. Even her fingers were lovely. Despite their calluses they were plump and pink. "I'm worried I won't ever marry. I do want a family and children, you see." She looked up sheepishly.

"You're a young girl. You have many years ahead of you to worry about that. For now your duty is to support your family by your labors."

"But what if I never marry?" She burst out, uninvited.

Like Sibel. Ela realized what she was getting at. Did Sibel have regrets about her life? If she did she'd never expressed them. If she'd asked Ela to find her a husband, then she would have.

Wouldn't she?

Maybe Sibel was a little too good at not speaking unless she was spoken to.

"I understand your concerns, and I find it almost impossible to believe that you won't marry." She didn't want to congratulate the girl on her spectacular good looks, as that would only encourage her to have airs above her station in life. "However, I must have your word that you will avoid any liaison with Drogo Blount."

The girl chewed her lip.

"I'll be speaking to him as well. If he can't maintain a respectable distance from you I'm afraid he'll have to leave the household, which will make his position in life most precarious. He owes a debt to a local landowner." She wasn't sure how much the girl or her other staff knew about his poaching difficulty, and she didn't want to spread rumors.

"I understand," she said in a tiny whisper. "I'm sorry for causing trouble."

"You've certainly troubled Cook, and I'd appreciate it if you would apologize to her when you have a private moment with her."

The girl looked like she'd rather die, but she nodded.

"Thank you. I know Sibel is happy to have you here and Sibel's happiness is very important to me."

"Thank you, my lady. I'm grateful for the opportunity."

ELA FOUND DROGO OUTSIDE, chatting with the boy hired to protect the sheep from loose dogs and poachers.

"Master Blount, may I speak with you?"

"Yes, my lady." He sprang up, enthusiastic and cheerful as always, though he did finish his conversation with the boy as he turned to walk toward her. "A fine day, is it not?"

"Fine enough, but I have a serious matter to discuss."

"Oh?" He looked infuriatingly unconcerned.

She turned to walk through the apple orchard that had recently been pruned hard, leaving the trees with jagged dark stumps jutting among their pale buds.

"Cook says you've been flirting with Hilda Biggs."

"That old woman wouldn't know flirting if it had her by the throat. I've just been helping the girl settle in by being friendly with her."

Irritation flared in her chest. "I've spoken to Hilda myself. She flushed crimson and all but admitted she intended to marry you."

"Marry me!" He let out a burst of laughter. "The poor girl must be lacking sense."

"Indeed. I told her to let go of that delusion." She felt a bit cruel saying it. No doubt he'd been married before at some point—or had he? Perhaps he'd just left a trail of broken hearts from England to the Holy Land and back.

"Because a knight and a kitchen maid are too far apart?"

Now Ela laughed. "That was hardly my reasoning. A beautiful young girl with her whole life ahead of her and a grizzled and half-worn-out man of battle are too far apart. At least for her happiness." She didn't rub it in about him being penniless and an accused poacher.

"Aye. 'Tis true. My wife was a serving maid, though." He smiled warmly. "Lovely girl, as pretty as Hilda—maybe more so!"

So he was married. "Where is she now?"

"Died in childbirth when we'd been married less than a year."

"May God rest her soul." Ela crossed herself. "That must have been devastating. Did the child live?"

"Ay, my son John went to live with my mother in Wiltshire. Would have been nice if I had an estate to leave him, but as it is I can't even afford to pay for him to train as a knight."

"You could train him yourself."

"Aye, if I could find means to support myself at the same time."

Ela debated the wisdom of finding his son a place in her household and quickly scolded herself for the indulgence. "We seem to have departed from our topic. You must keep away from Hilda."

"That'll be hard since I dine in the kitchen with the servants." His oddly hopeful gaze made her realize with a jolt that he was angling for an invitation to dine with her in the parlor.

He has brass balls, that's for sure. Her husband's remembered expression gave her a little frisson of sadness. "I'm sure you'll manage. You're here very much on a trial basis. Simon de Hal will be glad of the chance to try you for poaching if you don't wish to keep your position here."

She doubted Simon de Hal would care one way, or the other but it was hard to focus Drogo's mind. She didn't want him to think that her affection for him as her husband's savior gave him a free pass to treat her household as his harem.

No doubt he'd got that other serving girl into trouble back then and been forced to marry her. She didn't intend for such a misfortune to befall Sibel's beloved niece.

"I'll behave myself," he said wryly, looking out from beneath the lock of hair that hung over his gray-green eyes. "Cross my heart." He placed a none-too-clean hand across his heart.

"Since you are a knight I know I can take your word as your bond," she said hopefully. "How are the new litter of piglets faring?"

AFTER A FEW DAYS BACK HOME, Ela found herself growing restless. Gomeldon was now up and running, the mildew scrubbed from its walls, the chimneys drawing well, the gardens planted and the pond stocked with fish.

The cook wasn't the warmest character and seemed to scold Hilda more than necessary, but the new girl was still learning the routines and would soon settle in. Sibel was pleased to have her there, able to earn money to support her family.

Deprived of a great household to run, her civic duties wrested from her, her husband gone forever and her children busy with their own pursuits, Ela found herself itching to head to the castle. For one thing, Simon de Hal should be aware that a man living under his jurisdiction—and lately questioned in the murder of his own father—was engaged in peddling opium to a crowd of unsavory customers, and hiding his profits by disguising the true nature of his business.

But now she worried that Osbert Pinchbeck might tell de Hal how he'd discovered her there in a compromising position. She tried many times to imagine explaining her actions in a way that could salvage her reputation, but no matter how she twisted the tale she was still dressed in a man's hose and meddling in matters that were no longer her official business.

After much handwringing and no little prayer, she decided to ride to Fernlees to meet with Osbert Pinchbeck. The man who brought the wood said he'd just delivered a large load there and seen a wagon of goods and furnishings being unloaded, so it was fair to assume that Pinchbeck was back in residence.

She took Bill Talbot along as her escort so she wouldn't risk revealing her secret to one of her guards. Bill also had reason to fear exposure, since he'd lain on the floor in the throes of the poppy resin and quite taken leave of his senses.

He expressed some reservations as they rode in view of the manor.

Ela slowed Freya to a walk. "We're not going to *bribe* him. We're going to...offer an inducement to silence."

"An inducement involving coin?"

She did have a small purse concealed under her cloak, but she certainly didn't need to add accusations of bribery to the words that could be spoken against her. "I haven't entirely decided what we're going to do. I'm going to play it by ear."

They rode into the courtyard of Fernlees, which was indeed a hive of activity. Men were carrying furniture out of the house as well as into it, and wooden shipping crates were being ferried into the hay barn from a large wagon.

Ela didn't recognize any of the servants she'd spoken to before. Perhaps he'd replaced them already. "Is Master Pinchbeck about?"

"Who?" A man looked up from his task and squinted at her.

"The owner of the house?"

"He's inside, I reckon," said another man dismissively.

Ela dismounted and handed her reins to Bill. She took a deep breath and headed to the doorway, where the door was propped open to admit the steady stream of goods in and out. "Master Pinchbeck?"

"He's not here." A deep growl emerged from the depths of the house. "Who wants him?" A dark-haired man emerged from the gloomy interior. The hair on the back of Ela's neck pricked her. It was the same man she'd seen speaking with Pinchbeck in the opium den.

His greasy curls hung almost to his eyes, which were an odd light-brown color, like a dog turd. Everything about this man set her nerves on edge. His clothes were fine but had a tawdry air about them, the trim too gaudy and the colors too loud and clashing. The leather of his boots was tooled in a way she'd never seen before, and he wore rings on several of his fingers.

"Who are you?" she asked, before she could stop herself. The question came out more imperious than she would have intended, if she had intended to ask it at all.

"Well, now, isn't that the question I should be asking you?" She couldn't put her finger on his accent.

"I am—" Did she really want to tell him? That made no sense under the circumstances. "Where is Osbert Pinchbeck?"

"Gone abroad." His eyes drifted down over her body in a way that made her flesh crawl.

"For how long?"

"Long enough." He stared at her, daring her to ask more.

An eerie sense of danger pricked at her. She'd suspected some kind of business transaction gone wrong was behind the elder Pinchbeck's death, and that was before she knew the kind of business the Pinchbecks were involved in. The man before her might be the one who killed Jacobus Pinchbeck, then crushed his chest with the wheels of his own cart.

Her instincts screamed at her to turn and run. *Bill Talbot is right behind you.* Bill could see her as she stood here in the doorway. She tried to calm herself and think straight.

"Vicus Morhees at your service." He bowed low. His voice and gesture dripped with mockery. *Vitus Morees.* Those were the unfamiliar words written on the piece of parchment she and Giles Haughton had found on Jacobus Pinchbeck's lifeless body. Said aloud, they spelled his name.

He had no idea they'd seen that scrap, or that Haughton—hopefully—still possessed it.

Her stomach lurched. If this man was the killer she'd have to convince Simon de Hal to arrest him after he'd already declared that he had no further interest in the case. She glanced at his boots. Did they match the prints she and the coroner had seen in the mud? She couldn't be sure.

"Ela of Salisbury," she said coolly. Mostly because she was scrambling to figure out what to do next. Did he recognize her as the "man" from the opium den? If he did, he didn't let on. He'd been gone by the time she was exposed so he might not even have heard of the fracas.

The longer he stared at her, the more likely he was to realize he'd seen her before.

"Are you a guest of Osbert Pinchbeck?" *Or did you kill him with the intention of stealing his house and property?* Her heart hammered against her ribs.

"He's rented the manor to me."

She waited, hoping he'd expand. He didn't. "Are you in business with him?"

"In business? No." His eyes met hers unblinking and dared her to ask more. He glanced over her shoulder to where she was sure Bill Talbot sat watching him from the back of his horse. "Why are you on my doorstep?"

"As I mentioned, I'm looking for Osbert Pinchbeck. I have business with him." She tried to sound as calm as possible. There was no reason to reveal her true purpose to this man. And from the sound of it she didn't have to worry about Osbert Pinchbeck appearing in the neighborhood any time soon.

"As I've mentioned, Osbert Pinchbeck is abroad." He stepped back and took hold of the door as if he intended to close it in her face. "So if there's nothing further I can help you with…" His fake smile chilled her to the bone.

No doubt about it, this was a very dangerous man. She had an instinct for people, and it rarely served her ill.

"I bid you adieu." She did not bow. Just fixed him with a steely gaze for one instant longer than was sensible, then turned and swept back down the path toward her horse.

It was time to pay an urgent visit to Giles Haughton.

CHAPTER 13

Ela and Bill Talbot rode through the familiar crooked streets inside the castle walls and up to Giles Haughton's neat house with its overhanging second story. Once outside she dismounted her horse and gave the reins to Bill, then knocked on his polished wooden door.

His housekeeper came to the door, sleeves rolled up as if she was in the middle of something. She looked quite flustered by the sight of Ela. "Master Haughton's away, I'm afraid, my lady. He's up at the castle with Sheriff de Hal."

"Ah. Do you know how long he'll be?" Ela wondered if they were meeting urgently over a new murder, or simply feasting and tasting the newest wines from Burgundy.

"I'm afraid not, my lady. And the mistress is away visiting their son in Dinton."

Ela debated the wisdom of pursuing him to the castle. She'd have a legitimate excuse to poke her nose in and see what was going on in the halls of her ancestors.

But the prospect excited her so much that she instinctively knew it was a bad idea. "I'll wait for him, if I may." She smiled politely. She suspected his housekeeper would gladly tell her that she may not, but she knew that wouldn't happen. She was ushered into his small parlor and sat in front of the empty fireplace. She heard the housekeeper send an errand boy to fetch Haughton, and then she worked to build a fire.

"Please don't go to any trouble on my account," said Ela, earnestly. "I'm quite warm in my cloak."

"Oh, goodness! I didn't take your cloak. I—"

"I didn't mean it as censure. I need nothing from you." She smiled again. There was something reassuring about knowing that no one—well, almost no one—would ever dare be openly rude to you. She wondered how it would feel to knock on a door, not knowing if it might be slammed in your face.

Maybe it would be refreshing.

Still, she knew the benefits of her position and tried not to exploit them.

She sat for some time in front of a spluttering and unenthusiastic fire, feeling chilly since her cloak now hung on a hook in the wall. Then the door opened and Haughton burst in, red faced. "I'm so sorry you've been waiting. I got away as soon as I could."

Ela rose, feeling suddenly guilty. "I hope I didn't pull you away from important business. I didn't ask them to fetch you. I simply said I would wait for your return."

"I'm glad of an excuse to get away. Too much rich food and wine doesn't agree with me."

"Simon de Hal is enjoying his role as castellan, I take it."

"Too much if you ask me. Hopefully he'll settle down soon. I still can't believe he didn't want to continue the hunt for Jacobus Pinchbeck's killer." He removed his cloak and joined her at the hearth.

"I suspect he wanted to start with a clean sheet of vellum. However, I don't want to leave mine blotted, either. Bill Talbot and I called on Osbert Pinchbeck in London and he is operating a shop as a false front. Inside he has some dismal rooms where he serves opium to customers. There were some very unsavory characters there. The substance seems to deprive men of their senses, and they must hide themselves in such low places until the effects wear off."

"I've heard of such establishments overseas, but never in England."

"And now Osbert Pinchbeck seems to have disappeared."

"He's not at Fernlees, enjoying his supposed birthright?" Haughton looked surprised.

"No. One of the men we saw in London is now living there—renting the place, he says. I shudder to think of the villains he'll bring into our midst. Pinchbeck seemed quite afraid of him when I saw them together."

"How did you manage that?"

Ela stiffened. "Bill and I pretended to be patrons. Poor Bill gallantly ate the opium and was quite ill for some time. We were there for hours, and I had the opportunity to overhear some conversation."

Haughton stared. "I'm glad you're unharmed."

"It was perhaps an unnecessary risk in hindsight, but confirmed that Osbert Pinchbeck continues in the same trade after his father's death."

"Perhaps he was tired of his father controlling the supply and keeping much of the profit."

"Indeed, he had motive to kill if he wanted to run the business alone. Except that now he's vanished. The man in his house simply says that he's abroad. And this man is called Vicus Morhees."

Haughton's eyes widened. "The name on the scrap of parchment in our victim's cloak." He rubbed his chin. "Well, that's an explanation of some sorts. Though I don't know what it explains."

"If Jacobus Pinchbeck wrote the name down because

Morhees was the man he set out to meet that morning—" Ela hesitated.

"Then Morhees could just as easily be the killer." Haughton stared at her.

"Indeed. When Bill and I were in Pinchbeck's establishment, I noticed that Pinchbeck seemed rather cowed by Morhees."

"Afraid of him?"

"Wary. I got the impression that Morhees was in charge."

"Interesting. Morhees is starting to look increasingly dubious. He's taken over the manor and perhaps he's now disposed of the younger Pinchback and is running the business as well. It seems that your visit to Pinchbeck's lair was not in vain. If there's good reason to suspect that Morhees killed Jacobus Pinchbeck, I can bring him before the jurors."

"Do you need to ask de Hal for permission?"

Haughton straightened his back. "I'm the king's coroner. I conduct my own investigation and report back to the sheriff."

"So he can't command you to cease and desist?"

"He can command all he wants." Haughton stretched. "But he can hardly be seen to subvert the course of justice."

"Not when he's so new to the role." Ela realized she was hoping de Hal would commit some gross breach of conduct. Then he might be sent away and she could return to the castle and—

"The villagers near the warehouse said that two people had visited before us. If one was Osbert Pinchbeck—which would be logical since the warehouse was his father's and they were in business together—then the other could be Vicus Morhees."

Ela snapped herself out of her foolish reverie of de Hal's fall from grace. "Indeed. But why?"

"Delivering the product after importing it from overseas?

It's quite possible he was the Pinchbeck's supplier—hence his name in the cloak of a man going to Exmouth to meet a new shipment." Haughton stared in to the empty hearth. "Or stealing the product back after being paid for it. Perhaps he decided to do away with the middleman and reap all the profits? And with the father out of the way he planned to seize control and make the son disappear."

"But Osbert Pinchbeck had opium in his shop in London. He was quite the lord of his domain until Morhees turned up." Ela remembered how his whole demeanor changed once Morhees arrived.

"Perhaps Morhees let him think business would continue as normal until he had the reins firmly in his hands."

"And now he's rid of both Pinchbecks and running the foul business himself." Ela's blood boiled just thinking about it.

"I'll interview him and let you know what I find out."

A FEW DAYS later Ela sat before the fire in her bedchamber, embroidering Isabella's wedding trousseau while her greyhound, Greyson, snoozed at her feet.

"Mama, I'm almost at the end of this skein of green and I still have several more leaves to do." Isabella bent over the hem of a nightgown with concentration worthy of a monkish illustrator.

"We don't have any more of that exact shade, but we have a pretty moss green. Your leaves will be varied, like those in the forest."

"It won't look right, though." Tears sprang to her gray eyes. "Nothing will be right!"

"Isabella! You're not going to cry over embroidery thread, are you?"

The girl's lip quivered. She was so sensitive. Ela did worry about how well she'd handle the stresses of marriage and running a household.

"I have plenty of the blue and red left, but if I'd known there was so little green, then I'd—" A fat tear rolled down her smooth cheek.

"Oh, Isabella." Ela put down her own sewing and rose to hug her. "It's not about the thread, is it?"

Isabella's slim shoulders shook as she sobbed. Ela pulled out a handkerchief and gave it to her. Isabella dabbed at her eyes and blew her nose. "It's everything, Mama. Everything all at once. Papa dying, the move here, and now I have to pack everything up again and leave you all and move to Northumberland. It's so far away!" The last word ended on a hiccuping sob, and she thrust her face into the handkerchief.

"William de Vesci will make a fine husband."

"William de Vesci is one of father's wards and has a great estate to inherit. I know that's the only reason I'm marrying him."

Ela's eyes widened. Isabella wasn't usually so blunt. "You know I wouldn't marry you off to just anyone! He's a handsome young boy with a fine education, and, yes, a great estate doesn't hurt anyone. It's always a wrench to leave your home and family, but you'll get used to your new home before you know it."

"But what if I don't?"

"I haven't raised you to be self-indulgent. Just put your duty before all and you'll be fine." She didn't want Isabella to think she could cry and complain to her new family members.

Isabella blinked back her tears. "Do you really think he's handsome?" She looked up at her mother curiously.

"Of course! He's almost as tall as Papa already."

"But his legs are like willow stems, and he does stare so."

"He's still young. He's grown fast—like a willow—and has yet to build muscle. If he stares it's only because he's astonished by his good fortune in being promised to you." She was teasing, but Isabella didn't laugh. She cleared her throat. "Boys can be rather awkward while they're young, but he'll mature into a great man, especially with you at his side."

Isabella fiddled with her half-embroidered cloth. "Mama—"

"Yes?" Ela waited. Isabella was avoiding her glance. "What?"

"About my wedding night..." She shifted awkwardly. "Will I bleed very much?"

Ela's gut lurched. She still remembered the anxiety and pain of her own wedding night, and had no wish to revisit it. It might not have been so bad if her new husband wasn't reeling drunk, but what with the wedding festivities at the king's court— "You might not bleed at all, my love. I didn't."

Isabella looked alarmed. "Then they might think I'm not a maiden," she hissed in a frightened whisper.

"They know you're a maiden and raised in a pious home. In the old days sometimes girls had their maid hide a tiny phial of chicken blood to splash on the sheets but we're past such foolishness, thank Heaven."

"Will it hurt?"

"It might." She wanted to be honest so there were no surprises. "The more relaxed you can be, the better. Have a cup or two of wine beforehand, but not more or you might get confused or ill. And talk to your husband. Tell him you're excited and nervous. I'm sure he'll feel the same. I tried so hard to be brave and mature and my wedding night was rather a disaster, I'm afraid. I think I cried myself to sleep while your father lay snoring afterward."

Isabella's eyes grew wider and Ela worried that she might cry again. "I'm just telling you that so you don't worry if it doesn't feel like the most wondrous night of your life. Marriage is a journey, and there will be rocky bits on the way."

"I'm not expecting it to be enjoyable—I know it's sinful—but I know that pleasuring my husband is one of my duties as a wife."

Ela wanted to bury her head in her hands. She felt so uncomfortable talking about such matters. Why? This was her beloved daughter, and she should reassure her even at the cost of her own modesty. "Sex between a woman and her husband is a joyful act that celebrates their love and brings children into the world. Don't let worries about sin cloud your thoughts. Sex within marriage is never sinful."

Isabella stared at her hands, the last skein of green draping over her lap. "What if I'm not able to bear him children?"

"That's in God's hands, my love. There's no use worrying about it. Send up prayers, then leave it up to him."

They prayed together, and Ela sent up earnest entreaties that her daughter's marriage be happy as well as prosperous. Isabella parted for her bedroom, and Ela was about to climb into her bed when an odd notion came over her.

She pulled a cloak on over her nightgown and headed downstairs. Most of the children were asleep, and Bill Talbot often turned in early, but Will was downstairs watching Richard and Stephen play one of their long-drawn-out games of chess.

"Where are you going, Mama?" asked Will.

"Just going to check on something." She could hear someone moving in the kitchen. "Don't wake the household. I'll be right back."

She slipped out the door without a candle. The moon was almost full, and her eyes would adjust to the dark soon enough.

Had Drogo and Hilda heeded her warnings or were they breaking their promise right now?

She moved toward the barn, lifting her skirts so as not to trip over anything. When she got close she stopped and listened.

Nothing.

The night was blissfully peaceful. Even the little creatures of the forest must be tucked up in their burrows and nests. She was about to turn back for the house when she heard an odd sound. A sort of muffled groan.

Tiny hairs stood up on the back of her neck. Would they defy her so soon after her stern warnings about relations between them?

She crept closer, ears pricked. She could now make out soft moans, rustling and a wet sucking sound.

Her stomach turned. She shoved open the barn door, expecting it to make a dramatic noise, but the hinges didn't creak and it didn't scrape across the floor, so she entered silently.

She listened for the source of the sound and realized it was coming from the hayloft above. It wasn't very high, only about six feet up, and the ladder was right there. Without even trying to be quiet she climbed up and peered over into the darkness. She could already smell the two heated bodies writhing in the darkness.

She cleared her throat and listened with satisfaction as they froze.

"Someone's there." She heard Hilda's panicked voice.

"Nay, it's nothing." Drogo's voice was husky with impatient lust.

Ela wondered whether to climb further up the ladder but realized she was in a vulnerable position. One of them could push it away from the loft and send her crashing back to the floor. "Actually, there is someone here," she said drily. "And

I'd ask what in God's name you think you're doing, but it would be a rhetorical question."

Hilda let out a tiny shriek, and Ela could hear scrabbling sounds as she gathered her clothes around her.

Drogo groaned again, no doubt frustrated at his intense pleasure being thwarted.

"Why?" asked Ela. She was now fairly confident that neither would try to push her off the ladder, and she could see them outlined in moonlight from the window above the loft. "I'm providing you both with a decent living and a roof over your heads. I warned you to stay away from each other. And now you're sinning in the eyes of God under my own roof."

She could hear Hilda sobbing. As well she might. Ela had every right to send her back home to her parents.

"Drogo, what do you have to say for yourself? She has the excuse of being young and foolish, but you don't." She was surprised at her anger with him. Did he think nothing of potentially ruining a young girl's life?

"The curse of lust is a terrible thing, my lady. Please pray for my sins."

"Pray for your own damned sins. I've a good mind to turn you out on the road right now." An idle threat. She'd promised de Hal that Drogo would repay his poaching debt. She'd have to take him back to the castle where he'd get his hand cut off.

"It's what I deserve. I'll leave right now." He stirred. She could see his eyes gleam in the darkness.

"No!" called the girl. Was she already in love with him? "Take me with you!"

"So you can starve together?" asked Ela. "How would you support yourselves with no friends to help you. Did Drogo tell you he first came before me because he was arrested for poaching? If it wasn't for my intervention he might have hanged for it, and don't think he can't still hang for it. Then where will you be?"

The girl was now sobbing hysterically, and Ela felt her heart soften. Great beauty was often a cruel curse for a poor girl, dooming her to being used and discarded by a man who cared nothing for her hopes and dreams of marriage and family and a quiet life. "Go back to your bed in the kitchen and don't dare leave it on any other night or it will be your last night here." She climbed down off the ladder to let the girl descend. "Go!"

Hilda scurried away, tears glittering on her skin.

"As for you, I ought to let you hang."

"Aye. 'Tis almost surprising I haven't hung yet. Perhaps it would be better if I did. I don't deserve the kindness you've shown me."

She couldn't see Drogo's expression but he sounded deadly serious. Now her heart softened even toward him. "If you lay another hand on that girl I'll be the one to bring charges against you. You may recall that I promised Simon de Hal that you'd repay your debt for poaching his pheasants. You need to earn that money or you'll make me a liar. In the meantime you'd better mind keep your eyes and hands to yourself or you'll be back in the castle dungeon."

She climbed back down the ladder and stormed off, muttering to herself about how no good deed went unpunished. She could just let them carry on and deal with the consequences, but Ela saw the people in her household as extensions of her own family. The specter of young Hilda's prospects being ruined would keep her awake at night.

Maybe I should convince myself to care less about everyone and everything.

But even as she formed the thought she knew it was impossible.

CHAPTER 14

"I'm your mother, darling. That's why I'm here." Her mother handed her cloak to Sibel. She'd arrived—entirely without warning—with enough luggage for a month's visit.

"I'm thirty-nine years old, Mama. Nearly forty. And you were here barely a month ago."

"You're still my baby. And your husband was just cruelly taken from you. I know how devastating that is."

"You survived it three times." Once again she had sneaking suspicion that her mother was only here to push her into some advantageous marriage that suited her own aspirations.

"Don't remind me, darling."

"Where's Jean?" She didn't see her husband among the baggage.

"He's attending a tournament in Suffolk. You know how tiresome I find those big events these days. I thought I'd come spend some time with my grandchildren before they all grow up and leave home. And I can help you plan the wedding preparations."

Ela ushered her into the parlor. "You've breathed some life into this old place," said her mother admiringly. Ela had added some handsome carved furniture made by a local artisan and a beautiful woven tapestry of a girl with a white horse in a forest filled with birds and flowers. Her familiar tapestries and some of the furnishings from the castle had been out of proportion, and in addition had looked old and grimy against the freshly whitewashed walls of Gomeldon. She'd been forced to make an investment in her new home—even if it was temporary.

"We've settled in. Gomeldon suits me well for now."

Her mother sat down and smoothed her skirts. Hilda arrived with spiced wine for both of them.

"Goodness, that girl is a beauty," said her mother as Hilda hurried back to the kitchen to fetch some freshly baked treats.

"More's the pity. She's attracting attention from the wrong quarters," said Ela in a hushed voice.

"Not young Will?" Her mother looked alarmed.

"No." Ela debated whether to admit it. Her mother didn't much like Drogo. Truth be told, nobody did—except her. "Drogo Blount." She spoke in hushed tones.

"You should have left him at the castle behind to face justice."

Ela sighed. "I know William would have wanted me to help him so I gave him a position here. Just to get him back on his feet."

Her mother pursed her lips. "I wouldn't have credited you with such a soft heart. Or such a soft head. I'm not sure which it is." She sipped her wine. "You need to get rid of him."

Ela stayed silent as Hilda delivered a plate of star-shaped shortbread. "He's not a bad person."

"He's not a good person either. And since he's been

freshly imprisoned for poaching he's not going to get hired anywhere."

Ela bit into a piece of shortbread and chewed it. Crisp and buttery at the same time. If only everything in life were that perfect. "Do you know anyone who's skilled with the law?"

Her mother peered at her over her shortbread. "Skilled at doing what with the law?"

Ela laughed. "Exactly." She put down her shortbread. "If I could somehow prove Drogo to be the true owner of Fernlees, then it would get him out of my house and also remove the unsavory character who's suddenly moved there."

"That nasty Pinchbeck fellow?"

"Worse. There's a new renter who looks like a Spanish pirate and deals in opium."

Haughton's interview with Morhees had gone nowhere. He'd produced official looking contracts detailing the terms of his lease of the property and explained away the note on Pinchbeck's person by saying that he'd been waiting for Pinchbeck in Exmouth—where he had an iron clad alibi in the form of his innkeeper.

The alibi, which was corroborated by several other witnesses, made it impossible for Morhees to have murdered Jacobus Pinchbeck.

Morhees had later visited the warehouse, where he'd dropped the goods at Osbert Pinchbeck's request. Then Osbert Pinchbeck had removed them to London.

There were no grounds to arrest him, so she needed another way to get rid of him.

"What is opium?"

"Some nasty black lumps of boiled poppy sap from the far east. People eat it and go out of their minds."

"Why would anyone want to do that?" Her mother looked doubtful.

"I suppose for the same reason people dive into their cups for days on end. Either way the end result is not good, and Salisbury will be better off without this man in our midst."

Her mother inhaled deeply. "Well, I do know a man who went to Oxford. Very experienced in the law. He's noble, of course. A younger son of a great family. He was at the king's court for some years, though not the current king." She frowned. "He's retired, but a small matter like this might be entertaining for him."

"Can you put me in touch with him?"

"He lives in London. I often play cards with him when we're in town. I'll write to him today."

THE FOLLOWING WEEK, her mother's friend Walter Spicewell arrived to stay at Gomeldon while he investigated the documents regarding Fernlees. He was a man of about seventy, with wiry gray hair and darting blue eyes, sprightly and with a wry sense of humor.

He arrived in a carriage with a young footman driving, and explained that he was too old to ride the whole way anymore. Hilda served wine and the most delicate, flaky oatcakes Ela had ever tasted. Spicewell and Ela's mother were soon laughing and joking about a surprise visit to de Hal. "We can ride through the arch as if we're coming home from a day's ride, and we're both so elderly and infirm that we can't remember that the castle isn't my home anymore!"

"You wouldn't." Ela didn't want to overreact, but her mother was capable of almost anything.

"Oh, wouldn't I? What do you think, Spicy, dearest? Would my husband disapprove?"

"I suspect he'd slap his thigh and have a good laugh over

it. Never did like de Hal. Jumped-up little twit if you ask me. Greedy and not afraid to use the law to line his own pockets."

"Ela's going to be sheriff soon." Her mother didn't look at her but said it quite matter-of-factly. Ela stared. Was her mother proud of her determination? She'd never done anything but criticize her ambition before.

"Ela's father would be proud," said Spicewell. "He was a fine sheriff in his day."

"A very long time ago," sighed her mother. "But why shouldn't a woman be sheriff? I suppose I should have petitioned the king myself."

Ela found the idea preposterous. Which gave her sudden —and rather daunting—insight into how some people must feel about her seeking the role.

There were a few moments where the only sound was the crunching of oatcakes. Spicewell's attendants announced that his baggage was unpacked, and they settled into a much less controversial conversation about Isabella's and Will's impending marriages and what a fine match each one was.

THE NEXT MORNING, Ela and Spicewell set out to visit the records office, where any officially recorded documents about Fernlees were stored. Since she'd already looked into the matter she knew there were no records beyond the initial gift of the manor to Radulph Blount's ancestor. Her intention in hiring an experienced man of the law was to press a suit that the property legally belonged to Drogo on the basis of that original contract.

It didn't take long to find the deed again. The old man retrieved it from a dusty back room. "I've brought this record out more times this spring than any other document here," he exclaimed, as he slapped the scroll, now bound with a thin strip of knotted leather, down on the smooth table.

"Who else has asked for it?"

"Who hasn't? You, de Hal, Osbert Pinchbeck, Thomas Blount, and just yesterday Master Morhees."

Ela stilled. Osbert Pinchbeck's presence was understandable, though what he found—or hadn't found—should have let him know the manor wasn't his. According to the legal record it was never officially his father's, either. De Hal's request for the documents made sense, since he was called on to decide the fate of the property. Thomas Blount—whoever he was—had visited since he was trying to establish a claim as Blount's son. But why would Vicus Morhees show an interest in the ownership of the property if he was just a renter?

Ela burned to ask for details but restrained herself. She needed to stay focused on her plan, which relied to a great extent on the oversight and ignorance of others. "Has a change of ownership been recorded lately?"

"Not since the eighth year of King John's reign."

So de Hal had either neglected or postponed the transfer of the property to Osbert Pinchbeck since his pronunciation that Pinchbeck was now the owner. Perhaps he was still awaiting payment of whatever bribe Pinchbeck had offered? Either way it would be a disappointment to Morhees, who seemed to be in the process of wresting Pinchbeck's worldly goods from his clasping and possibly bloodstained hands.

This left a clear path open for her plan. "So the property still belongs—officially at least—to the rightful heir of the original owner of Fernlees."

"That's what the law implies," said the old man.

"Indeed it does," agreed Spicewell. Ela had described her plan in great detail and he'd only said he'd see what he could do. "And the legal heir is Drogo Blount."

"That's not what Thomas Blount said," muttered the old man. "He said he was Radulph Blount's firstborn son."

"He's an imposter," said Ela. "We don't know his real identity, but Drogo Blount was born Thomas and he's the true heir. His birth is recorded in the parish records." Luckily Drogo was born at Fernlees and christened Thomas Drogo Blount. She'd had the Bishop's clerk dig those records up from where they were now stored behind the new cathedral. Drogo's memory of William's favorite song had assured her that he was indeed the true Thomas Blount, so the other must be a fake.

Ela noticed Spicewell shooting her a glance, and she remembered that he'd told her to let him do the talking. She resolved to hold her tongue.

"Sir Thomas Drogo Blount is my client," said Spicewell, in a grave official tone she hadn't heard before. "And he asserts his ancient right to his ancestral property."

"I heard Simon de Hal made a decision that should go to Pinchbeck because your client was an accused poacher."

"My client is now a free man living in the household of Ela Longespée, Countess of Salisbury." He continued, intoning his pronouncement like the judge at the assizes. "And the aforementioned Pinchbeck has fled the county and rented the property to a person of ill repute."

The law clerk's eyes widened.

"We see no reason why there should be a trial since the existing documents explicitly state that the property belongs to my client legally," continued Spicewell.

"That's a matter for the sheriff to determine," said that clerk slowly. He seemed to realize that something was up, and he didn't want to be caught in the middle.

"We shall make an appointment with him to discuss the matter. No doubt you'll be called to attend with this document, so guard it with your life."

Ela looked at Spicewell. What an odd thing to say. Still, he had decades of experience.

"I take my responsibilities seriously," the old man replied. "And this office is under lock and key and guarded around the clock. It contains all the property records for this part of the shire."

Spicewell bowed. "I appreciate your assistance."

Once they were outside and mounted, Ela apologized for speaking out of turn. "I hired you because I don't want to be the mouthpiece for this matter. It seems a conflict of interest."

"I understand your thinking. Your mother told me it's become a personal matter to get Drogo Blount out of your house."

"True, but I want him elevated to his true status as a brave knight in retirement, not forced to beg in the streets or pilfer someone's pheasants." She sighed. "When this matter first arose, there was talk of him fighting Jacobus Pinchbeck in a trial by combat. Pinchbeck would have used a champion, and likely Drogo would have been killed. On reflection, I think it's barbaric that the strongest man should win, regardless of each person's true claim to the property."

"Ah, but is what we're attempting really any different? You've hired me to be Drogo Blount's champion on the field; it's just a different field."

Ela looked at him. "Surely a battle of wits befits us more than a battle with swords."

"There are many who'd find a battle with swords more honest." His eyes crinkled into a smile.

Ela sighed. "Do you think we can win?"

"It will depend on de Hal and his commitment to the disposition of Fernlees. He does have the final say after all. Don't take this the wrong way, but I think you should stay completely out of the matter and leave it up to me."

"I do believe you're right." Much as it pained her to stay home and embroider her daughter's linens when important issues were under discussion at the castle, she resolved to do just that.

~

THAT AFTERNOON, Spicewell sent a message to the castle and he was invited to dinner there. Ela and her mother sat at home, discussing—at her mother's behest—the marriage prospects of all her other children. Ela tried not to smart with curiosity about what was taking place at the castle as it grew dark and then late.

"Walter Spicewell will probably stay overnight there, I suppose." Ela said as she bit off a skein of blue silk.

"I'm sure de Hal could provide him with an escort if the need arose, but dear Spicy is so amusing that de Hal might keep him there for days."

"It was kind of him to come at such short notice."

"I think he's glad of the chance to sharpen his wits on a difficult case. He enjoys a challenge."

"I suppose it's similar to the way my dear William enjoyed the challenge of a joust or a sword fight. I never could understand why he'd put himself at such risk for sport."

"It's in their nature, dear. Men have courage running through their veins like blood. The good ones do, anyway."

"I wonder. There's always a lot of blood and courage wasted on a battlefield when perhaps a clever man of the law could have negotiated a bloodless solution to the conflict."

"You speak like a merchant's child, not a daughter of the nobility. You're descended from the men who won this land by the sword." Her mother stabbed her embroidery with her needle. "Your father would be—"

She was interrupted by a sharp knock on the door.

Ela looked at her mom. "I suppose it's Spicewell." Something in her gut told her it wasn't. "But why wouldn't the guard announce him?"

Ela rose from her chair and put down her sewing. For reasons she couldn't explain, her heart was thudding. The knocking came again, louder this time.

She hurried across the flagstone floor and slid back the heavy iron bolt at the bottom of the door. It was stiff and a little rusty and took her a few seconds to pull it, during which the knocking came again, more frantically.

Ela hesitated, hand on the latch. "Who's there?" She heard a quaver of fear in her voice and it scared her more.

The only response was a desperate pounding. Now Ela's mother was on her feet, standing next to Ela by the door. "We must call someone. Cook!" Her mother hurried toward the kitchen. "Sibel! Hilda!"

As the frantic banging continued, Ela lifted the latch. The door flew open and Hilda crashed into the parlor, hair streaming loose about her face, completely naked.

CHAPTER 15

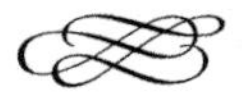

Ela let out a shriek of surprise before she could stop herself. "Hilda, what are you doing?"

The girl didn't answer her, but clutched at her like she was the last floating spar from a sinking ship. Ela held her for a moment, fear rising in her heart. "Hilda, what's going on?"

She pushed the girl back from her and as Hilda's hair swung, Ela noticed with a start that her face was dirty, smeared with— "Is that blood?" Hilda's wide eyes stared up at her. She still hadn't spoken a word.

"Hilda! What in heaven's name are you doing?" The cook rushed forward in her nightgown, her long gray hair streaming down her back.

Ela had managed to separate herself from Hilda and frantically grabbed one of the half-embroidered linens to cover her nakedness. Sibel rushed over with a cloak she'd snatched from a hook and wrapped it around the girl.

Ela's mother stuck her head out the open front door. "Guards! Guards! Attend us immediately!"

Footsteps on the stairs heralded the welcome arrival of

Bill Talbot, sleepy eyed, with his hair standing on end. "What's the ruckus?"

"Hilda appeared at the door in a panic, completely naked. I think she has blood on her."

"Is she hurt?" Bill hurried forward to examine her, but Ela quickly warned him she was still naked under the cloak. Hilda's silence was unnerving.

"Let me examine her," said Sibel softly. She led Hilda into the small passage behind the parlor. Ela could hear her talking softly to Hilda, but heard no response. "She seems uninjured, but this is certainly blood spattered on her face and chest," she called out.

"Heaven preserve us," exclaimed Alianore.

Ela crossed herself. "Where are the guards?"

Bill hurried to the door and called out again. There was no response. "Let me go see what's going on. May I have a lantern? I'm going to get my dagger." Sibel rushed to fetch him a lantern and came back with it lit and ready, just as Bill came down the stairs with his dagger unsheathed.

"Do be careful, Bill." Ela felt alarm coursing through her body. "There could be someone out there."

"I'm damned sure there's someone out there," replied Bill firmly. "And I intend to find out who."

Will and Richard had appeared down the stairs, and Ela's mother hen instincts told her to shoo them back up again, but they weren't babies to be coddled now so she restrained herself. They all poured outside into the night, just as the moon disappeared behind a cloud.

"Guards!" called Ela. She walked toward the entrance from the road, where one of them was supposed to stay at all times. It was eerie not being able to even see her feet on the path, and she worried about tripping over something.

There was a wooden stool where the guard sat when no

one from the house was outside, and Ela found it in its usual place, empty.

"Why would he abandon his post?" asked Alianore, making her jump.

"What are you doing out here?"

"The same thing you are. You can't expect me to wait inside for a killer to arrive."

"Oh lord!" she heard a voice from over toward the barn. "A body."

"Someone's killed the guards," whispered Alianore. "What if he's still here?"

"Do go inside, Mother." Ela hurried over to the male voice that had called out. She could see the planes of Bill's face in the light from the lantern. "Who is it?"

"It's one of the guards, but he's breathing. Let's carry him inside."

Two of the servants helped lift the heavy body, and they brought him into the kitchen and laid him down on someone's bedding.

He was indeed breathing, mouth wide open. She saw no wounds. Oddly, his eyelids were open and his eyes rolled back. "Is he drunk?" She leaned in to smell his breath, but it didn't have a reek of liquor. "Let's leave him here and look for the other one."

They went outside again. This time she stayed with Bill and his lantern, and they soon found the other guard slumped against the outside of the barn. He, too, was breathing but didn't rouse even when Bill slapped his face quite hard.

"Where's Drogo?" Ela wondered why all the commotion hadn't roused him. Then a horrible realization occurred to her. "Hilda must have been with him."

She hurried toward the barn, heart thumping. Bill pushed

past her and pushed the barn door open. "Drogo? Where are you?"

As Bill swung the lantern around, it cast deep shadows among the beams and cobwebs.

"He sleeps up in the hayloft," said Ela quietly. She had a very bad feeling about this. Bill bravely walked toward the ladder, and climbed it with the lantern in one hand.

"Jesus wept." His voice came out in a hoarse growl. He wasn't even all the way up in the loft. He climbed the rest of the way while Ela waited in fretful silence. "He's dead. Throat's been slashed. There's blood everywhere."

Ela felt as if her own blood had drained from her body. How cruel that this should happen just when she was working to get Drogo's life—and his manor—back for him. She knew she cared about Drogo more than she should. His cavalier attitude and boyish charm reminded her of her husband. Now the loss of her husband seemed magnified as if her pain could echo off the wooden barn walls.

She heard a tiny whimper escape her, and she felt arms around her waist. "I'm not going to faint," she said brusquely, pushing them away. "May God rest his immortal soul. Don't bring the body down yet. We must raise the hue and cry and send for Giles Haughton."

The metallic smell of the blood stung her nostrils, uncanny and awful.

"I'll go," said Bill. Ela wanted to protest. With the guards asleep—or in a trance of some kind—who would protect the household if the killer was still at large? "Will can fetch his sword to defend you."

Ela reluctantly agreed. A boy ran to fetch a horse and tack it up. The entire household was now huddled outside in their nightshirts in the dank spring air. "Come inside, all. There's nothing we can do for Drogo now."

~

IT SEEMED an age before Bill finally returned with Haughton. The entire household was still up and abuzz with tension. The guards showed occasional signs of stirring, but neither could be roused enough to speak. Hilda sat on a stool in the corner of the kitchen, still wrapped in the cloak, staring mutely, as if scenes of unspeakable horror played behind her eyes.

Will, proud of his new commission, stood outside the house with his sword unsheathed, ready to spring into action every time a leaf rustled.

At last Ela heard the horses outside and hurried out to greet the coroner. "God be praised that you're here safe. I'm so sorry to drag you from your bed, Master Haughton. And on such a dark night as this." The moon had never reappeared from behind the bank of clouds.

"It was not easy finding the road, I'll admit." He eased himself down from his mount, looking a little stiff. "But murder won't wait until morning."

"The killer still walks abroad," said Ela quietly. "We don't know who it is."

"I hear Will is protecting the household, and he's a capable young man."

"He should be with all the years of training I've given him," said Bill. He seemed unflustered by the awful events of the night and even his long ride both ways. "I'll take over now and let him rest."

Ela guided Haughton toward the barn. They each carried a bright lantern prepared by Sibel. Ela held her breath as they reached the door, as if her lungs might keep out the scent of death. "He's up in the loft," she breathed.

Haughton climbed the ladder first. He didn't say a word at the top, but she watched him take in the grisly sight. Then she gathered her courage, picked up her skirts in one hand and climbed the ladder after him.

Ela averted her eyes from the body until both of her feet were safely off the ladder and on the platform of planks. The surface was strewn with old hay from the last time the barn was used to store fodder over a winter. She allowed her eyes to adjust to the lantern light before she dragged her gaze back to Drogo's lifeless form.

The sight of him made her knees buckle. There was blood everywhere, covering his face and chest and arms and hands, as if he'd struggled while he died.

"The artery in his neck was severed," said Haughton, bending over him. "He was killed from behind."

"How can you tell?"

"The angle of the blade. It slashed from front to back. It's not a long cut, but it's in just the right place. He bled out fast."

"So poor Hilda must have been lying under him and his blood sprayed over her as he was slashed with the blade."

"What?" Haughton looked at her.

"That's how we learned of the murder. She came to the house, banging on the door, quite naked and splashed with blood."

"Did she see the killer?"

"I don't know. She hasn't uttered a word since. She just sits and stares like she's possessed." Ela crossed herself.

"I've heard of such cases. Where the sight witnessed was so horrible that the person couldn't speak about it. I've never seen it in all my years as a coroner, though. Hopefully she saw enough to identify the killer. There was some moonlight earlier."

"She's lucky to have escaped with her life."

"Did you know she and Drogo were...having relations?"

Ela nodded. "Unfortunately I did. I'd spoken to them both in no uncertain terms, telling them to stay apart or lose their positions. Clearly the lust between them was stronger than common sense."

"They might have been, uh, engaged in the act when he was killed. If he was on top of her, got his throat slit and died instantly, she'd have to struggle out from under his dying body, and that would explain why he's sprawled half on his side like this."

Drogo's legs were positioned almost as if he were trying to run while lying down. Ela felt the urge to cross herself again, but she resisted it. She didn't want Haughton to think her a cloistered nun who needed to be shielded from the world.

"If the killer climbed the ladder to the loft, unobserved, while Drogo and Hilda—" She cleared her throat. "How would they not hear him?"

"There's a window over there." Haughton looked at the wall at the end of the loft. The window was an unglazed square opening with just a few ragged strips of its leather covering remaining. "Maybe he climbed up from the outside, then he could have entered and crept up on them from behind."

"Or he could have been waiting in a corner of the loft the whole time."

Haughton looked about the loft. "That seems less likely. The space isn't that large and there's nothing but the cruck framing to hide behind. I reckon he listened from outside until he heard them making the beast with two backs, then he took his chance."

"Why did he let Hilda live when she could identify him?"

"Maybe he didn't intend to."

Ela heaved a sigh. "Poor Drogo. He wasn't a lucky man."

"Some would say he was. Many a man would be happy to die doing what—" He stopped and coughed awkwardly into his hand. "Excuse me, my lady. Almost forgot myself."

"I see what you mean." She tried to say it lightly, but it came out odd. She rather liked that he'd talked to her as if she were one of the male jurors. "Still, I suspect he'd rather be alive to inherit Fernlees."

Haughton was checking Drogo's hands, possibly for signs of self-defense. He looked up. "I thought Fernlees went to Pinchbeck the younger?"

She inhaled slowly. "It did, in theory, but no deed has been recorded. I've retained an experienced man of the law to explore the issue of Drogo's rights more fully."

Haughton stared at her. "I see." He probably thought—like everyone else—that she'd put too much time and effort into a man they all saw as a liability. He frowned. "I wonder if that attracted the attention of the wrong person."

Ela blinked as thoughts rushed her mind. "You think Drogo was killed over Fernlees?"

"Why else would someone kill him?"

"But who would even know about it? My lawyer only arrived here the day before yesterday."

"Word travels fast." Haughton examined the sides and back of Drogo's head.

"Did you tell De Hal about Morhees renting Fernlees and Pinchbeck disappearing?"

"I mentioned the events, yes." Haughton looked a bit sheepish.

"He was uninterested?" Ela could already imagine Haughton voicing her concerns and de Hal changing the subject immediately."

"I'm afraid so."

"Well, he'll have to show some interest now there's another murder." Indignation flared in her chest. He couldn't just ignore a death on her estate, could he? "I'll ride to the castle tomorrow and make sure to focus his mind on the matter."

Haughton looked doubtful. "He's likely to say that Drogo Blount got what he deserved."

Ela stared. "Do you believe that?"

"Not at all. No one deserves to be murdered, and I take it as my sacred trust to investigate the means of their death and help bring their assailants to trial. But—based on my observation of his character—de Hal is going to see Drogo as a poacher who probably should have been hanged anyway."

"He should arrest Morhees and question him about Pinchbeck's whereabouts." Ela relished the picture of Morhees in the castle dungeon.

"On what grounds?" Haughton pulled a piece of linen from his bag and wiped his hands, which were smeared with Drogo's blood.

Ela hesitated. She recalled her own reluctance to arrest people on mere suspicion. She had nothing against Morhees so far except a distaste for his manner—and the fact that his name had been found in a note on the dead man's body. "I see what you're saying."

"And why would Morhees kill over the manor if he's just a renter?"

"A long leasehold can be as good as ownership if the terms are favorable," she said with conviction.

"True." Haughton folded his soiled linen and put it back in his bag. "We'll have to leave the body here for the jurors to examine in the morning. At least if we want enough witnesses to have a decent trial."

"Of course." She hated to leave poor Drogo here, naked and defenseless. "Can I cover him with a blanket."

Haughton pursed his lips for a moment. "Better not to. The blanket will soak up the blood and alter the appearance of the scene."

She wanted to argue that the dusty old hay would do the

same, but held her tongue. She rose to her feet. "Let's go find Hilda. Perhaps she's settled and is able to talk by now."

BACK INSIDE THE house Ela called for a bowl of water for Haughton to wash his hands.

"How's Hilda doing?" she asked Sibel.

When Sibel looked up, Ela saw tears in her eyes. Sibel's lip quivered, and she clearly didn't trust herself to say anything.

Ela's heart went out to her. "She's lucky to be alive."

Ela and Haughton went into the kitchen, where Hilda sat on a low stool in the corner. Someone had wiped the blood from her skin and dressed her in a borrowed shift. Her own was still in the barn somewhere. Her hair hung wet about her shoulders, where they must have tried to mop the blood out of it.

Haughton looked at Ela, and she took it to mean that she should approach the girl first. Ela went up to her and took her hands. They felt oddly cold and lifeless. Hilda stared past her toward the fire.

"Hilda, can you hear me?" She gently squeezed the girl's hands.

"She's been struck dumb," said the cook, who stood to the side with her hands twisted into her apron. "I've never seen nothing like it."

"She's in shock, poor lamb." said Haughton.

"I'm not sure how much of a lamb she was out there in the barn with that fellow," continued the cook. "I did warn you—"

"Not now, Cook," said Ela. They could hardly gain the girl's confidence if she expected to be berated for her sins in front of the household. "She's the only person who can tell us who the killer was." She moved back so Haughton could come closer.

He crouched down so that he was eye to eye with Hilda "Did you see his face?" Hilda just stared past him before the fire, like she was in another world. "He's still out there somewhere, and we can only catch him if we know who he is."

"We tried splashing her with cold water," said the cook.

"Perhaps some wine will loosen her tongue," suggested Haughton.

"The servants usually drink ale," said cook with disapproval.

"Please fetch a cup of wine," said Ela. The cook was getting on her nerves, which were already in tatters. "And something sweet." If they could tempt the girl to use her mouth for food and drink, maybe her tongue would find words again.

But efforts to get her to sip the wine or eat a sweetmeat met with more mute staring.

"The poor girl will starve to death before she talks at this rate." The cook folded her arms. "She won't be of much use in the kitchen like this."

"Cook, I will thank you to keep your thoughts to yourself for now. If I require your opinion I shall ask for it." Ela spoke sharply. At this point her authority was being disrespected and she felt the need to assert it. "Please prepare something for Master Haughton to eat."

The cook looked like she wanted to retort but managed not to. She bustled away to the pantry.

"Perhaps we should try to shock her out of it," suggested Ela.

"As if it were a bout of hiccups?" said Haughton wryly.

"She was shocked into this state. Though I suppose she did manage to run to the house so she was still in her right mind."

"I suspect time is the only medicine that will heal her. And we don't have that with a killer abroad. Now the hue and cry has been raised the sheriff knows there was a murder in his jurisdiction and his men will be baying for blood."

"I suggest they ride to Fernlees and see if Master Morhees has blood on his hands." What if de Hal chose to ignore the matter? She felt herself grow heated at the prospect. "And Osbert Pinchbeck must be located. He was Drogo's true rival for the ownership of Fernlees."

"I'll be sure to mention all of this when I speak to him tomorrow." Haughton stared at Hilda.

The girl's unusual beauty was even more haunting in her current expressionless state. Ela noticed Sibel standing stiffly in another corner of the kitchen, barely holding back tears. Perhaps she blamed herself for bringing her niece into this situation that had led her first into one disaster and now another.

"I'm sure she'll recover soon," Ela said, trying to reassure her. "Perhaps after a night of sleep." She wasn't sure how any of them were going to sleep after this. For all they knew the killer still lurked near the manor.

"Have the guards come to yet?" Ela realized they were nowhere to be seen.

"I kicked those louts outside," said the cook, returning with a slice of pie and a flagon of ale for Giles Haughton. "Drunk as skunks, they were."

Haughton sprang to his feet. "Where are they?"

The cook gestured to the back door of the kitchen with her thumb. Ela cursed herself for forgetting all about the guards until now. Sibel opened the door, and Ela hurried out into the dark again. "Guards, where are you?"

A voice almost at her ankles made her jump. She realized the two men were sitting slumped against the side of the building.

"Get up!" What did they think they were doing, lounging on the ground? Haughton held the lantern up, illuminating their blinking, bleary-eyed faces.

One of them attempted to rise, leaning heavily on the building wall, but the effort proved too much for him. The other didn't even shift position.

Ela was furious. "You're hired to protect us, not drink yourself senseless when there's a killer roaming the manor. What did you drink?"

"Just ale," said the first one slowly. "But there must have been something in it because..." His voice tailed off. The other man just stared ahead of him like Hilda. If Ela believed in witchcraft—which she didn't—she'd begin to wonder if they were all under a curse.

"Who gave it to you?"

"Drogo."

CHAPTER 16

Ela turned to Giles Haughton. "What on earth?"

Haughton blew out a breath. "They've been drugged with something. Could be rat poison for all we know. But why?"

"Drogo might have wanted them out of their senses so he and Hilda could go about their foolishness without being noticed. The guards are supposed to patrol the property." Ela stared at the dark outline of the barn, where Drogo's body lay. "And now he's dead because there was no guard to keep a murderer at bay."

"Has Drogo given you ale before?" Haughton asked one of the slumped guards.

"Once or twice. I've never felt like this, though."

Ela crossed her arms over her chest. "If the murder hadn't happened they might have just slept it off and never known anything was amiss. From the sound of it our house has been unguarded before. The Lord only knows who's crept about among these bushes while we were all tucked in our beds, foolishly thinking ourselves protected. You deserve to be horsewhipped."

The more alert one hung his head. "Begging your pardon, ma'am. I thought it was just ale."

"Can you really not rise to your feet?"

"Everything's moving. The earth is shifting, the wall is tilting—"

Ela noticed Bill Talbot standing nearby. She looked up at him. "Sound familiar?"

"Indeed it does."

"It could be opium," Ela said to Haughton. "The resin might have been broken up and put into the ale."

"Or melted and stirred in," said Bill, looking down at the incapacitated guards. "They drink it as a brew in the Holy Land."

Haughton looked thoughtful. As well he might. He knew about the warehouse. He knew about Pinchbeck's shop in London. He knew about the sinister new renter at Fernlees. The opium trade seemed to be at the heart of everything going wrong in Salisbury.

As if he'd heard her thoughts, Haughton suddenly asked, "How does Drogo Blount connect to the opium trade?"

Ela shook her head. "He wasn't supposed to leave the manor, but I suppose he might have since he clearly had no trouble circumventing the guards." She frowned, thinking hard. "And he did seem to have more life in him since his release from the castle. Now that I think about it, his limp seemed less pronounced and he certainly had enough vigor to pursue Hilda. Perhaps he's been taking the poppy resin?"

"He may have been a user even before coming here. Did he know Morhees?"

"I have no idea. I never discussed Morhees with him. And who knows what Drogo got up to when I was away in London."

"A very bad business," murmured Haughton. Ela felt a sting of censure, as if he was referring to her patronage of

Drogo. "I'll be back in the morning, when they've sobered up, and I'll bring two jurors to hear their testimony."

Ela smarted again, as if her testimony would be irrelevant now that she wasn't acting sheriff. Which was probably the case. "Do have some pie before you go."

"I thank you, but nay. Eating at this time of night doesn't sit well with me."

THE NEXT MORNING Sibel went early to tell Hilda's family that she'd had a shock and been struck mute. Ela had debated going herself to break the news, but decided that might be too much. She didn't want them to see her arriving with her retinue and worry that Hilda was dead.

Ela's mother had endured a sleepless night peppered with nightmares and couldn't wait to depart for the familiar safety of her heavily fortified home and husband. She vowed to pick up Spicewell on her way past the castle and take him with her and Ela didn't try to argue. Spicewell's mission—to secure Fernlees for Drogo—had evaporated before the morning dew.

Hilda had dark circles under her eyes in the morning. She did eat, but listlessly, as if her bread and cheese were leaves and grass.

Her parents arrived on foot late that same morning, in high dudgeon. Clearly word of last night's murder had escaped into the neighborhood—hardly surprising since the hue and cry was raised.

Ela ushered them into the parlor, where Hilda was installed by the fire in a high-backed chair. "Yes, I'm afraid she was witness to a murder. We suspect she can't speak because the sight of the killing has shocked her into silence."

Hilda's parents were ordinary-looking people a few years

older than herself. Her father was a sturdy man of medium height with a greasy cap over graying brown hair. Her mother—Sibel's older sister—was stout and plainly dressed in a worn blue gown, with a wimple that covered much of her face. Still, Ela could see that she was the likely source of Hilda's unfortunate beauty.

"You say it happened in the barn? What were she doing in the barn at night? I thought she worked in the kitchen."

"Yes. She does work in the kitchen." Ela looked at Hilda, hoping that she might find the strength to comment. "I'm afraid she had gone to the barn to visit a…man."

"What do you mean, a man? Who was this man who got killed?" Hilda's mother fidgeted. Ela thought it strange that neither of them had tried to address or even embrace their daughter.

"His name was Drogo Blount. He was a knight in my service."

"And why under God's heaven would a lovely girl like our Hilda be left alone with him in the darkness of night?"

Ela swallowed. No parent would want to hear what she had to say. "The cook had warned me they were having a… liaison. I spoke to them both very firmly about it and told each that their position would be terminated if they continued. Sadly they didn't listen."

She glanced at Hilda again. The girl just sat there staring as if she could hear music in her head instead of their words.

"How old was this Blount?" asked her father gruffly.

"Forty or more, I suspect," admitted Ela. "I told her she must have no hopes for him as a husband."

"Our daughter is good enough for any knight," her father retorted.

"I'm afraid it was he that wasn't good enough for her."

She didn't want to speak ill of the dead. Poor Drogo's bloodstained corpse still lay in the barn, awaiting the arrival of one juror who was a baker and couldn't attend until his bread was baked.

"Well, I'm sure my little girl would never do anything against God's commandments."

Ela quickly scanned the stone tablets in her head. "I don't believe she did. He wasn't married so there was no adultery. The sin of lust is not mentioned in the commandments." She looked at Hilda again, hoping this frank talk might jar her into defending herself.

"Lust! Hilda's an angel. She'd never so much as look at a man she wasn't married to."

Ela drew in a slow breath. Did the girl's parents really need to know she was naked in Drogo's arms at the time his throat was slit? "I'm afraid she had crept out to the barn in direct defiance of my forbidding her to do so."

The girl's mother let out a whimper and pressed her face into her veil.

"I won't hear you speak ill of my daughter," said her father firmly. "We'll take her home with us right now."

Ela was about to heave a sigh of relief. Then she remembered that Hilda was the only witness to Drogo's murder. "I'm afraid the coroner will need to speak with her when her voice returns. She should remain here for now."

"In a house where her reputation is slandered and her virtue in constant danger?" Her father looked around as if the manor crawled with opium-addled seamen. "I think not. Come, Maud, let's take her."

Hilda's parents each took one of her arms and lifted her from the chair. She stared at them wordlessly, then flopped back down.

"We can hardly carry her seven miles across the fields."

"Nay. I suppose she'll have to stay for now." They both looked at Ela with deep suspicion.

"She shall be under constant watch. I really don't know

how she crept out when she was sleeping in the kitchen with at least two other people at all times. The cook must sleep like the dead."

She realized too late how wrong her comment sounded. She crossed herself. "God willing she'll regain her speech soon and help us find Master Blount's murderer."

"Sounds like he deserved it if you ask me."

"No one deserves to be savagely murdered."

"You'll still pay her?" Her father looked at Hilda doubtfully. She stared at the window in the opposite wall, seemingly insensible to their presence.

"Yes. She'll be paid. And her aunt Sibel is here to make sure she's happy and taken care of. Sibel is a highly valued member of our household. I don't know what I'd ever do without her."

They looked at each other. "Well, we'll be off then," said her father.

"Perhaps you should talk to Hilda." Ela wondered at their lack of affection and concern. "Maybe remind her of home and her brothers and sisters. Something you could say might bring her out of this trance."

Hilda's father looked pained. He shuffled a step or two closer to her. "Hilda, dear. Your little brothers miss you. Do you remember little Daniel? He's been crying at night since you left."

Hilda simply stared, the light from the window playing across her comely features.

OVER THE NEXT FEW DAYS, Hilda gradually became more responsive, started to speak and resumed her duties in the kitchen. But she couldn't remember anything about the night of the murder.

"You do remember Drogo Blount?" Ela sat with Hilda and Giles Haughton in the parlor one morning. Haughton was no closer to finding the killer and wanted more information. The girl nodded and tears sprang to her eyes. They'd had to explain to her that he was dead and gone, and she seemed to understand it.

"When was the last time you saw him?"

The girl blinked and looked down at her hands.

"I know you weren't supposed to be seeing him. You're not going to get in trouble for that again."

Hilda shifted in her chair. Still staring at her hands, she spoke softly. "I kissed him that afternoon behind the oak tree near the sheep pens. It was very quick. I just went outside to gather some chamomile for Cook."

"But you don't remember going to the barn after dark."

Hilda shook her head. Her eyes wide and fixed right on Ela's, she seemed to be telling the truth. Perhaps the Lord had chosen to spare her the awful memories of that night by erasing them from her mind.

"Do you remember seeing anyone else that day? Maybe earlier that afternoon or even in the morning? Anyone unfamiliar about the place?"

Hilda thought for a moment, then shook her head.

"Was anyone acting strangely?" asked Ela. There was the grim possibility that he'd been killed by someone on the manor.

Hilda's lip twitched.

"Anything you could tell us will help," encouraged Haughton. "Even the tiniest detail."

"It's not a person, but I did notice a ladder had been moved to reach the loft window outside the barn." She blinked nervously. "At first I thought Drogo put it there to sneak out more easily, since that side of the barn faces away from the house. I meant to ask him about it, but I never—"

Her lip quivered again, and a fat tear rolled down her cheek.

"Who else might have had reason to move a ladder there?" Haughton asked Ela.

Ela shook her head. "The barn wasn't in use except by Drogo. It was a place to put the animals in poor winter weather or to store forage over the winter." She paused and frowned. "So the killer was here before the night of the murder and planned the whole scenario."

"For all we know the killer supplied Drogo with the opium to addle his own wits as well as those of the guards. He could even have had him put the ladder there himself on some pretext." Haughton crossed his arms. "I wonder if he expected to find Drogo asleep and was surprised to find him with company."

"So the killer is someone with access to opium." Ela pressed a finger to her mouth.

"The mysterious Master Morhees once again has a raft of witnesses placing him in Exmouth. The sheriff himself confirmed his presence there. Morhees created a disturbance in the town square that afternoon and was fined a shilling for it. He was in the sheriff's jail when the murder was committed."

"An impressive alibi. And Osbert Pinchbeck?"

"Hasn't been seen—neither hide nor hair. His shop in London is closed and barred."

"We need to talk to that old man at the door. He'd know where Osbert Pinchbeck is."

"Gone and no one seems to know who or where he is."

Ela let out a sigh. "He did seem old. Too old to scale a ladder and slit a man's throat, even if he did have the means to make the long journey from London."

"Is there anyone here on the manor that would have motive to kill Drogo?"

Ela shook her head. "We're not a large number. Most of the staff here have worked for me for a long time. The cook is new but came highly recommended."

"What about the guards?"

"They were chosen because they'd served faithfully at the castle for years. They drank the ale thinking it was simply ale, which all the servants drink with their meals. They had no reason to believe it was drugged."

Ela admitted that the manor was not walled, so someone might have gained access through the woods. Hilda was eventually sent back to her work with no one the wiser.

"At least she's regained her senses. Perhaps the memories will come back in time."

After she was gone, Haughton leaned in. "There's been a development." The tone of his voice was so different that Ela startled a little.

"What?"

"Thomas Blount has laid a claim to Fernlees."

Ela frowned. "The other Thomas Blount? How did you hear this?"

"From Simon de Hal. He was complaining that this matter is like a tiresome terrier nipping at his heels and he never wishes to hear the name Blount again."

"Perhaps Spicewell's investigations knocked over the hornets' nest and de Hal has realized that he can't simply pronounce the property to be Pinchbeck's if there's a legitimate legal claim against it. That was Spicewell's purpose in visiting the castle."

"Indeed. But apparently this claim from Blount—or whoever he is—predates Spicewell's arrival. It came from London by messenger. It seems this other Thomas Blount had the same idea you did and hired an expensive man of the law to represent him."

Ela stared. "Who is this man calling himself Thomas Blount?"

Haughton frowned. "The only Thomas Blount in the parish records is the one we knew as Drogo. He grew up in this neighborhood and several people have now vouched for him as the same person, though time and his warrior's life certainly took a toll on his health and appearance. This new one has crawled out of the Fernlees woodwork like a worm. De Hal wanted to tear up his claim, but Blount had said in the letter that if his claim was ignored he planned to take it to the king."

"The king? Who does he think he is? He's not even a knight, like Drogo. Or is he?"

Haughton shrugged. "I'm the coroner. Investigating such matters lies outside my purview." He looked at her with meaning.

"I think I understand you. You haven't been given the means to investigate, but you think that I should."

His eyebrows lifted almost imperceptibly. "I realize you have absolutely nothing to gain from such an inquiry at this point."

True. She would spend her own money on messengers, clerks, lawyers, and for what? "But you know that I consider the pursuit of justice to be an end in itself."

That familiar gleam shone in his eyes. "Exactly."

Ela felt something swell in her chest. She hoped very much that it wasn't pride.

"I shall send a message to Walter Spicewell, who's now at my mother's home, asking if I may engage his services again. If he's willing, we shall see what he can find out about this other Blount's claim and about the man himself."

"De Hal would be annoyed to learn this matter is still active."

Ela felt a tiny smile tug at her lips. "I know."

CHAPTER 17

On Sunday, the family attended services at the cathedral. Ela rode her horse, Freya, and her children piled into the covered carriage pulled by two stout grays. William and Bill Talbot rode behind. It had just rained but the weather was bright, with sunlight sparkling from every leaf and puddle as if to dazzle her.

Ela tried to steady her nerves as the cathedral tower appeared. It had only been five days since Drogo's gruesome murder, but already the news had spread throughout Wiltshire. No doubt her name was on everyone's lips.

Being publicly ejected from her ancestral home was bad enough. Now they surely knew she'd invited a known poacher into her household only for him to be murdered under her roof. If the servants had gossiped—which they usually did—they might know that he'd lain with her serving maid as well.

Freya splashed happily though the puddles, oblivious to her mistress's distress. They dismounted outside the west gate, and the servants took the horses while she led the children into the cathedral, head held high.

Bishop Poore stood at the door, greeting the nobles as they arrived, and she bowed and kissed his ring as she passed through. She'd visited the day before to discuss Drogo's burial, and they'd arrived at an expensive but satisfactory arrangement. She'd sent out inquiries for the whereabouts of his mother and his son but heard nothing back so the burial would have to go ahead without them. Bishop Poore had been gracious enough to praise Ela for her charity rather than scolding her for her folly.

They took their seats inside the nave, still in the front row where they'd sat since the cathedral first opened for services. She kept her head turned forward, toward the magnificent altar, willing herself not to turn and look for the presence of de Hal.

The beauty of the place moved her. Even half built, with scaffolding still in place, the great cathedral felt like a tiny piece of God's kingdom on earth. And now that her dear husband's body lay here the cathedral felt like a second home. Which was odd considering how bitterly she and her husband had opposed its creation because it meant losing the old cathedral inside the castle walls. She did miss the spiritual home of her childhood, but she had to admit this cathedral was grander and finer by far.

She worked hard to keep her mind focused on the service and the lessons, and to receive the sacrament with the humility and respect it deserved. Still, her heart dreaded the moments after the service when she and the other nobles would gather outside to wait for their horses. It was the one time of the week where families from across that part of Wiltshire saw each other and exchanged greetings and invitations.

She'd been showered in condolences for her husband's untimely death over the past two months. The last few weeks had brought quiet commiseration for her move to Gomeldon, which humiliated her. Naturally she couldn't announce that she'd soon be back at the castle. They'd think her either arrogant or mad. Or both.

Maybe she was.

And now a murder in her household?

Once the service was over and the final psalm had been sung, Ela ushered the children out ahead of her. She'd told the ostler to be ready with the carriage and Freya as quickly as possible so that she could avoid unnecessary socializing, but other nobles invariably did the same and there was always a crush of horses and carriages.

Ela had schooled her staff not to shove to the front or demand special privileges just because she was the countess, and she could hardly change her tune now.

She was outside, searching the throng for Freya's bright head, when her old friend Catherine de Brealt hurried toward her. "Ela, my darling, how are you bearing it?"

Catherine meant well, and her kindness warmed Ela's heart, but she didn't want to get into any kind of detailed discussion of her woes. "We are all in God's hands." She attempted a smile as she squeezed her friend's hands. "Has young Simon recovered from his fever?" She knew this to be a safe inquiry because she'd seen the boy in the nave.

"Yes, all praise be to God."

Ela quickly steered the conversation to Isabella's and William's weddings, which allowed her friend to congratulate her instead of weep with her.

After a few similar encounters she managed to mount Freya and ride away with the children following behind in the carriage.

She released an audible sigh of relief as they left the cathedral grounds. Only one person had mentioned Drogo and not by name. They probably didn't even know his name. Hopefully, the matter would soon fall to the bottom of the gossip barrel, at least until the killer was caught and tried.

~

BACK AT HOME, Ela felt cheerful and refreshed after both the ride and her communion with God in such a beautiful place. She handed Freya to the groom and went to help her children down from the carriage.

She was surprised to see the youngest in tears. "What's the matter, Ellie?"

"They were telling lies about you!" sputtered the girl through tears.

Ela glanced at her older children, who all looked somber enough to strike fear in her heart. She ushered them quickly into the parlor so as not to create gossip among the servants.

"What was said to you? Master Blount's death was not my fault or the fault of anyone except his killer."

"It's not that, Mama," said Richard. "They were spewing outright untruths." Red spots of anger colored his cheeks.

"They were," agreed Stephen. "They said you were dressed up as a man and pretending to be one!"

Ela froze. "Who said such a thing?"

"Everyone! All the children were joking about it," said Petronella. "I told them that lies are evil and will split their tongue."

"I told them the sheriff would have them arrested for spreading falsehoods," said Nicholas.

Ela reached deep inside herself. She'd promised herself that she'd never lie to her children. "It's not a lie."

The stunned silence made her knees buckle.

She inhaled deeply. "I did it with good reason." Was that a lie? She wasn't sure. "We're searching for the man who killed Jacobus Pinchbeck, and while I was in London

I dressed as a man so I could enter his establishment. A woman would have no reason to go there and could never gain admittance." She wondered how word had got out.

They all stared at her like she'd grown another eye.

"Because I was able to go there, I now have more insight into Pinchbeck's business."

More silence.

"Did you catch the killer?" asked Stephen at last.

"Not yet, but we're getting close." She hoped that wasn't a lie.

"You put on a man's clothing?" Petronella looked incredulous. "With your legs uncovered?"

"I wore hose. And the tunic was quite long." Her children did not look impressed.

"They're gossiping because you're not married," said Stephen. "People talk about a woman without a husband."

"Your father was all the husband I need or want. I do not intend to take another, and people will just have to get used to the idea."

"You could become a nun," suggested Richard. "You could even be an abbess."

"One day, if the Lord permits, but for now my most important job is to be your mother. I can't live in a cloister and raise you at the same time."

"Don't ever do that again, Mama." Isabella looked deadly serious.

Ela felt a surge of annoyance. "Is it really such a terrible thing? I'm a woman and a mother, but my intelligence is as keen as any man's. My hunger for justice and my desire to see the will of God enacted here on earth is as strong as any man's. If a citizen of Salisbury is murdered, I want to know who did it as much as any man. I simply pursued the investigation as best I could. Do you really think I should confine myself to the narrow role assigned even to women of high birth?"

"Yes." Richard and Stephen answered at once and in unison. Petronella and Ellie nodded in agreement. Isabella's tight-lipped stare spoke volumes.

Ela's heart sank. No doubt their disapproval just reflected their milieu. She'd raised them to be dutiful and obedient members of that society. Had she done her daughters a disservice?

"Well, I'm sorry that my actions have become fodder for gossip and have embarrassed you. But I believe God has charged me with doing his work here on earth and if that involves me sometimes doing something unusual or even alarming to you, then I shall do his work before I look to my reputation."

They regarded her in a respectful if unsettled silence.

"You still wish you were sheriff, don't you, Mama?" asked little Nicholas.

"Yes." She took his chubby chin between her thumb and finger. Her heart swelled with pride that he knew it so well. "Yes, I do."

"Women can't be sheriff," said Richard firmly. "It's not allowed."

"Untrue. Nicola de la Haye, Will's future grandmother-in-law, has been sheriff of Lincoln."

"Has she really?" Petronella looked astonished.

"She really has. So it's not impossible. Don't you think I'd be a good sheriff?"

Their silence deflated her enthusiasm.

"I'm sure you would be, Mama, but we'd be teased mercilessly," said Stephen.

"Christ endured mockery on the cross," she retorted. "But he never weakened. You must learn from his example."

DROGO'S FUNERAL was a pitifully small affair. The bishop led them in prayer in a side-chapel at the cathedral and only Ela and Will and Bill Talbot were in attendance. She'd sent invitations to a handful of other knights who might remember Drogo but had received regrets that they were unable to attend. She felt bad that he'd been buried without word reaching his living relatives—if indeed they were still living —but they couldn't keep the body unburied any longer with spring well on the way.

Ela had forbidden Hilda from coming in order to preserve the poor girl's reputation. She might be heartbroken and lovesick now, but in time she'd be ready to find a husband and the less anyone knew about her involvement with Drogo, the better.

She'd contemplated staying home herself, but decided that would be a display of weakness. If people wanted to talk about her, then let them. She wasn't ashamed of her actions in trying to help Drogo, or even—on reflection—of her ruse to penetrate the secret world behind Pinchbeck's shop. If the idle gossips of Salisbury wanted to wag their tongues about her, then let them. The Lord alone could judge her actions.

Drogo was a knight of the realm and deserved a proper burial, and fortunately Bishop Poore agreed. At Ela's prompting Bill Talbot said a few words about Drogo's career and how he'd saved the great William Longespée in battle. He was laid to rest in a quiet corner of the graveyard where Ela fervently hoped he would finally rest in peace.

AFTER DROGO'S funeral Ela rode to the castle to meet with the sheriff about finding the murderer. She didn't want

Drogo's murder—and the identity of his killer—swept away like the rushes from the floor of the great hall.

De Hal was out hunting when she arrived but she was assured he'd be back soon, so she accepted a cup of wine and made polite, innocuous conversation with Bertrade de Aldithley and her husband, who had come to pay his respects to the new sheriff.

Being back in her old hall but not mistress of it was uncomfortable and itched her like a hair shirt. Even the familiar servants seemed unsettled by her presence, hovering awkwardly around her as if waiting for orders.

When de Hal finally returned, dressed in clothing trimmed with fur and gold and surrounded by his ebullient hangers-on, he didn't notice her. At last the porter approached him and pointed her out. She witnessed his slight frown of irritation before he rose to greet her with a forced smile on his face.

He strode over, politely kissed her hand and murmured the usual pleasantries.

"I'm sure you know why I'm here," she replied.

"My coroner mentioned that you were concerned with the disappearance of Osbert Pinchbeck and were unhappy with the new occupant of his property." He lifted his chin. "And now I'd imagine that the violent demise of Drogo Blount has joined your concerns."

"Indeed. I'm concerned that the murderer—or murderers if there are two—be brought to justice." He could hardly ignore the second murder, which had taken place under his jurisdiction.

"I'm as concerned as you are, except that we have no suspects to arrest. Morhees was under arrest in Exmouth at the time of the second murder and was witnessed there at the time of the first, and Osbert Pinchbeck hasn't been seen in Salisbury—or anywhere else—for weeks."

Ela drew in a deep breath. "The man calling himself Thomas Blount has made a new claim to Fernlees, so he's a prime suspect in Drogo's murder."

"Impossible. Fernlees belongs to Pinchbeck now."

"Not if he can prove a claim in the courts, which my own legal advisor suggests is entirely possible. Especially since Pinchbeck can hardly defend his own claim if he's nowhere to be found." Did de Hal really think his own pronouncement superseded all wills and codicils? He must be dazzled by his own splendor.

"Is this new Blount in Wiltshire?"

"As far as I'm aware, he's in London."

"Then he can hardly have murdered Drogo." He pronounced the name with distaste. "Unless his arm is as long as the river Thames."

"He might have hired a proxy. Or traveled here and returned immediately. He has the strongest motive."

"I fail to understand why." De Hal looked exasperated. "Since Drogo isn't the owner of Fernlees. Spicewell certainly went a long way toward convincing me that he should be, but the fact remains that he never was, and now never will be the owner of Fernlees."

"Since Blount was making his own similar claim to Fernlees—claiming, in fact, to be the true Thomas Blount—I'd imagine he saw Drogo as an obstacle to be eliminated."

"Who is this other Thomas Blount?"

"I don't know. But he's convinced a lawyer to represent him—a lawyer that Walter Spicewell knows and respects—so his claims can't be entirely without merit."

De Hal let out a sigh. "Well, if this second Thomas Blount returns to Salisbury to make such a claim, then my coroner will interview him."

Ela bristled. "It would be better for Giles Haughton to travel immediately to London and interview the man calling himself Blount and those around him while the memories of his associates are still fresh. If he doesn't speak to him for two weeks or more, his friends will have forgotten whether he was at home or not on any particular night."

"My coroner can't be spared for such a long journey. He has business to attend to here in Salisbury. He's preparing the jury for the upcoming assizes."

Ela doubted this since the previous assizes were barely two months ago. Did he intend to thwart her efforts to find the killer just because he could?

One thing he couldn't do was prevent her from hiring Spicewell to keep her informed about the fate of Fernlees. He also couldn't prevent her from going to London herself.

CHAPTER 18

London, June 10, 1226

"Isabella, do stop sighing." Ela was growing increasingly exasperated with her daughter as their carriage rolled along the bumpy cobbled streets. Her morose and distracted behavior had worn Ela's nerves to shreds during the long journey. "We're not selling you into slavery."

"She's just nervous, Mama," said Will. "I'm nervous too, but I'm being a man about it."

"The weddings aren't for a month! Most girls would be thrilled to take a shopping trip to London." Ela prayed that Isabella wouldn't sulk and pout with her new husband. She wasn't a child anymore, and she had no reason to be unhappy about this marriage to William De Vesci. This nonsense had gone on far too long.

Bill Talbot was with them again. This impromptu mission to London was ostensibly to purchase wedding finery and expensive gifts for her future in-laws, but mostly to investigate the mysterious Thomas Blount and seek news of Osbert Pinchbeck. Heavy rain since Chiswick had driven Will and

Bill to seek shelter in the carriage while their horses traveled behind it.

Ela had brought Hilda instead of Sibel and told Sibel to enjoy some leisure time in this beautiful June weather. Sibel had been worked off her feet by the move and adjustment to their new home and deserved a rest.

Ela pulled out the most recent letter she'd received from Spicewell and read a line aloud. "Thomas Blount asserts his rights to the manor of Fernlees as the only surviving natural heir of Radulf Blount, etc." She looked at Bill. "Don't you think Blount has a nerve to assert his right so soon after Drogo's death? Does he realize it makes him look like a murder suspect?"

"If he has an alibi it will be impossible to prove that he's behind it," said Bill.

"Spicewell says Blount has a house not far from the fish-market. He rents it but has considerable pretentions according to his spies."

"Pretentions that would seem quite genuine if he was lord and master of a manor."

"But how can Radulph Blount have two sons called Thomas? It makes no sense. And since I've found from local records and the reports of my neighbors in Salisbury that Drogo was his true son, this one must be an impostor."

"They do look alike," said Will, staring out the window at the rainy streets through a gap in the curtain.

"Drogo and that man?" Ela stared at him. "They don't look at all alike."

"They do have similar features," said Bill Talbot. "The cut of their nose and mouth, and the shape of their ears."

"But they have entirely different hair color and one is half a foot taller than the other." She hated that it was the imposter who towered over Drogo. "I wonder what hair color Radulph Blount had?"

"Dark," said Bill decisively. "I remember him. It had some gray in it even back then, but it was near black."

"Drogo was dark. This mysterious Thomas is blonde. So he's unlikely to be his natural son."

Will laughed and dropped the curtain back over the carriage window. "Mama, I'm tall and fair and Isabella is petite and dark-haired. Are we not from the same father?"

Ela blinked. "I suppose you have a point. Spicewell says this second Thomas has a different mother. Though why she would call him Thomas when there was already a Thomas—" She blew out a breath. "Even the rain doesn't stop the smoke here. It comes right in the windows."

"You can hardly put window glass in a carriage, Mama," said Isabella. Ela had almost forgotten her capable of speech. "It would break."

"It would indeed. In fact my bones may break if this cart rattles any harder over these stones."

Will pulled the curtain back again. "We're almost there. I think I recognize the streets."

"Each street in London is dirtier and uglier than the last. And it's even worse in the rain."

"You're complaining a lot, Mama," said Isabella. "I think you might be worse than I am."

"I beg your pardon, my loves. I have a lot on my mind."

"We all do," said Isabella. "We must be gentle with each other."

THE NEXT MORNING was dry and bright as Ela attended Spicewell in his chambers near the courts of law. His rooms were spacious, with fine furniture and tapestries and a floor of inlaid stone. Spicewell himself welcomed her, and a servant brought them wine in silver cups.

"I'm surprised at your continued interest in the manor of Fernlees," he said, as they sat in front of a tall window with a view over a courtyard with a fountain in it. "Since Drogo Blount is no longer alive and eligible to inherit."

"Part of my interest lies in wanting to know who killed him, and the rest in wanting to oust the noxious tenant and his foul business from Wiltshire. Now that I know his trade, Osbert Pinchbeck and his cohorts are not men I wish to have as neighbors."

"Without a promising intended heir to the property, which you offered in the form of Drogo Blount, I cannot say who will turn out to be the ultimate owner. I can only follow the trail of documents. Unless you'd like to assert a claim to the property. Given your family's long association with the environs and your role as countess—"

"Oh, dear, no. That would be most unseemly. I realize you feel the need to justify your fees, but the information alone is worth coin to me." She looked around his luxurious quarters. "At this point I have many questions and no answers, and my most burning questions concern the identity of the man who calls himself Thomas Blount."

Spicewell tilted his head back. His halo of whitish hair barely moved. "Thomas Blount is indeed his real name. As I mentioned in my letter he's the illegitimate son of a woman called Wilfreda."

"Born while Radulph Blount was married to Drogo's mother?"

"Yes. He and Drogo are almost exactly the same age. The elder Blount maintained his mistress Wilfreda, who was a barmaid at the time of their meeting, in an upstairs room near the London premises of his business."

"He had a business? I thought he lived on the proceeds of the manor."

"He inherited a trade in fleeces but did not profit from

the venture. He was a profligate and a gambler, as you know."

"Why would Wilfreda call her son Thomas when his other son was also called Thomas?"

"Wilfreda's Thomas was actually born first. When Radulph Blount's wedded wife suggested calling his son Thomas, after her own father, could he protest that her rival had already chosen the name for her bastard?"

Ela blinked at his rough language. "So the illegitimate Thomas was firstborn. You've learned a lot."

"Wilfreda is from a class of people whose lips are easily loosened by ale. She herself is still alive and works as a professional mourner."

"She attends funerals?"

"Yes, and wails piteously at the graveside to provide atmosphere."

Ela fought the urge to cross herself. Such playacting seemed quite sacrilegious. "Do you think she gave her son Thomas the idea that he was the rightful heir to Fernlees?"

"She says she didn't."

"You spoke to her?"

"One of my associates did. I have men in my employ who are far easier to confide in than a hoary old man of the law." He twisted a big gold signet ring. "She told him that Thomas is chasing a wealthy widow and came up with the idea of pursuing the manor as a means to win her favor."

Ela frowned. "Do you think he heard of the death of Jacobus Pinchbeck—which would have reached London quickly given his business here—and saw an opportunity?"

"Yes. And he persisted in his suit even after de Hal decided in favor of Osbert Pinchbeck. He's been haunting the offices of my fellow in the law, trying to drum up a case that he is the rightful owner of Fernlees."

"Because he's Radulph Blount's firstborn son?" Ela wanted to scoff at the idea that an illegitimate son might have a claim to his father's property, but her own husband was an illegitimate son who'd been generously favored by his royal father.

"As lawyers we're often asked to pursue cases that seem at first glance to have little merit. A case, like a wren's nest, can be built slowly and gradually from many tiny fragments that each alone would not amount to anything."

"How is he funding his suit? What does he do?"

"He cultivates the air of a man of means, but he seems to be a clerk of sorts for a merchant who moves cargo between here and Antwerp. It's possible that he's borrowed money to finance the venture."

"And who is this widow he's wooing?"

"Her name is Beatrice Panton. Her husband was a merchant who imported linen from Flanders and went down with his ship two years ago."

"And Blount's feelings for her are reciprocated?"

Spicewell lifted his hoary brows. "Perhaps she's lonely. I know little about her, and she does not seem to be someone my associates can ply with liquor in a tavern. She lives in her own house and does not frequent amusements. She barely leaves her home, according to my spies. She seems prosperous enough. I'd imagine that Blount would seem a good deal more attractive to her if he owned a manor."

"But he has no chance of success in gaining the manor, I presume?"

Spicewell leaned back in his chair. "On the contrary. Given the untimely demise of two rivals and the disappearance of another, I'd say his chances appear more promising every day."

Ela blinked. Was this surrogate Thomas Blount owning Fernlees an improvement over Osbert Pinchbeck owning Fernlees and renting it to Morhees? Neither option appealed. She reminded herself that her job was to discover who murdered the two victims, not decide the disposition of their property.

"I believe I'll go visit Mistress Panton."

Spicewell's jaw drooped. "But why?"

"I wish to learn more about her and her relationship with Thomas Blount. He's managed to escape the coroner's notice by his absence, but he has motive to kill both of the men who've died. He seems to be turning over every stone to get his hands on this manor. He would have no chance at it if Jacobus Pinchbeck were alive, nor if Drogo Blount was still here. By bringing this suit he's jumped to the top of my list of suspects."

"You have a list?"

"I do." Much as she already admired Spicewell she did not mean to spread word of Salisbury's unfortunate entanglement in the opium trade. "But since the coroner is not at liberty to come to London to pursue Thomas Blount for questioning—"

"Why not?" Spicewell leaned forward.

Ela drew in a breath. "The sheriff requires his presence at Salisbury." She also did not want to acquire a reputation for speaking out against de Hal. Spicewell was well connected in society, and it was wise to be circumspect in her dealings with him. The vice of gossip could infect even the best of men.

"I see." She suspected he understood everything. But perhaps that was an air he'd cultivated during decades of court appearances. "You wish me to follow Thomas Blount's efforts to acquire Fernlees?"

"Yes. I'd like to know every detail of the suit and anything you learn about him and his associates. And if you hear any news of the missing Osbert Pinchbeck I'd be most grateful for that information as well. Where might I find Beatrice Panton's house?"

ISABELLA CHEERED SOMEWHAT at the sight of the fine jewels she might choose. The jeweler brought his wares to Alianore's house, in the presence of a heavily armed guard. Ela helped Isabella choose two pretty rings, one a ruby and one a sapphire, a delicately wrought gold pin for her cloak featuring two lovebirds, and a fine belt of gold chain interwoven with pearls.

"I feel like a princess," she said, examining the flash of the gems on her fingers. "Thank you, Mama."

They visited Alianore's favorite clothier and ordered new gowns and cloaks for both Isabella and Ela, and new tunics for Will. He sold them embroidered ribbon that would save them hundreds of hours of painstaking stitching in decorating the cuffs and collars of various garments. They also purchased some hose in garish hues that Will swore all the young noblemen preferred that season.

The city's finest cordwainer—who shod the king himself—measured all their feet, ankles and calves and promised delivery of their new shoes and boots to Gomeldon within the month.

Their final shopping destination was the armorer, where Will was measured for a new suit of chain mail armor. He'd grown almost four inches since his last suit was made, and it was time to hand it down to his brother. As Ela's husband had observed, one should not wait for war to be declared before purchasing armor. She was glad Will would be well protected if the fragile peace they'd enjoyed lately wasn't to last.

It was still only midafternoon. Isabella begged exhaustion and wanted to return home. Will wanted to visit a friend who lived a short distance upriver. Ela decided to take Bill Talbot and Hilda along with her to call on Beatrice Panton.

CHAPTER 19

"Are you going to wear a disguise?" Bill Talbot did not like her plan to visit Mistress Panton.

"I shall go as myself." She arranged her veil about her shoulders. "Most people are flattered by a visit from a countess. They shouldn't be, but I've yet to be turned away."

"I'll come in with you." He still looked doubtful.

"That won't work. She'll hardly confide her womanly secrets in me with a man in the room."

"It's not safe for you to go into a strange house alone."

"As Countess of Salisbury I'm rather too visible to be made to disappear."

"That's what you think." He rubbed his chin. "When people are desperate they don't act according to custom or good sense."

"Why would she be desperate? I'm not going to accuse her of murder. It's simply a social call."

"But you don't know her." Bill's forehead creased.

"I intend to remedy that. We shall travel in the coach, and you can wait outside in it."

"I'm bringing my sword."

"Of course you are. You won't even go to the privy without your sword."

"You're making sport of me, but I consider it my duty to keep you safe."

"Which is not the same thing as keeping me a prisoner in my house. This murder investigation is at a standstill. If I don't act now we may never pinpoint the killer. Drogo died on my manor, and I take that very personally."

He heaved a sigh. "I do wish I could come in with you. Perhaps I could woo the Widow Panton myself." Mirth danced in his eyes.

"Then Thomas Blount might try to kill you."

"And I'd dispatch him to meet his maker. Problem solved."

"I don't know if he's the killer. The last thing I need is for you to toy with the emotions of a lonely widow and then elect yourself judge, jury and executioner. Just sit quietly in the coach like a good brave knight."

Hilda sat silent through their exchange. The girl hadn't been herself since Drogo's death. Ela wasn't sure if it was the shock of seeing the brutal murder or the loss of her lover. Probably both.

"Hilda, you will accompany me inside and I'm quite sure they'll offer you refreshments in the kitchen. I want you to listen carefully to any conversation and learn everything you can about the household. How many servants are there? Does she entertain company? Anything you can gather might be a key to solving Drogo's murder."

Hilda brightened at that prospect. "I shall do my best."

"Good. Observe the details. Anything you see might be important."

Bill shook his head and sighed, clearly wishing he could wash his hands of the whole effort but far too loyal to do so.

A servant came to the door before Ela had even alighted from her carriage. Hilda, with a little whispered prompting, hurried to the door to introduce her mistress. The servant looked stunned and hurried inside to report their presence.

They stood outside the door for a few awkward moments, then a young male servant ushered them in.

"My mistress will be with you presently. May I fetch you some wine?" The boy was about Hilda's age and did a fine job keeping his eyes off her, which was quite a feat.

"That would be very kind." It occurred to her that he might think Hilda was her daughter. The girl's clothing was plain but fine quality and looked similar to her own unfussy attire. "Might my maid take refreshments in your kitchen?"

"Yes, my lady."

He ushered Hilda down a passage that led to the back of the house. Ela had time to look around the spacious parlor. The wood floor was swept until it shone and partly covered with a woven carpet, which seemed a grand extravagance. A tapestry with a scene of ships in a port ornamented the wall opposite the windows. The windows themselves were of good size and well glazed. The whole room had a feel of comfortable opulence, and Ela reflected that Mistress Panton's late husband must have been successful in his ventures.

At last the lady of the house made her appearance. Her entire dress looked fresh and uncreased as if she'd just donned it—which maybe she had. She was about five and thirty, with big dark eyes and a full mouth. Her hair was hidden behind her perfectly smooth white veil and wimple, but Ela would guess that it was a rich dark brown.

"I do apologize for keeping you waiting, my lady. I am Beatrice Panton."

"God be with you, Mistress Panton. As your boy may have informed you I am Ela of Salisbury."

Beatrice bowed, clearly quite flustered by the honor of a

visit from the nobility. "I suppose you're here because of Thomas."

Ela blinked. Did Beatrice know she was here to inquire about his whereabouts on the night of the murder?

"He told me about his old family estate near Salisbury and that he'd visited you recently at your castle. He said it's a fine place with a commanding view over the countryside."

"Indeed it is." She managed a smile. So, he'd helped his mistress imagine a social visit to Salisbury Castle, where he was guest of the countess, not a suspect in a murder. "I don't come to London often and I know so few people here." She decided to continue in the same vein Thomas had started to mine. "I'm newly widowed myself, and I thought I'd come make your acquaintance."

Beatrice looked delighted, if a bit surprised. "How kind of you. Are you hungry? The cook has made a mushroom tart."

"Oh, thank you, but I just ate." She could hear Bill Talbot admonishing her to avoid being poisoned. She was already making efforts not to actually drink her wine. "But I'd appreciate any advice you have on adjusting to widowhood. My husband is gone since March. Do you find it lonely?"

"Sometimes." Beatrice sat opposite her in a carved wood chair. "My husband traveled a lot on business, so I was used to his absence, but it's quite another thing to know he'll never be home again."

"How long ago did he die?"

"It's been nearly three years."

"Ah, so long."

"I know a year is the usual period of mourning, but I've not been beset with appealing suitors. Most men prefer a malleable young girl with no experience of the world. I think they find us seasoned wives rather intimidating."

Ela laughed. She was warming to Beatrice. "Understandable. We know the ways of men well by now and they might find we are too skilled at managing them while they think they are managing us."

Beatrice's dark eyes sparkled. "Yes! And for some reason once you're a widow, the hoariest old men with eyebrows like bristle brushes come out of the woodwork. I have had two proposals."

"I suppose they think you'll be dazzled by their string of breweries or their fine stone houses and not notice their hunchbacks." If a man with a string of breweries approached Ela her father would likely rise from his grave to slay him for his insolence, but this merchant's wife wouldn't know that.

"Indeed!" Beatrice laughed. "It's enough to humble a woman. I admit that when Thomas Blount first started to woo me my first thought was, "What's wrong with him?"

"How did you meet?"

"He came here on business. His firm had consigned some cargo to my husband's ship and it was lost. They wanted a signature to claim on the insurance."

Spicewell had told Ela that Blount was a clerk for a shipping firm, so this made sense. She wanted to ask more, but didn't want to betray that she really didn't know him at all.

"I take it his company was more enjoyable than his predecessors."

"Oh, yes, and a man who owns a shipping firm is much preferable to one who owns a tannery or a bakery."

Ela just managed to stop her mouth dropping open. If Blount was pretending that he owned the shipping firm, then he was engaged in a deliberate deception. No wonder he so badly needed a manor to maintain the illusion.

"Aren't you worried he'll travel too much?"

"Oh, I'm used to that." She smiled. "I enjoy my quiet time to spend in reading and needlework. And prayer, of course."

Ela wondered if those were her true hobbies. It wouldn't surprise her. Beatrice Panton seemed like a nice enough woman. "What do you read?" Many women, even of her own noble class, could barely read their own name.

"Our Bible is my most prized possession. My husband bought it for me as a gift on our fifth anniversary. He wanted to reassure me that he was happy with our marriage even though we weren't blessed with children. Would you like to see it?" Beatrice looked so excited at the prospect that Ela could hardly refuse. Beatrice hurried away to fetch the Bible. Ela heard her climb the stairs and walk in a room overhead.

Ela took in a deep breath. She didn't like deceiving Beatrice Panton. But clearly she wasn't the only person doing so. The more she learned about Thomas Blount, the less she liked him. And she suspected she'd be doing Mistress Panton a great favor by exposing him when the time was right.

Beatrice came back down the stairs carrying a thick volume bound in tooled green leather. She graciously placed it in Ela's lap and they leafed through it together. It was a careful copy in black and red ink, with all four gospels and the psalms. The illuminations, though few, were inventive and colorful and she could well imagine spending many happy hours with such a treasure.

"You must miss your husband greatly."

"I do. He was a kind and thoughtful man. Ours wasn't a romance like the minstrels sing of, but we were quietly happy together." She took the offered Bible back into her arms and hugged it to her chest. "And he left me well provided for."

Which likely explained Thomas Blount's keen interest in her. Though Beatrice Panton was certainly pretty and pleasant as well. And some men in midlife preferred a woman unlikely to burden them with the responsibilities and expense of a brood of children.

"Do you think Master Blount is serious?" asked Beatrice,

after she's placed her Bible on a table across the room. "About marrying me, I mean. He's hinted and teased, but there's been no proposal." She blushed. "I can't believe I'm confiding in you so quickly, but there's something about you—"

She came and sat down again. "And it's not often I get to speak with a woman in my position. My dear mother is dead some seven years and my only sister lives in Norfolk."

Ela ached to tell her the truth about Blount, but that wouldn't serve the purpose of trapping him in any lies, deceptions or crimes he'd committed.

"I have no reason to believe he isn't serious in his intentions. Do you feel he would be a good match for you?"

Beatrice hesitated. "He seems a kind companion who I'd enjoy sharing meals and conversation with."

Ela sensed her hesitation. "Are you worried about sharing...other things?"

"My bed?" Beatrice blushed. "I can't say I'm excited at the prospect. But he surely won't expect to have children with me. Or will he?" Concern creased her brow.

"I can't say but I doubt that's his main objective." Ela shuddered at the prospect of sharing her bed with any man but her husband. How some women—her mother included—adapted to one new husband after another baffled her. A man of forty or so could have bedded a dozen women and might easily be poxed. And his wife would have no way of finding out until she was already wed and it was too late to refuse him.

Unless she bedded him first. A trial of sorts. Ela wondered if Beatrice had allowed Thomas Blount into her bed and was just playing the demure widow.

"Has he ever spent the night here?" she asked in as warm and sympathetic a manner as she could muster.

Beatrice looked shocked. "Of course not! What must you

think of me?" She looked at her Bible as if she'd like to hold it in front of her to ward off the accusation.

Ela immediately felt terrible. "I'm so sorry. I didn't mean to offend. I simply meant that…as mature women…we…we —" She didn't know where she was going so she closed her lips and started anew. "I hope that things work out for the best."

Beatrice's placid expression had changed. Her look was suddenly sharper, and had a glare of suspicion. "Why are you here? Did Thomas send you?"

"No! I was in London and thought I might call on you, as a friend."

Beatrice looked doubtful. "I wonder if he didn't send you to discover secrets about me. Let me assure you, there are none!" She rose, clearly flustered. "I must bid you adieu. I attend Vespers every day, and I must get ready."

Ela rose, feeling like she'd stepped in something. Which was silly since she'd come here to get information, not to make a new friend. Still, she liked Beatrice more than she'd expected. "Thank you for welcoming me into your home. I'm sorry I shocked you with my frankness."

"'Tis no matter. May God go with you."

Ela muttered a few more pleasantries as she donned her cloak and headed for the door. Hilda was summoned from the kitchen and joined her outside, where Bill was impatiently waiting with the carriage. She and Hilda climbed in, and they trotted away.

Ela heaved a huge sigh of relief at being back in her own space, even if it was a moving carriage. "I'm afraid I offended her." She let out a nervous laugh.

"What did you say?"

Ela blinked. "Something I won't repeat in mixed company." She shook her head. "But Mistress Panton seems a perfectly decent woman. I admit I'm surprised by that. She appears modest and pious."

"What were you expecting?" asked Bill.

"I'm not entirely sure. Perhaps I'd pictured a courtesan of sorts, decked with gold and jewels from her admirers."

Hilda giggled. Ela turned to her, a little surprised since she and Bill were speaking in French and, as far as she knew, Hilda spoke only English. "Did you learn anything from the servants?"

"I couldn't learn anything when the housekeeper was there. She was awful strict with the others. But when she went to fetch the meat for dinner, I was left alone with the kitchen girl and I asked her all kinds of questions."

"Like what?"

"Did Thomas Blount ever spend the night?" Hilda looked pleased with herself.

"And did he?"

"Never. Not for want of trying, she said. He's full of flattering words and affectionate gestures, she said. But her mistress always shoos him away before bedtime."

"Well done." She now felt confident that Beatrice was telling the truth and that her outrage at Ela's question was justified. "Now we know Blount is lying if he claims that he stayed here on the nights of the murders."

"The girl said he's very keen on her. Always telling her about his shipping firm and how successful it is, and how he's inherited a manor in Wiltshire. He said his father was a knight and he was going to train to be one but he went into business instead. She was asking me how rich he was!" Hilda spilled her news with breathless excitement.

"What did you say?" Perhaps Beatrice Panton had her spies, too.

"I told the truth, that I didn't know."

"Good girl. I don't want her suspicious of him yet. It may

be interesting to watch them and see if he tries to draw her into his scheme somehow."

"You seem to be assuming he's the murderer," said Bill. "What about the opium business? He has no connection to that."

"This opium business has long fingers. How did Drogo obtain the resin to drug the guards? I make no assumptions that Thomas Blount is innocent of connections to the opium trade as well."

Bill stared, clearly trying to make sense of it. And failing. He shook his head as if trying to expel buzzing bees. "What do you intend to do next?"

"We need to lure Thomas Blount back to Salisbury, where he can be questioned by Giles Haughton and arrested if necessary."

"How do you plan to do that?"

Ela leaned against the padded seat back. "By giving him exactly what he wants."

CHAPTER 20

The next morning Ela visited the shop of a silversmith and ordered a cup inset with precious stones as a gift for Nicola de la Haye, her future daughter-in-law's grandmother. Idonea's parents were both deceased so there was no need of gifts for them. She also bought an array of finely worked serving platters for the other set of in-laws. William de Vesci's father was also dead—killed by an arrow just a year after signing the Magna Carta with her husband—but the boy had close living relatives on both his Scottish and Northumbrian sides. She then visited a joiner and ordered a carved chest to hold Isabella's trousseau.

She attended the Sext services at midday and prayed for patience with Isabella, who was still skittish and irritable when the subject of her wedding came up. On her way out she stopped and lit a candle to Mary in a side chapel and said a prayer for her husband's soul.

Her eyes filled with tears as she allowed herself to grieve her great loss. A man in his prime, William was cruelly torn from her and his beloved children. The unfairness of it made her want to scream.

How must the Holy Mother have felt as she witnessed the terrible miscarriage of justice committed against her only son? Surely she must have ached to challenge the Roman authorities or rail against the God of her forefathers? Instead she quietly accepted her fate and trusted that her son had suffered a cruel death in order to save the world.

She must pray harder for such patience and forbearance within herself.

Still, if she couldn't pursue her husband's killer, she certainly intended to solve the murder of the man who'd bravely risked his life to save William's. So that afternoon she headed out, with Bill Talbot in tow, to Thomas Blount's place of business. She'd intended to bring Hilda to see if she had any recollection of him—as Drogo's murderer—but poor Hilda had come down with something and was very ill.

"Why are we going to his workplace instead of his home?" Bill rode alongside Ela as they wove through the people and horses on the crowded streets down by the docks.

"Blount told Beatrice he owns the company. Spicewell says he's a mere clerk. I wish to see for myself."

The building was a sprawling two-story structure of wood on a stone foundation, with part of it seeming—at least from the street—to jut out over the river. There were three doors of varying sizes, but only one ornamented with a carved surround and an iron knocker. Ela and Bill handed their horses to the guard, who followed them, and went to the main door.

She rapped firmly and waited for a few moments before the door opened and she found herself face to face with Blount himself.

He stared at her, apparently struck speechless.

"Good afternoon, Master Blount. You remember Sir William Talbot, of Salisbury?"

"I...indeed." He made no move to invite them in. "To what

do I owe this—" He was trying to be polite but not sure how far to go with it.

"May we enter? There's a light drizzle starting, and I don't want to get my cloak wet." The drizzle was imaginary, and he looked past her as if he might hope to contradict her.

"What is your business here?"

"We came to see you, of course." She smiled, as if it was perfectly natural for her to call on him. "I hear from my lawyer that you're soon to be declared the natural owner of Fernlees."

His face brightened. "If all goes well. My lawyer says my prospects are promising." Perhaps he suddenly saw her as a potential new neighbor—and friend—because his whole demeanor changed. "Won't you come in?"

Ela nodded her thanks and they went in through the doorway to a small, dark chamber with a desk in one corner. The walls were lined with shelves, each one filled with bound books of different sizes. The chamber appeared to be an anteroom, leading into the heart—or bowels—of the building, and Ela walked toward the door on the opposite side.

"This is my counting room." He gestured to the desk, which itself was cluttered with books and scraps of parchment and much blotched with ink.

"Your business deals in shipping goods to Europe?"

"Exclusively to and from Antwerp."

"Gemstones?" She knew the city had fine stonecutters and jewelers.

"Uh, no. Not gems. Mostly linens, lace, ribbon from there, fleeces and tanned hides from here."

For no particular reason Ela felt certain that he was lying. Perhaps every merchant in England was pretending to import flutes or length of ribbon while secretly raking in profits from more valuable items. "And you own this company!" She said it brightly, as if she was impressed. "May we see your wares?"

"Uh..." His gaze fled to the door into the rest of the building. "I'm not the sole owner. A...a partner. And I'm afraid they're busy unloading cargo right now so we'd be in their way."

Ela didn't believe him. If there was a substantial ship docked behind the building, she'd have seen the mast as they approached.

"How fascinating. Perhaps we can watch from the street," she said, mostly to see what he'd do.

"Do have a seat." He pulled out the scarred wooden chair from in front of the desk. Now he'd have to detain her until his imaginary ship sailed to prevent her from discovering him in his lie. That should give her time to learn more about him.

"I went to visit Beatrice Panton," she said quietly, eyes on his face.

He paled. "Why?"

"To make her acquaintance. She was pleased to meet a friend of yours." She waited for this to sink in.

"Naturally I told her that I'd been in Salisbury and met you at the castle," he spluttered.

"Of course. And soon you'll be a near neighbor," she said pleasantly. His growing confusion amused her. "She was a kind hostess. I do hope your intentions toward her are honorable."

"They most certainly are!" The words exploded from his mouth with such force that Ela almost scooted her chair backward. "She's a very fine woman. In fact, she's the main reason I'm so anxious to claim the manor. She deserves a quiet home away from the smoke and grime of London."

"She certainly does. I'm not sure how anyone lives here full time. The noise is incessant. And the smells!"

"One does grow accustomed to it. I've lived here most of my life." He looked rather offended.

"I know. My lawyer, Walter Spicewell, has looked into your past and determined that you are indeed a son of the late Radulf Blount."

He blinked. "Why would you—?"

"As Countess of Salisbury I take a personal interest in the disposition of every manor in the vicinity. I wish to see Fernlees in the hands of its rightful owner, and I feel that a terrible wrong has been done in bestowing it upon Osbert Pinchbeck."

"I'm so glad you agree." Blount rubbed his hands together. "My father would have wanted the manor to return to the family."

Ela wanted to retort that he'd likely have wanted the manor to go to his legitimate son, Drogo, but she couldn't be sure of this. If Radulph Blount had a long relationship with this Thomas's mother, it was entirely possible that he had a closer and more affectionate relationship with his illegitimate son than with his legitimate one. Such a thing was far from unheard of.

"What steps are you taking to ensure the return of the manor to your family?"

"The lawyer I hired has found all the original documentation granting the manor to my family. He has the lifetime deed that my father made to Jacobus Pinchbeck. That and the fact that a change of ownership was never properly recorded —which is not unexpected in the case of a temporary transfer of property—points to the Blount family as the rightful owners. Since I am now the sole survivor, that means I should inherit the property."

Ela fought a sudden urge to raise the possibility that Drogo Blount might have an heir who could make a claim.

But that would hardly add to her knowledge of Thomas Blount and might place the young heir's life in danger.

Her current goal was to learn as much as she could about Thomas Blount, share it with Giles Haughton, then draw Blount to Salisbury to face the facts. To learn more, she decided to tug on his rope a little.

"It seems that you're well on your way to owning Fern-lees. Some might accuse you of stepping over two corpses to get there. Aren't you worried that people will think you a murderer?"

He didn't look rattled. Clearly he anticipated this line of questioning. "Not at all. I'm hardly a murderer." He held out his soft, ink-stained hands as if they somehow proved his innocence.

"Is there someone who can vouch for your whereabouts on the night that Drogo Blount was murdered in my barn?"

He looked down at the floor, and for a moment she thought she'd caught him off guard. Then he looked up at her with a soft gray gaze he'd probably laid on Beatrice Panton more than once. "I don't like to say. It involves the reputation of another."

Ela wanted to roll her eyes. "I know you weren't with Beatrice Panton." She wouldn't necessarily take the lady's own word for her innocence, but the servants corroborated it.

"As I said, I wouldn't like to say." He had the audacity to look rather pleased with himself.

"Another woman?" She stiffened her back. If he claimed to be in another woman's bed she felt it her duty to protect poor Beatrice from him.

"Not another woman." He cleared his throat. "You wish me to besmirch a good woman's character?"

"Indeed I do."

"You are neither judge nor jury, so I shall not."

"You say you were with Mistress Panton, but you don't wish to name her." It wasn't a question. "Let's go to her house and ask her."

"Never!"

"Because to do so would spoil her opinion of you and ruin your plans to marry her wealth...I mean her good heart?"

"Because she's a pious and respectable woman who'd rather die than see her good name dragged through the mire."

"So she'll deny that you were with her, but that won't prove your guilt, because it will be assumed she's merely protecting her reputation."

The man lied almost every time he opened his mouth. She knew he must be itching to throw them out of this anteroom, but once outside they would see he'd lied about the ship being unloaded.

Being a liar made life so complicated and difficult.

"And who can vouch for your whereabouts on the night of Jacobus Pinchbeck's mysterious death? Where he left home but was found back there, chest crushed by his own cartwheels?"

"I've never believed that was anything but misadventure. Have you never had an accident with a horse?" His anger had reddened his face.

"Not one which involved a cart rolling over me." She crossed her arms over her chest, glad Bill Talbot was there. If he weren't Blount might be plotting how to kill her right now and dump her body in the Thames. "So no one can vouch for you on the night Pinchbeck was killed?"

"I would never ask her to do that."

Ela sighed. In addition to lying he was trying to save himself by besmirching Beatrice Panton's reputation, and without good reason from what Hilda discovered.

The door into the interior of the building suddenly swung open. "Tell Wilson the load is three casks short."

Blount jumped half out of his skin. The door hadn't opened enough for Ela to see who was behind it, but the person had addressed him like he was a servant.

The door opened and she found herself staring at a short, rotund man in a red tunic whose thick brown hair naturally formed a tonsure not unlike a monk's. He stared from Ela to Bill then to Blount.

"This is Ela of Salisbury and Sir William Talbot," stammered Blount.

"And I am John Crain," he said, after a moment where they all waited for Blount to introduce him. "The proprietor of this establishment. To what do I owe the honor of your visit?"

Ela was tempted to dig a deep hole and toss Blount into it, but that might permanently sink her plan of luring him back to Salisbury. "We came to visit Master Blount. We have mutual friends in Salisbury." She smiled pleasantly. She knew she was bestowing capital on Blount because now his boss would think he had noble friends.

Blount himself looked deeply uneasy. As well he might.

"Is the ship unloaded yet?" She couldn't resist asking.

"Oh, yes, nigh on two hours ago," said Crain. "Smaller load than we expected. Loaded up and set sail back to Antwerp already."

Ela glanced at Blount, whose mouth had shrunk into a flat line. "Good news," he rasped, clearly wishing the floor would open and swallow him.

"The linen bales for Robert Weft are up on the top floor. Be sure he removes them before the week's end as we need the space for the fleeces coming from Dorset."

Blount nodded.

"And write a letter to Morhees telling him that if the bill isn't paid by Whitsun I'll send a bill collector after him."

Ela's ears pricked at the name Morhees. "Vicus Morhees?"

Crain stared at her as if she were a horse that suddenly spoke. "That's the one. You know him?"

"I've made his acquaintance. Is he a customer of yours?"

"Only once and he won't be again. Quick to order and slow to pay."

"Was he importing or exporting?"

Crain stared at Ela. "What business is it of yours?"

Ela's back stiffened. She wasn't used to such rudeness. Of course, this merchant owed no fealty to a liege lord and had no reason to bow and scrape to nobles.

"I'm leaving for Richmond. The boy is scrubbing the dock. Lock up when you leave." Crain turned and left with a curt nod to Ela and Bill."

Ela blinked as the door closed behind him. "Did you know Vicus Morhees is the current resident of Fernlees?"

"What?" Blount looked incredulous. "How is there anyone there?"

Ela's heart beat faster. "What do you mean? Why wouldn't you expect Osbert Pinchbeck to be there?"

Blount's mouth worked for a moment. "He's abroad."

"Abroad where?"

Blount turned and paced across the small room, picked up a worn volume and turned it over in his hand. "I don't know."

"Then how do you know he's abroad?" She cocked her head. "He can hardly have just disappeared."

Blount shrugged. "Not my business."

Ela wondered if Osbert Pinchbeck was being held somewhere against his will.

And what relationship did Blount have with Morhees? "Did you arrange the trade with Morhees?"

"No. I just recorded the cargo in my ledgers. A load of baskets from Bruges."

More lies, no doubt. "Why would anyone import baskets when we make the finest ones in Europe here in England?" Ela wondered if the baskets were filled with opium.

Blount's shoulders were creeping higher with every minute. "Not my business to care."

"Did Jacobus Pinchbeck import through this business?"

"Never. Always shipped into Exmouth as far as I know. Again, it's not my concern."

"Why would he dock goods at Exmouth, then send them overland to London?"

"He wouldn't. That would make no sense." Blount looked scornful. "No one would do that."

"So he must have been shipping the goods somewhere else?"

Blount put the scuffed volume back down and dusted his hands on his tunic. "You must leave. I have work to do."

"Where did Pinchbeck get the goods for his shop?"

"I have no idea." Blount had opened the front door and stood holding it. "I bid you adieu."

But there was something else she'd wondered about. "How well did you know Drogo Blount? You're half brothers. You must have met before."

"Whether we did or no is none of your business." He gestured for them to leave.

Ela wanted to remind him that when she first encountered him he'd said that Drogo was an impostor. But calling out his lie might frighten him away from coming to Salisbury and didn't serve her purpose. Ela glanced at Bill, who suddenly put his hand on the hilt of his sword as if to defend her honor.

"We shall leave." She rose and hurried to the door. "I'll

seek the answers to my questions elsewhere." She swept past Blount and out into the street.

The late-afternoon traffic was heavy. A donkey laden with bales of something almost knocked her down as she emerged and looked around for the guard with their horses.

"He's likely around the corner, trying not to get trampled." Bill gestured for her to go ahead of him. She knew he hated to have her out on the streets, where an urchin might swipe at her brooch or ring.

"I'm dissatisfied with how little I know of his business. What is really in that warehouse?"

"We learned he's not an owner or even a partner.

"Almost every word out of his mouth is a lie. Do you think he's in the opium trade as well?"

Talbot ushered her forward. "I can't say. And the trade itself is not illegal, though it seems to lend itself to secrecy and subterfuge."

"I suppose that's true with any item of value." Ela was relieved to see the guard, still mounted, calmly holding their two horses out of the fray in a narrow alley between two buildings.

"I'm glad you've managed to keep the horses calm. This area is far too busy for comfort."

"They had their moments, but I'd rather deal with an unruly horse than an unruly human any day of the week." The guard was a gruff older man with a north country accent. Ela found his presence soothing and reassuring.

Bill helped her mount. It was a relief to be safely back in her own saddle and up above the fray. He rode ahead and the guard behind her, and soon they were trotting along the streets while people scurried aside to avoid them.

"Have a care!" she called—half to Bill and half to an old woman swathed in grimy brown homespun who barely avoided his horse's legs—but her words were lost amid the clatter of iron horseshoes on the cobbled streets.

~

THE NEXT MORNING Ela called at the jeweler and commissioned seals for both William and Isabella, to reflect their new status in life. She asked for Isabella's to be ornamented with both the rampant lions of Longespée and the cross of De Vesci, to symbolize the joining of two great families. She intended them to be a surprise wedding gift for each of her children, that symbolized them stepping out from under her wings and taking charge of their own lives.

After the jeweler, she visited Spicewell at his chambers. The old man looked amused—or was it bemused—that she'd called on both Thomas Blount and the object of his intentions.

"I fear you're sticking your fingers into a rat's den, my lady. What is to be gained from meddling in Master Blount's affairs?"

"I gained the knowledge that Thomas Blount is an opportunist and a liar."

"This came as a surprise?" He lifted a white brow.

"No, but the sheer audacity of his falsehoods—the foolishness of them—makes me think he will be easy enough to trap if we can but lay the snare correctly."

Spicewell leaned forward and tented his hands on his desk. "Did you gain evidence that he's your murderer?"

Ela stiffened. "Not yet. But he has such a compelling motive. He needs the manor to woo his intended. She doesn't seem naive or adoring enough to accept him without it."

"What of Osbert Pinchbeck? Are you surprised he hasn't come forward to assert his claim?"

"Not if he's overseas. No one seems to know where he is."

"Do you really believe he's overseas?" His pale lashless eyes narrowed. "Call me a cynical old coot, but I believe that Osbert Pinchbeck is dead."

"What makes you think that?"

"He inherits his father's business and manor, then abandons them to the hands of others?"

"But in his shop I overheard Morhees telling him it was just for a while."

"Did Morhees announce his intention to move into Pinchbeck's fine new home in his absence?"

"Well, no, but I only overheard the briefest snippet of their exchange."

"I feel confident that Osbert Pinchbeck is currently the food of either worms or fishes."

Ela shuddered. "How can you be so sure?"

"Osbert Pinchbeck waited his whole life for this moment. Finally he had everything in his grasp. He's not a man with five manors to choose one for himself and lease out the others. He could move—at last!—from his cramped rooms above the shop into a spacious house with a well-laid garden—"

"It's not that spacious. And as for the garden…. Fernlees has long lacked the attentions of a caring mistress."

"If Osbert Pinchbeck was to appear in my room today I would know myself in the presence of a ghost."

Ela frowned. What if he was wrong and Pinchbeck was their murderer? He had motive enough to murder his father, based on how pleased he'd seemed to assume his new role. "Could your people find him? Alive or dead?"

"Perhaps, with enough time and effort, but is your money well spent on the search? As your lawyer I'd advise you to look to your own affairs and let the sheriff use the king's coin to hunt down the living and the dead."

Her skin pricked with irritation. If only she had a sheriff's license and resources to seek him. "Then who would have killed Osbert Pinchbeck? Thomas Blount, to gain clear access to Fernlees? Or Vicus Morhees, so he could step into his shoes and enjoy his profits."

"Or someone else entirely, for reasons you have yet to discover? Again, I caution you to save your funds."

"I wonder how much of a businessman you are to refuse it." She put a small purse of coins—all gold—on the desk. "Finding Drogo Blount's killer is worth considerable expense to me. However briefly—and however ill-advisedly—I considered him a friend and he brought me solace at a time I dearly needed it. I want his death avenged."

Spicewell reached for the purse and weighed it gently in his palm. "Your folly is my bounty."

CHAPTER 21

Life at Gomeldon seemed to move as slowly as a cloud across the blue June sky. There was much to anticipate but little to do except wait. Ela knew Spicewell was doing everything in his power to encourage Blount's lawyer to goad him to Salisbury to claim his prize.

Preparations for both weddings were well underway, but since she was hosting neither one—a relief in many ways—Ela had no responsibilities other than to deliver the bride or the groom along with their respective baggage and an array of expensive gifts, which she'd already bought on her visits to London.

She was stitching an intricate pattern of grapevines onto yet another new garment for Will when the cook shuffled in, clearly in a huff.

Ela looked up, unsure whether to celebrate the interruption to her boredom or shrink from the litany of complaints about to scald her ears.

"Begging your pardon, my lady."

"Yes, Cook?" She kept her expression neutral.

"It's Hilda."

"Is she worse?" Poor Hilda had picked up something in London and couldn't seem to shake it.

"Not worse but not better. Not any use to a body, though. She can't even stir the pottage without retching and she's taking up space in the kitchen, lying on her pallet all day as well as all night."

"I've given her ginger tea and cloves to calm her stomach. I tried an emetic to purge whatever ails her. She's been treated with hot and cold compresses and even leeches. She doesn't seem to be in danger. She has no fever. I can see no alternative but to wait until it passes out of her system."

"In about nine months." The cook's mouth settled into a hard line.

It took a moment for her meaning to sink in. "Oh no. Do you really think so?"

"What else could cause such vomiting without other symptoms?"

"I never vomited like that during my...times."

"Myself neither, but I've heard of it happening. Might be the little bastard hatched out of her sins poisoning her from within."

"Cook! I'll thank you not to use words like that ever again in my house."

"Begging your pardon," she replied, with no hint of remorse, as she crossed her arms over her ample chest.

"We don't yet know what's amiss. Why don't you send her to me and I'll ask her some more questions." She frowned. "You haven't said anything to her, have you?"

"What? And give her more reason to wail and sob and flail all night long? No, thank you very much."

Ela reflected that it was a shame this cook made such fine work of plain ingredients. Her cooking was the only admirable thing about her. Except her honesty, she supposed. "Send her in. Gently! Don't say anything. I'll probe her with some questions and see if your suspicions are correct."

The cook nodded gruffly and swished out of the room. Ela drew in a deep breath and crossed herself.

When Hilda walked in, her pretty face green and wan and her fillet crooked, Ela asked her to bring a chair to sit at the window with her.

She surveyed the girl surreptitiously before reminding herself it was far too early for her to be showing. "How are you feeling?"

"Not better, but not worse, my lady." Hilda looked reluctant to sit down with her. "It just comes upon me like my stomach is gripped by a fist."

"Have you noticed any other…symptoms?" She struggled for a delicate way to ask. "Have your, er, your nipples changed at all?"

"My—" Hilda glanced down at her breast. Ela quietly noted that her chest did appear slightly fuller than before. She lifted her face, which was now a deeper shade. "They are rather sore, now that you mention it. It hurts to lie on them."

"And redder in color?"

Hilda nodded, eyes widening. "Yes, almost like raspberries. And swollen. Is it very dangerous?"

"I do hope not," Ela stalled for time, trying to think of a way to break the news gently. "Your symptoms seem to indicate a fairly common ailment."

"Do I have the plague?" Tears sprang to her bright eyes.

"Goodness, no! There's been no plague for—" She couldn't even remember the last outbreak. "It's a condition unique to women." She wished Hilda would just catch on so she didn't have to say it.

The poor girl blinked, tears clinging to her long lashes. "Will I die?"

"No." Well, she couldn't promise that. It was as easy a way to die as any. "You will get larger, however. And in approximately nine months' time…."

She looked at Hilda hopefully.

Hilda stared back, apparently more confused than ever. "What?"

Ela reached out and took hold of Hilda's hands, which stiffened with apparent terror. "We can't be certain, since it's still early and anything could happen." She squeezed Hilda's poor cold hands. "But it seems you are with child."

Hilda blinked. Her mouth opened. Then closed again. "I can't be."

"Yes, you can."

"I can't. I'm not married."

Jesus, help me. Ela felt her eyes roll to the ceiling. Did the poor girl have no idea how babies were made? She held fast to Hilda's hands. "When you were with Drogo…in the barn loft—"

Hilda's confused and frankly terrified face stared back at her.

"What you did together…. That's how babies are made."

"But we only—" Her eyelashes fluttered in confusion. "We kissed and—"

"Did you…kiss with the lower parts of your body as well?"

"Well, yes. He said it would feel nice. And it did." Two fat tears rolled down her cheeks. "Why did he have to die?" Her words turned into a wail.

Ela felt hot tears rising to her own eyes. The situation was too awful. The poor girl not only devastated by the loss of her lover but also pregnant with his child—who would be forever nameless because his father no longer lived to make an honest woman of her.

Part of her wanted to horsewhip Drogo for putting the poor girl in this position, but the rest of her wanted to avenge his death for both of them. "You won't feel so ill for the whole nine months. You can go back to your parents' house and rest for a while. Would you like that?"

Hilda nodded.

"Your parents did want to take you home right after the murder so I suspect they'll be happy to have you back." That seemed so long ago. She hoped they wouldn't be too angry about her condition. "The ostler can drive you there this afternoon." She squeezed Hilda's hands again. They were still ice-cold. "Before you go, did you remember any more details from the night of the murder?"

Hilda looked down at her lap. "I wish I did. I don't know why I can't."

It was almost like her mind had painted over a piece of memory that was too awful to recall. Painted it in black so that no one would ever know the details.

"Don't worry about that now. Just think of a good way to break the news to your parents." Ela wondered if she was expected to break the news herself but decided against it. They'd been hard toward her and soft toward Hilda after the murder, so her presence might only anger them. "Go pack your things. I'll summon the wagon."

HILDA WAS BACK FROM HER PARENTS' house before dinnertime. Now quite hysterical with sobbing, and still retching despite her empty and exhausted stomach, she had to be supported back into the house by the frightened stable boy, who was barely older than she was.

He helped her into the kitchen, where Ela could hear the exasperated cook trying not to snap at her as she gave her a bowl of pottage.

Ela ate her dinner in the dining room with her children, thankful that none of them had ever known such distress as poor Hilda. At least she could offer the poor girl a home here. She could do light duties until her baby was born.

Sibel was unusually quiet and seemed to be taking Hilda's ruin very hard. Ela suspected she felt terrible for having brought the instrument of such sorrow into their home and she resolved to set Sibel's mind at ease somehow.

That night Ela could hear the girl's sobbing and moaning despite her own heavy bed curtains, the closed door and a floor between them. She finally gave up and resolved to spend some time at her prie-dieu, asking for God to show the poor girl some mercy by easing her distress.

She was halfway through the fourth decade of her rosary when she heard the cook snap and yell at Hilda to mind herself or sleep outside in the barn. Hilda let out a wail, and Ela decided that she'd suffered enough.

She donned her house gown and hurried downstairs, without even stopping to light a candle. "Cook! Please don't torment Hilda. She shall never, ever have to sleep in the barn."

Hilda lay on her side on her pallet in the corner, curled up in a ball, still shivering and sobbing. It was worse than when she sat in a silent stupor. "Hilda, come with me." Hilda didn't even seem to hear her. She leaned down and rubbed the girl's arm. "Come upstairs with me."

"Go on with you, girl!" snapped Cook. "Heed the mistress, for the love of God!"

Ela wanted to scold cook but decided to focus on Hilda. She managed to get the girl on her feet and guide her upstairs. She was shaking like a leaf, quite inconsolable. Now that the numbing shock had worn off, the pain of her loss and her looming predicament gripped her like a fever.

Ela guided Hilda into her bedroom and sat her on the single chair next to the bed that Sibel sometimes used. She lit a taper above the mantel, then fetched a soft handkerchief from her chest and sat on the bed while she softly dabbed at the girl's flushed cheeks, making soothing noises, until at last her sobs subsided.

"Why are you being so kind to me?" asked Hilda when she finally found her voice.

"It hurts my heart to see you in so much pain."

"My dad said I deserve it for bringing shame on myself and the family." Her shoulders hunched up and another sob rose through her. "And he's right. You warned me. You told me not to sneak out with Drogo, and I didn't listen to you. Why aren't you angry at me?"

"I'm past anger. There's no point in it now. What's done is done and we can't turn back time."

"But you could punish me by turning me out onto the road and letting me starve." Hilda stared right into her eyes as she said this, as if it was a perfectly legitimate option.

"Do you think our Lord would want me to do that?" Ela stroked the girl's hair.

Hilda blinked. Her eyes were bloodshot from weeping. "No," she said softly.

"What do you think he would want?"

Hilda seemed to think this over. Her lip quivered. "Would he want me to become a nun?"

Ela inhaled deeply. The poor girl was trying hard to give a right answer. "Only if you felt the calling, which you don't. I think he'd want you to do your best to manage the difficult circumstances you've found yourself in, and I feel sure he'd want me to help you."

"The cook is fed up with me." Hilda clearly felt no need to

hold back. Things were bad enough already. "She'd throw me out on the street if she could."

"If anyone goes out on the street it will be the cook," said Ela, without meaning to be so blunt. "But keep that to yourself. We'll all starve if I can't find someone to replace her first."

Hilda's eyes widened.

"Perhaps you could sleep in Isabella's room until she goes away to be married. It's not long now, and we can make you a more comfortable bed there rather than a pallet on the hard kitchen flags."

"Won't she mind?"

"I think she'll like having a girl her own age to talk to." Isabella was a kind girl who wouldn't shrink from an act of charity. And—while she certainly wasn't going to suggest it, if Hilda could tell Ela how much she'd enjoyed being "kissed," perhaps it would lessen Isabella's terror at the prospect of relations with her husband. "And you can help her finish preparing her trousseau and packing it. Her wedding is barely six weeks away."

Hilda's eyes filled with tears. Ela knew she was thinking about Drogo and the wedding she'd never have.

"No one will ever marry me now."

"That's just not true. Women with young children marry every day. What would happen to widows if that weren't the case?"

"Their children weren't conceived in sin." Her lip trembled again. "God will punish my baby for my sins."

"Nonsense." Ela thrust the handkerchief into Hilda's hand as a big tear rolled over her cheek. "The Lord would never punish an innocent baby for its parents' sins. Did you know that my late husband was born out of wedlock?"

"He was?" Hilda's eyes opened wide.

"Yes, he was. And he lived a good, productive and happy

life. Not a long enough life to satisfy me," she tried to smile. "And he didn't let the circumstances of his birth stand in his way."

There was no need to mention that her husband's father was King Henry II. The girl would learn that soon enough once she started to gossip with the staff about being in good company.

"I wish I could have married Drogo." Hilda stared into the darkness. "Even though you told me I couldn't."

Ela reflected that Drogo wouldn't have taken advantage of Hilda if he had honest intentions toward her. There was no need to rub that salt into her wounds now. If he were alive, Ela would have done her best to pressure him into giving the girl and her baby his name despite his dubious character.

And if he'd inherited Fernlees, as Ela intended, perhaps Hilda would have inspired or helped him to manage it competently enough and she would have raised her baby as a little lord or lady of the manor.

Suddenly Ela felt like she had no idea what was right and wrong anymore. But she did know the deep aching pain of suddenly losing the man whose star guided your life. She knew what it was like to lose your love to cold-hearted murder. She knew how it felt to be surrounded by people, but more alone than you could ever imagine.

"Life is full of strange twists and turns, and sometimes it's best not to peer too far into the future. Why don't you come lie down in my bed and get some rest. It's big enough for both of us."

Hilda looked surprised and was perhaps too intimidated to refuse. She was already dressed for sleep, and Ela helped her under the covers then climbed in herself from the opposite side.

"Your kindness means more to me than you can imagine."

Hilda spoke so softly Ela could barely hear her. "I never thought that my own parents—" She broke off and Ela heard a sob rise in her chest.

"Don't think about it. They had a shock. I'm sure they'll settle down eventually." She wasn't at all sure of it, but she didn't want Hilda becoming desperate again. "What grand-parent can resist a new baby?" Hilda could face tomorrow better on a night of sleep.

And so could she. For who knew what fresh horrors tomorrow might bring?

CHAPTER 22

"But, Mama! Why?" Isabella was not nearly as charitable as Ela had anticipated. They stood in Isabella's small but pleasant chamber, with its blue curtains and view over the fish pond and plenty of room for another bed beside her own. "She was howling like a banshee yesterday. Something's wrong with her."

"She's distressed." She'd never fully explained the situation with Hilda and Drogo to her children, even the older ones, but surely everyone in the household knew she'd witnessed his murder and arrived naked at the door. Did she have to spell it out? "She needs comfort and prayer."

"Then let Petronella look after her. Prayer is her specialty."

Ela felt herself frown. "Isabella, I'm asking this of you because you're a woman." She leaned in and lowered her voice. "She's pregnant."

Isabella stared. "But how? She's not married."

Really? Had she left her own daughter so ignorant to the workings of human sexuality? "You do know how babies are made, don't you? I could swear I explained it to you—"

"In mortifying detail. Yes, Mama. But you also said it only happens between a woman and her wedded husband."

Ela sighed. "Ideally, yes. But if a woman and a man aren't wedded, and they perform the same…acts." She swallowed. Why were such matters so hard to discuss when they were the very root of all life? "Then the woman will still grow his baby in her womb whether they're married or not. That's why I always impressed upon you the importance of being married first."

"I see." Her gray eyes filled with…something. "Is this Drogo's baby?"

"It is."

"And she's sad because he's dead so they can't be married."

"Exactly." Ela felt relief flood her heart as Isabella's whole demeanor softened.

"Poor Hilda. She's such a beauty and no one will ever marry her now."

"That is not at all what I need you to say to her!" Ela pressed a hand to her forehead. "She might be the perfect fit for a widower with young children of his own."

Isabella looked skeptical. Then sighed. "Don't worry. I'll be kind to her. She can sleep in here. I can't sleep myself half the time, worrying about what life will be so far away from my home and everyone I know. We can console each other."

"Thank you, my love." She squeezed Isabella's hands. "God will reward your kindness."

She hurried out of the room and back into her own chamber before Isabella could have second thoughts. She'd thought to retrieve her favorite prayer book and spend a few moments in quiet contemplation, but she found Sibel in there, folding a nightshirt that she could have sworn was already folded to perfection.

"I'm sorry to bring so much trouble into the house," Sibel

said in a half whisper. "I'm mortified that her parents won't take her back."

"Parents don't look kindly on a girl giving away her maidenhood without a marriage contract to protect her. Poor Hilda. Luckily, she can stay here so there's nothing to worry about."

"I'll make sure she's useful."

"Don't you worry about her. She's not your responsibility. She's mine at this point, and I intend to find the killer of her child's father." She picked up her prayer book. "Did you enjoy your time off while we were in London?" She wanted to change the subject.

"I did, my lady." The odd tone of her voice made Ela look up from her book. "I went to the fair at Amesbury, and I even danced." Her eyes glittered, and her voice trembled slightly.

That struck dread into Ela's heart. She silently vowed not to interfere with Sibel's happiness for her own convenience. "How lovely. Did you meet someone new?"

"Not new, exactly, but I got talking with Piers Warren. I used to see him all the time a few years ago when he owned his shop inside the castle walls."

Ela racked her brain and conjured a memory of a kind man who'd sold jars and barrels and bottles. "I remember him. Has he moved his shop?"

"Down to the new town, near the cathedral. I didn't even know about it. It's on a side street. He said business is brisk and he's rented some meadows and a flock of sheep to graze them."

"How nice for him to enjoy such prosperity. Was he the one you danced with?"

"Yes he was. And a fine dancer he was, too. Quite light on his feet." She looked giddy as a teenage girl talking about her first love.

Doubts crowded Ela's mind. "Has he been married?" She

wanted to make sure Sibel wasn't going down a foolish path with the first man to glance at her—like Hilda.

"He was. Married eight years, but his wife died in childbirth two years ago. It was to be their first but the little boy didn't survive either."

"How sad." But possibly good news for Sibel. "Did you make plans to see him again?"

"He suggested it, but I told him I'm very busy here at Gomeldon."

"Well, for goodness sake, we must ride out to new Salisbury and put the poor man at ease."

Sibel looked rather stunned. "You wouldn't mind me seeing him again?"

"Mind? I'd be delighted. I've stolen enough of your life already." She placed her book back in the chest. "I'm deadly serious. Let's go into town right now. We can purchase some of his wares, and I will discreetly turn a corner so you can make your plans. You may have off whatever time you need. I have Hilda to attend to me now. See? She's already becoming useful."

All aflutter, Sibel donned a fresh wimple and they set out on horseback, with Sibel riding Petronella's dead-quiet bay pony. Sibel chattered quite uncharacteristically about Piers Warren and how he'd leased his shop space from the bishop by providing for his needs and then built the shop with his bare hands. It was obvious they'd already spent some hours in conversation.

Ela reflected that, pretty and kind as Sibel was, she'd have married years ago if she'd had even a tiny sliver of opportunity. Hopefully it wasn't too late.

The blow of losing two of her children and her faithful companion to marriage in one short year would be hard to bear, but she'd manage somehow.

Piers Warren was quite flummoxed by the arrival of Sibel

on horseback at his shop, followed by Ela and her entourage of guards. He hardly knew what to do with himself, and Ela tried to put him at ease. She fingered his wares and bought a basket that fit over the arm for gathering herbs, and some bottles for making herb-infused oils for cooking. She then excused herself and went outside for a walk around the cathedral, leaving Sibel to make her plans.

The guard followed Ela to the cathedral close. She intended to ride around three times, which should give Sibel enough time to plan her next outing but not enough to get herself into trouble. Scaffolding covered the outside of the great cathedral, and a crew of masons were hard at work chiseling blocks of stone and raining stone chips and dust down on the ground below. She was halfway through her second circuit when Giles Haughton trotted up to her on his bay palfrey.

"My lady!" He saluted her. "God's blessings on you. May I have a few words?"

Ela pulled up her horse. "How did you know I was here?"

"I was heading to the castle, and one of the soldiers said he saw you headed this way."

Ela wondered at herself being talked about but decided not to inquire further. "And you came looking for me?"

"Good news. Thomas Blount is arriving tomorrow to petition Simon de Hal to grant him Fernlees."

"That is good news." Her horse responded to her excitement by jigging in place. "Will you be able to arrest him or hold him for questioning?"

"I spoke to de Hal about that this morning, and he was in agreement that he should be arrested."

"Thanks be to God." Ela'd been a little afraid that de Hal might refuse just to slight her. "I'd like to come when he's questioned, and bring Hilda. If she sees him she might recognize him as the murderer."

"She's back to normal?"

Ela hesitated. She didn't want to reveal Hilda's condition. The pregnancy was still early and might not stick. "Not exactly, but she's regained the power of speech."

"I shall tell him I summoned you to be present as the complainant. The murder happened at your manor."

"Indeed. What time is he coming?"

"I believe he arrives tonight. If you come early in the morning I hope to be in full control of the situation."

Ela wanted to glance back at the guard, who sat on his horse within earshot. She hoped that nothing would happen to warn Blount or prevent him from arriving safely within the castle walls, where he could be detained.

"Is there a chance that Blount won't be in the dungeon tonight? The thought of him walking abroad in Wiltshire frightens me."

"We have men on the London road waiting for him to make an appearance," said Haughton confidently. "He won't escape. You can sleep quietly tonight."

"I thank you. May God protect you and I'll see you in the morning."

When Ela arrived back at Warren's well-ordered shop, Sibel was waiting outside, chatting animatedly with him in broad daylight as if to dispel Ela's fears that he'd take advantage of her. A pleasant featured man of medium stature, Warren seemed to have grown a foot taller since she'd left.

Ela made conversation about the carvings underway on the cathedral. Sibel, with a shy glance at Warren, asked if she might have the next afternoon free to walk with him and Ela readily agreed.

As they rode back Sibel chattered gaily about baskets and bottles and black-faced sheep. Ela tried to reassure herself that she'd survive without her closest companion of more than twenty years—and so soon after the loss of her beloved husband.

Or maybe they'd quarrel on Friday. Maybe Piers Warren would find Sibel too old to bear his children. Maybe Sibel would decide she'd prefer to live in a castle, or at least a rambling manor house, rather than in two rooms above a shop.

By the time they arrived back, Ela's head was spinning and she'd resolved not to interfere in any way but to leave the matter up to God and his will for herself and Sibel.

THAT NIGHT ELA watched with relief as Isabella welcomed Hilda into her bedroom and helped her settle in.

Ela spent some quiet time at her prie-dieu and climbed into her bed. Sibel had scented her sheets with lavender, and the aroma soothed her and eased her passage into rest. She barely registered Sibel coming in to close the window against nighttime drafts, but still managed to whisper thanks and wish her a restful night.

She was deep in the land of dreams, floating on a boat over choppy seas and trying to hold up the tilting mast all by herself against a hard wind, when a blood-chilling scream shocked her awake.

CHAPTER 23

Ela flew out of her bed. "What's amiss?" She rushed to the door and pulled it open. Doors opened all over the house. Isabella appeared in her doorway, two doors down from Ela's. "Hilda's gone!"

"Gone where?" Was the girl ungrateful or foolish enough to run off into the night?

"Out the window! There was a man, and he told me he'd kill her if I screamed." Isabella's face was a mask of terror. "And I screamed!"

"Guards! Bill! Will! There's an intruder—catch him!" Ela yelled out the orders and rushed past Isabella into her bedroom. The diamond-paned window swung open to the outside and Ela, leaning out, could just make out a ladder below, which had been knocked to the ground to prevent pursuit.

"Blount! He must have come for her." Panic gripped her chest along with guilt that she'd thought poor Hilda guilty of running off. "We must raise the alarum."

She prayed that they'd catch him on the property and

could present him to Simon de Hal as a trussed hog in the morning. She ran downstairs, tugging on her robe. The servants were all up and bearing candles, and she gratefully took one and headed outside. The six guards—she'd hired more—ran hither and thither.

"Hilda!" Ela called into the night. "Don't let him take you! Cry out to us and we'll save you!" She rushed toward the woods, which was the way she'd enter if she were an intruder. The thicket of ancient trees lay only fifty yards or so from the house on one side and extended down to the road. "Hilda! Where are you?"

Her ears pricked as she could swear she heard a meek reply.

"Hilda, are you out here?"

Again she heard a noise. "Guards! This way! I think she's here." Ela forged into the woods, holding out her candle. "Call out to me, Hilda, we're coming!"

Was the man still there with her? He might try an ambush. "Bill? Where are you?" He was the only one she truly trusted to protect her. She heard him call back from the far side of the woods, out by the road.

Branches grabbed at her hem and roots tripped her, but again Ela heard the faint sound, like a cat. The sudden grip of a hand on her ankle made her shriek.

"Hilda!" The girl lay on the ground, her mouth tightly bound with stout rope that forced her lips apart. Her wrists and ankles were also tied, but she'd managed to free one hand from behind her back. "Praise be to God! Are you hurt?"

Hilda tried to reply but couldn't make a sound with the gag in place. Bill crashed through the woods from the far side. "Bill, do you have a knife?"

"I have my sword."

Ela held her breath while he cut carefully through the bounds. Hilda was crying and gasping and quite hysterical by the time she could finally move her mouth.

"Who was it?" Ela asked.

"I've never seen him before." Sobs wracked her. "He trussed me and flung me over his shoulder. He told me and Isabella he'd slit our throats if we made a sound."

Ela stared. How would this man—if it was Blount or some other—know which room to climb up to? The manor had at least seven rooms on the second story alone.

"Did he have light hair or dark?"

"I'm not sure. He bound my eyes." She pulled up a rag with a knot still tied in it that lay around her neck. "I only got a glimpse of him when I first woke from sleep with him standing over me, and it was dark. He had dark eyes. I'm sure of that."

Ela frowned. Blount had light blue eyes. Of course, the darkness could make anything look dark. "Bill, did they catch him?"

"I don't think so. I should have stayed awake myself."

"We need to raise the hue and cry. Haughton said they had spies awaiting Blount's arrival on the London road. They planned to put him in prison as soon as he arrived at the castle. How could he sneak over here in the night?"

"He must have not gone to the castle yet. But why would he attempt to take Hilda?"

"Because he doesn't want her to testify against him. He doesn't know she can't remember anything about Drogo's murder."

"But why take her? Why not just kill her quickly and sneak out again?" Hilda let out a whimper, and Bill apologized for his bluntness. "And why drop her here in the woods?"

"I got my hand loose and tried to scratch his eyes out. I know I hurt him." Hilda's chest heaved. "I think that's why he dropped me. Then I heard you calling me."

"Do you know which way he went?" asked Ela.

She shook her head. "I couldn't see anything."

"How far was he hoping to carry a grown woman slung over his shoulder? He must have a horse nearby." Blount was tall but not especially strong looking. She'd heard no sound of horses until just now, with the guards scrambling to chase him and to alert the castle.

Bill had freed Hilda's legs now, and she rubbed at her ankles. Ela could see abrasions left by the ropes. "Can you stand?"

Hilda took her hand and managed to raise herself up. Ela wondered if all the shock would make her lose the baby, and whether that would be a further crushing blow to her or a blessed relief.

"Are you able to walk back to the house?" Hilda nodded, and they walked back slowly.

"I'm staying on guard outside for the rest of the night," said Bill. "He might try to come back. And with your permission I'd like to have words with the guards."

Ela inhaled deeply. The guards should be sent away without pay. Or worse. "Someone alerted Blount that Hilda was in Isabella's room. Be careful. There's someone on the manor who's in Blount's pay. Let's just try and get through the night without further incident."

And she'd worried about not having a good pretext to come to the castle and accuse Blount.

Now she just prayed he'd be there—in custody—when she arrived.

Ela commanded that all six guards ride to the castle in the morning with Bill there as a safeguard. Will remained behind to protect the household. Hilda rode alongside Ela.

The castle stablehands took the familiar horses with warm greetings, and the porter ushered her into the hall with his characteristic serious expression. Ela was relieved to see Giles Haughton already there.

The familiar castle hall looked different with her family's old tapestries removed and the tables arranged in a different pattern than she'd have chosen. The rushes on the floor needed changing, and she could smell the spilled wine and ale from last night's carousing. De Hal's well-fed henchmen sat here and there, some already drinking, others picking their teeth or looking bored.

After the preliminary pleasantries were out of the way she immediately asked if Blount had been arrested.

"Oh, yes," said de Hal. "Giles Haughton had obtained a warrant for his arrest, and it took place as he entered the castle gates. He's in the dungeon right now."

"He arrived this morning?"

"Late last afternoon."

Ela stared. If Blount was in custody here since yesterday afternoon, then who had broken into the house to take Hilda?

"Has he been questioned?"

"Not yet. Master Haughton wanted to wait until this morning."

Ela silently thanked him for that.

"I have three men of the jury here as witnesses," said Haughton. "We can go down and question him when you're ready."

"Have him brought up to the hall," said de Hal. He didn't want to climb a ladder down into a malodorous dungeon when he could listen to the inquisition from his comfortable chair while munching on dried figs.

"In the meantime, I'd like all six of my guards arrested."

"What?" De Hal and Haughton spoke in chorus.

"We've had two different people enter my property on their watch. Drogo Blount is dead, and last night someone attempted to abduct my maid Hilda Biggs from my daughter Isabella's bedroom. Their failure demonstrates something more than simple incompetence, I think."

"Agreed," said Haughton.

De Hal looked perplexed. "But you chose those guards yourself."

"I did. There may only be one bad apple in the barrel, but I believe they deserve punishment for their failure. I would like to select six new garrison soldiers as my guards."

She looked him steadily in the eye.

"These soldiers are the king's garrison. They must be battle-ready at all times."

"All the men of my household are at the king's disposal in time of need. The king is close cousin to my children." She enjoyed reminding him of her family's status.

"I suppose six men can be spared." He issued the command to arrest her guards. Ela tried not to feel bad for any of them, even those she'd known for years, because of this repeat gross dereliction of duty. What use was a guard that couldn't keep out an intruder?

The tables were arranged in a U shape, with de Hal seated in his grand chair in the middle. Haughton and Ela sat on one side and the jurors along the other. Ela described the events of the previous evening and summoned Hilda over to the table to watch the proceedings. "Whoever took her must have been strong. He carried her right across the lawn and into the woods and apparently was making for the road."

"She's a slip of a girl," said de Hal dismissively. "Any man here could carry her. And it can't have been Blount, that's for sure. He was down in the dungeon the entire time."

As they waited for Blount to appear, Ela half expected a servant to come running in and announce that he'd vanished.

That didn't happen. A surly-looking Thomas Blount, his blond hair uncombed and his fine clothes rather the worse for his night in the dungeon, appeared between two soldiers. "Why have I been arrested? I came here to claim my birthright!"

"Silence!" barked de Hal. "You'll speak when you're spoken to, prisoner."

Ela heard a whimpering sound that make her turn and look at Hilda, who was suddenly trembling and staring at Blount.

"Do you recognize him?" Ela asked her.

Tiny sounds issued from Hilda's throat.

"Is this the man who killed Drogo?" Ela placed a gentle hand on her arm.

Still staring at him, and now shaking like a leaf in the wind, she nodded her head. "It's him," she whispered finally. She grasped Ela's arm and stared at him. "I know it's him."

Ela wanted to cross herself in gratitude for the return of Hilda's memory. "We seem to have our murderer, gentlemen."

"Who is this girl?" demanded de Hal, looking at her as if she'd just asked him for alms.

"Hilda is my maid," said Ela. "She happened to be in the barn at the moment that Drogo Blount was murdered."

"What was she doing in the barn?" De Hal peered at her. Hilda's lip began to tremble. De Hal's expression turned somewhat derisive. "She is a pretty girl, I'll say that."

"I saw him kill Drogo with my own eyes." Hilda suddenly

found her voice, and it sounded loud and clear. She stared right at Blount. "His blood sprayed on me as the knife cut Drogo's neck. He came after me and tried to kill me, too, but he couldn't catch me because I ran to the house."

"She came pounding on the door, covered in blood," said Ela, praying that she wouldn't have to mention Hilda's nakedness.

Blount had turned white. He probably hadn't seen or noticed Hilda when he first came into the hall. Or hadn't recognized her under such different circumstances. But now he knew she was the witness who escaped his knife.

"She's lying!" he yelled. "I never saw her before!"

"Wasn't Drogo Blount killed at night?" asked de Hal. "If so, how did she see him?"

"The moon was full at that hour," said Hilda. "It shone in through the window in the hayloft. It was almost bright as day."

De Hal cleared his throat. "Master Haughton. You saw the conditions in the barn on the night of the murder. Would you consider it possible for this girl to have seen the killer's face clearly enough to identify it?"

Giles sat up in his chair and leaned forward. "The moon was hidden behind cloud by the time I arrived that night, but I'd say it's possible, if she had good enough eyesight."

"I was in London when he was killed."

"You have no witnesses to that effect," retorted Ela. She turned to de Hal. "I already interviewed the woman he claims to have been with. And Hilda spoke to her servants. He was not at her house on the night of the murder or any other night."

"What woman is this?" De Hal seemed intrigued.

"Her name is Beatrice Panton. She's a widow. Blount has been courting her and no doubt hopes to win her heart by becoming the owner of Fernlees." Ela looked from de Hal to Blount. "Which is why he had motivation to kill both Jacobus Pinchbeck and now Drogo Blount. He may well have killed Osbert Pinchbeck as well."

"What? I never killed anyone! It's all lies! The woman is mad!" Blount's face was white as cut stone and his eyes darted around the room as he looked for someone—anyone—to believe him.

"Osbert Pinchbeck is dead?" Haughton asked Ela.

"We have no evidence of it, but he's nowhere to be found. My lawyer's men report that his shop in London is closed up. A man called Morhees is living in his house here."

"At Fernlees?" asked de Hal.

"Yes," said Ela. "He claims to be renting it from Osbert Pinchbeck."

"So, by your claim, you're hoping to turn this man Morhees out of Fernlees?" asked de Hal of Blount.

"Yes. Fernlees is my birthright. My father wanted me to have it." He spoke as if he could still turn the situation around and go forward with this plan.

"So..." De Hal leaned back in his chair. "When you rode to Fernlees yesterday, did you know Master Morhees was in residence or was that a surprise?"

Blount blinked, and looked flustered. "I didn't go there yesterday. I came straight to the castle."

"You're a liar. I had you followed from the moment you entered Wiltshire. You rode straight to Fernlees, spent some considerable time there, then came to the castle just before dusk, where we promptly arrested you."

Ela stared at de Hal, astonished and pleased that he'd actually taken the matter this seriously.

"He could have had a conversation with Morhees, possibly about abducting Hilda!" exclaimed Ela.

"Oh, he had a conversation with Morhees. He was followed to the edge of the property by two of my men who were hiding in a covered cart filled with sacks of flour."

Blount started to look panicky again. "I wanted to see my future home. I went to tell him that he must get ready to move."

De Hal lifted a brow. "My men admit they couldn't hear your conversation. They said it was spoken in hushed tones, as if you wanted to be sure the servants didn't overhear."

"So it wasn't a confrontation?" asked Ela. "Like you might expect if one man orders another to leave his property?"

"Not in the least. More of a whispering between conspirators."

Ela looked from one to the other, trying to take this in. Morhees and Blount working together? When she'd called on him in London, Blount had seemed stunned that Morhees was living at Fernlees. "So Morhees could have come to my house last night to steal Hilda. He should be arrested and brought here."

"Did you kill Jacob Pinchbeck or did Morhees do it?" Giles Haughton asked Blount.

"I never killed anyone." Blount's voice was shaking. "I don't know about any of this. I came here to claim my birthright."

Giles Haughton leaned forward and pinned Blount with his hard gaze. "Two men are dead for certain and one is missing. You are currently under suspicion of killing all three of them. Don't lie to us. Did you kill them all or did you have an accomplice in Morhees?"

Blount looked from him to the silent, stunned jurors. Then to Ela. Then to Hilda.

"Are you willing to hang for another man's crimes?" asked de Hal. He plucked a fig from the earthenware bowl on the table and ate it slowly and deliberately, as if it might be one of Blount's internal organs.

Blount looked like he was about to soil himself. His hand shook and even his knees seemed unsteady. "Morhees planned it." His voice was a breathy rasp. "He wanted the Pinchbecks' business."

CHAPTER 24

Ela stared at Blount. The great hall was so quiet that even the mice must be holding their breath. "Do you know the nature of the Pinchbecks' business?"

"Opium," he spat out. "Hidden inside cheap trinkets and fripperies. They ferried a fortune in the stuff across the roads from Exmouth to Oxford and other places as well as London. They never docked in London. Too many spies. They kept their wares in a big barn in the woods somewhere. I don't know where."

"I know where," said Ela coolly. "And so does Master Haughton. But how do you know all this if you weren't involved? I hardly think Morhees would share his business plans with a virtual stranger, especially if he intended to have you hang for them."

"I have...associates who looked into his business for me."

Ela kept her face expressionless. "Sir William Talbot and I have attended Master Blount's place of work and Master Blount is but a lowly clerk for a merchant house."

His face hardened. "My mother works in a tavern frequented by the sort of men Morhees and the Pinchbecks associate with." He spoke without hesitation, and this time her gut told her it was the truth. Especially since it was not the kind of thing a man would brag about.

"Your mother is a barmaid?" asked de Hal, with a sneer of derision.

Blount lifted his chin. "She is. An honest woman who raised me with little help from my father."

"Who was unfortunately still married to his lawful wife," muttered de Hal. "I've never met a more reprehensible group of individuals."

Ela fought the urge to murmur that was because he hadn't been sheriff very long. "How did you become acquainted with Morhees?"

She watched Blount's Adam's apple bob as he swallowed. "He overheard me speaking with my mother in the tavern about how my father had just died and his manor Fernlees—my birthright—was in the hands of a man who'd cheated him out of it.

"Fernlees was not and never will be your birthright," contradicted de Hal, obviously exasperated. "You are a bastard son and have no right to it!"

Giles Haughton cleared his throat. "Perhaps our prisoner assumed that if all the relevant heirs were wiped from the face of the earth, he might make a bold claim."

"Perhaps Morhees convinced him of that," said Ela. "He could have seen an opportunity to gain control of the Pinchbeck's business by having Blount do his dirty work. Blount kills Jacobus Pinchbeck, and Morhees somehow disposes of Osbert Pinchbeck, then Blount kills Drogo to clear the way to his inheritance."

"I didn't kill Jacobus Pinchbeck!" cried Blount. "Morhees told me that Osbert Pinchbeck killed his father. He wanted me to spread the rumor so Osbert would be arrested and out of the way."

A stunned silence fell over the room. He'd effectively confessed to a conspiracy.

"Then where is Osbert Pinchbeck?" asked de Hal.

"Morhees told him he was under suspicion and that he'd have to lie low for a while. Said he'd rent the property from him and take care of it in his absence."

"And Pinchbeck believed him?" De Hal scoffed. But he was leaning forward, figs abandoned, listening intently.

"Didn't have a choice, did he?"

"So Morhees took over his business and his house. But then why would he encourage you to claim the house if he wanted it himself?"

Blount blinked. Ela could feel Hilda trembling behind her. Her anger at this man boiled inside her, but she vowed to sit quietly and let him dig his own grave.

"Jacobus Pinchbeck died with Morhees name written on a note he carried," said Haughton. "He must have been on his way to meet Morhees, who told Osbert Pinchbeck when and where to waylay him."

"Osbert might even have put Morhees name on his father's body himself, to redirect suspicion," muttered de Hal. "There's no honor among thieves."

"Why did he bring Jacobus back into his own drive and not just leave him dead on the road?" asked Ela.

"He needed time to leave the area and get back to London undiscovered. He could hardly leave his father's dead body on the London road. Since he returned the cart and its owner to its rightful place the death wasn't discovered until first light." Blount's voice was strangely expressionless. He seemed to finally realize the swamp he'd waded into.

"And I suppose Osbert Pinchbeck knew the property well enough to do it easily," said Haughton. "He was motivated by a desire to inherit both the property and the company."

"And had no idea that Morhees was goading him on so he

could stitch him up and take both," said de Hal. "Where is Osbert Pinchbeck now?"

"How would I know?" said Blount sullenly.

"And Morhees persuaded you to kill Drogo Blount?" Giles Haughton stared at Blount.

"Why would Morhees want to do that?" the prisoner retorted, without actually denying it. "What did he have to do with Drogo Blount?"

Good question, thought Ela, frowning. But he'd killed him and Hilda had witnessed it.

"I suspect Morhees saw it as a way to sweep both you and Drogo Blount out of the way, and with Osbert Pinchbeck missing, he could keep living at Fernlees and retain control over the Pinchbeck's business, all while keeping his hands clean of the murders."

"So he made you his fool?" asked de Hal, looking at Blount. He ate another fig, slowly tearing it with his teeth. "You tried to make a deal with the devil and now you're about to twist in the wind for him."

Blount couldn't seem to summon the energy to protest. His dreams of a manor and an heiress wife had collapsed like a house of cards.

"But who tried to kidnap this girl?" He pointed at Hilda.

"Morhees." His shoulders lifted slightly, as if he were proud that Morhees had kept his part of the bargain.

"He agreed to it after you passed by his house, to eliminate the witness. But why? It's in his interests for you to hang and be out of the picture."

Blount didn't have an answer for that.

"Perhaps he didn't intend to succeed," suggested Ela.

"Then why come at all?" asked de Hal. "He could leave the girl where she lay."

"Ela's house being invaded last night virtually guaranteed she'd be here at the castle this morning—with the girl," said

Haughton. "Thus ensuring Blount could be accused of Drogo's murder and could thus be no more trouble to him."

Ela saw no reason to mention that Hilda's memory had been absent this whole time. But one thing puzzled her. "But now Blount is here naming Morhees as the mastermind behind both killings."

Haughton's brows lowered. "Morhees has no blood on his hands and solid alibis for both killings. His accuser is a reprobate and a liar. Perhaps he hopes to walk free and keep the manor and the business."

Blount's eyes darted around as he realized the trap he'd stepped into.

De Hal ordered a group of ten soldiers to go arrest Morhees forthwith. Ela said a prayer that they'd succeed.

"Jurors, do you have any questions?" De Hal looked at the men, who'd been sitting in intent silence this whole time.

Stephen Hale, the cordwainer, asked a question about Blount's whereabouts on the night of the murder. Ela listened for him to say he was in London, but he didn't even try to lie. "You know where I was. But I say to all of you that Drogo Blount was a man willing to sell his soul for a lump of the poppy resin. He didn't deserve a manor or any of the honors that come with it. I did the shire a favor by ridding it of him." Ela wanted to protest that she'd never seen signs of opium use in Drogo. Looking back, she could imagine that he craved relief from the injuries he'd sustained while fighting for king and country, so maybe he'd used the poppy without her knowledge. Truth be told, Drogo had a lot to answer for, but he didn't deserve to be murdered in cold blood over a piece of land.

A younger juror, a tanner with black hair and piercing blue eyes, asked about the method of murder and how much Drogo had suffered.

Blount lifted his chin. "It was a quick slash to the neck

like any man would use on a sheep or a calf. Painless as could be." The juror shook his head like he was looking upon the devil himself.

"Have you ever killed a sheep or calf?" asked Haughton.

Blount hesitated. "Nay, I've lived my life in London. Morhees schooled me on where to cut for the most blood loss."

Haughton shook his head in disgust. "And the girl was there?"

Ela glanced at Hilda. She stared at her knotted hands like she was trying to block the proceedings from her mind.

"Aye. I didn't see her until it was too late. She was lying right under him." He shot her a leering glance that sent a surge of fury through Ela. Thankfully Hilda didn't look up. Ela hoped she wasn't slipping back into the deaf and dumb state she'd been in right after the murder.

"Any further questions?" De Hal looked around the room. No one spoke. "Then save this information carefully in your minds for the assizes. Blount will be tried for his life. In the meantime he'll remain locked in the castle dungeon."

"What about leniency for revealing Morhees role?" asked Blount.

De Hal snorted. "You'd better pray for leniency from your creator, because you'll be seeing him soon enough."

Ela felt tension creep up her spine despite the reassuring news. Drogo's killer would meet his day in court and likely hang for his crime. But Morhees was still at large and if anything he was the worse criminal. "Morhees must be arrested quickly, before he's warned and escapes."

She remembered that she'd heard Sibel closing her window in the night. It occurred to her with a chill that it was probably Morhees, climbing to the wrong room by mistake. He knew where she slept.

Blount had been hauled to his feet by the guards in readiness to return him to the dungeon, but another question for him suddenly prodded her. "How did Morhees gain entrance to my manor, past the guards?"

He just stared. His shoulders had dropped and his whole demeanor changed. His fate seemed to be descending upon him like a heavy rainstorm.

"Perhaps they were bribed with the same potent substance that lured Drogo," said Giles wryly. "It seems to turn sane men into brute beasts who fall prey to their own cravings."

"They shall be put to an inquisition," said de Hal. "Don't trouble yourself further about it."

Ela reflected that she should be pleased with the progress made today and not push de Hal too far by wanting to oversee every detail of the investigation. "I thank you, sheriff." She wanted good words about her involvement to reach the king's ears. "But what of Fernlees? Drogo mentioned a child. Shall I have my lawyer investigate this child and pursue a possible claim for the property?"

"If that's how you wish to spend your coin," said de Hal as he reached for another fig. "I hardly see what you stand to gain from it."

"Not all gains are material." Providence had blessed her with abundance and the wits to keep it. Founding and funding a monastery was not the only way to court favor with the Lord.

Though that was on her agenda for this year as well.

She glanced at Hilda, who'd raised her eyes just enough to watch Thomas Blount being led away by the guards and who now looked like she was ready to slip back into her catatonic state. "I must return home. I'd appreciate being informed when Morhees is captured."

"I shall come tell you myself, my lady," said Haughton. Ela fought the urge to glance at de Hal to gauge his expression.

She had no official role in the proceedings, but without her involvement Thomas Blount would be taking control of Fernlees instead of preparing to meet his maker.

Still, she knew too much of the world to expect de Hal's thanks for what he probably still saw as tiresome meddling.

ELA SPOKE SOOTHING words to Hilda on the way home and made her go to bed with a bowl of hot gruel as soon as they arrived. The poor girl seemed exhausted, mentally and physically. Pregnancy alone could be draining, but narrowly escaping an abduction then staring in the eyes of a murderer .... She prayed that Hilda would recover.

ELA WALKED IN THE GARDENS, admiring the fast growth of the herbs and young vegetables. The birdsong and buzzing of the bees soothed her soul. She felt almost restored from the wrenching events at the castle when Sibel arrived home on foot.

"You walked all the way from town? What kind of man is this to let you find your way home?"

"He walked with me every step of the way." Sibel's face was radiant. Which could just be the effect of spring breezes on her cheeks. "We just said goodbye at the gate."

"Why didn't you invite him in?"

"I did but he had business to attend to at his shop."

"He's going to walk all the way back there?"

"It's not far. He enjoys walking. As do I. And the weather is so fine today." Sibel's mouth kept wanting to turn up into a smile.

Dread crept into Ela's heart. "Is there something you need to tell me?"

"We had the opportunity for a long talk today." Sibel wasn't wearing a cloak, but she still looked hot and flustered. "We spoke about our lives and what we hoped for and what we feared."

"What do you fear?"

"Regrets." Sibel looked sheepish. "Feeling that I've missed out on life by being too timid."

"I understand that."

"You're an example to me. You're bold about claiming things that are important to you."

Ela looked up from the sprouting chives feeling like she'd been slapped by her own maid. "Bold? I shall chasten myself forthwith."

"No, my lady! It's meant purely as a compliment. I so admire how you run your life and your household."

There was an awkward silence in which Ela wondered if thanks were appropriate for something that didn't sound like a compliment. Sibel fussed with her wimple, pulling it away from her neck as if to cool herself.

"He's asked me to marry him." She looked at the crushed stone path while she spoke. Then she glanced up, a mix of exhilaration and fear in her eyes. "I told him that I must ask your permission."

"Why? I'm not your liege lord to order you about as I see fit." *Even if I am bold.* Misgivings clawed at her, for Sibel as well as for herself and her Sibel-less future. "Do you want to marry him?"

Sibel looked like a girl of sixteen in the throes of her first infatuation "I do. I realize we don't know each other well, but he seems a good and kind man and I've heard no ill reports of him. I think we might be happy together."

Ela's heart squeezed—gripped by something that she

hoped was happiness. "Then you must marry him, and with my blessing. You deserve only the best."

"I can bring Hilda with me. I asked him and he said she could live with us. You can see how kind he is."

"That is generous of him, and so thoughtful of you to look for a home for your niece. But then who shall attend to my needs?" She didn't want Sibel's new marriage burdened by the expense and gossip that attended a young pregnant girl. She also didn't want Sibel to feel like she'd left Hilda as a burden to her.

"But she's ill so often right now."

"That will pass," Ela took Sibel's hand in hers and squeezed it. "Don't trouble yourself about me or Hilda. Look to your future. May it be blessed."

Happy tears shone in Sibel's eyes. "Thank you, my lady. I wonder if I'm still young enough to be blessed with children?"

"Many a woman has had a baby at our age. I shall pray for you. And a marriage can be joyful without children. You'll share each other's companionship."

A pang of loneliness pierced her as she said it. She kept herself too busy to feel it keenly much of the time. But there were moments when she remembered William's smile, or a teasing word, or a tender kiss on the cheek, and she missed him so hard.

Sibel looked like she wanted to offer words of comfort or solace but thankfully she was wise enough not to. Ela didn't want to be reassured that she could marry again.

"So many weddings! The world is filled with the promise of new beginnings. You should chase after him on the road and tell him to plan the date!"

Sibel startled and looked ready to spring into action. "Nay, we've had enough excitement for today. Tomorrow will be soon enough."

"You want to leave him on tenterhooks overnight?"

Sibel gave an oddly mischievous glance. "Some say that men enjoy the chase and it's best not to make it too easy for them. Since I've all but run after him so far, making him wait until tomorrow will keep him intrigued."

"I'm surprised to hear such calculation coming from you. It seems you're ready to handle the challenges of managing a husband."

"Managing? You make it sound as if a husband was like a flock of sheep."

Ela laughed. "Oh yes, and sometimes you shall feel like the busiest sheepdog in the shire. Especially if you have children." Suddenly filled with emotion she took Sibel to her breast and held her close. "You've been at my side through so many trials and joys. Please come to me first if you need help or advice with anything at all."

"Thank you." She felt Sibel's chest heave with a small sob. "My lady."

~

"Vicus Morhees is gone." Giles Haughton stood in her doorway late that afternoon, his hat in his hand.

Frustration surged through Ela. "How? They rode out to get him before word could possibly reach him."

"He might have realized the net was closing in, even if there's no blood under his nails."

"He must have spies at the castle." She sighed. "Sometimes I feel I can trust no one. How can we find him? He might be in London, or Exmouth, or anywhere."

Haughton nodded. "Simon de Hal will send a letter to the relevant sheriffs and ask them to keep watch for him. He'll be returned here if he's apprehended."

Ela felt hollow. Morhees might be on a ship to Spain by nightfall.

"I doubt he'll be back," offered Haughton in a way that sounded like she might think it a consolation.

"Did he take his effects?"

"Not all, but most. His clothes and chattels are gone. Some sticks of furniture remain."

"Those probably belonged to Pinchbeck. Also gone. And it would all have been Drogo's if he hadn't been so cruelly murdered."

"Do you really think Drogo deserved such a prize?" Haughton looked intrigued.

"Who am I to judge him? I hate that he took advantage of poor Hilda. But men are often prey to desires that are best subsumed in a marriage and he didn't have the means to take a wife. Maybe he would have made her a good husband."

"Your attitude is a model of Christian charity." Amusement twinkled in his eyes.

"You mock me, sir," she was only half joking.

"I admire you greatly, my lady. It was clever of you to mention Drogo's heir, so de Hal could not seize Fernlees as a reward for the pains this case has caused him."

"You give me credit for more cunning than I possess. At the very least Drogo's child must be notified of his father's death."

Ela wrote to Spicewell to inform him that Thomas Blount was as good as dead, and to ask him to find Drogo's heir. She also wrote to Beatrice Panton to inform her of her suitor's predicament. She wasn't sure whether Beatrice would weep into her pillow for her lost love, come charging up to Salisbury to plead for his freedom, or cross herself and thank the saints that she'd avoided the marriage.

Instead, she wrote to Ela, politely thanking her for the information and asking if perhaps she knew what had become of her Bible.

Ela remembered how much store Beatrice put in her Bible and suspected it was her most valuable possession materially as well as spiritually. Beatrice explained that she'd lent it to Blount so he could carry the Lord's grace with him on his journey.

Ela's heart sank. It was far more likely that Blount had used her Bible to finance his journey to Salisbury and his planned foray into the life of a landowner. Quite possibly he'd sold it to Morhees on his stop at Fernlees. Ela thought it unlikely that Beatrice would ever see her beloved Bible again, and that only increased her anger with the liar, cheat and cold-blooded killer currently rotting away in the castle dungeon.

She resolved to go there and question him.

CHAPTER 25

That afternoon Ela rode to the castle with Will—always restless and ready for action—in tow and told de Hal of the theft. She asked to question Blount about it and soon found herself being led to the dungeon.

"Can't they bring him up here?" Will seemed alarmed by the idea of her descending into the lightless depths.

"I suspect it's too much trouble. Aren't you curious to see what the dungeon looks like?"

Will looked sheepish. "I've been down there once. I asked one of the guards to let me see it. It's a grim and ghoulish place."

"It's hell on earth. That's why I'd never put anyone down there lightly. Remember that when you are sheriff."

Will brightened. "When will that be?"

Ela chastened herself for bringing it up. "All in good time, but for now, let's descend to see Blount."

It was awkward climbing down the ladder into the bowels of the castle in her long gown and the floor down there was unpleasantly wet. The rushlight borne by the guard escorting them barely seemed to pierce the darkness.

Around she could hear prisoners shifting in the shadows and could smell their unwashed bodies.

The guard led them to where Blount was chained to the wall. Sitting slumped on the floor, he barely looked up as they approached.

"May God forgive you," she said quietly.

He didn't reply.

"I wrote to Mistress Panton."

He flinched and sat straight up. "No! I don't want her to know about this."

"You wanted her sitting up and waiting for you, anxiously expecting a letter with good news? Wondering where you are? You wanted her to learn of your predicament through idle gossip?"

The flame cast long shadows across his grimace. "I suppose not."

"She asked about her Bible." She watched him shut his eyes tight. "Where is it?"

"Fernlees. Morhees has it. I gave it to him for safekeeping." More lies. She'd expected nothing less.

"He's gone and the Bible isn't there."

"Gone where?"

"I was hoping you could tell me." She could hardly believe that de Hal hadn't sent someone down here to ask him where Morhees had fled to. Though Blount would hardly know. He was simply Morhees's puppet.

"Why should I tell you? I'm to hang either way."

"The judge might show clemency."

"I don't know where he went. I barely know him. I wish I'd never met him."

"Beatrice Panton was very fond of her Bible. She showed it to me when I visited her. It was clearly one of her most treasured possessions." Ela crossed her arms over her chest. "She was never going to get it back, was she?"

Blount slumped against the wall, his head hanging slightly. He'd been so caught up in his magnificent plan of claiming his manor and marrying his rich widow that he likely hadn't stopped to consider the consequences of stealing and selling her Bible. No doubt he hoped to spend her coin to buy her a finer one. "Were you going to tell her that you were robbed by highwaymen?"

"Leave me alone." He snapped at her like an angry dog.

"Who might Morhees sell it to?"

Blount didn't reply. Then he looked up. "Morhees doesn't have it. I sold it to a man in the alley behind St. Bride's in London who deals in old books and manuscripts."

"If you have an ounce of goodness left in you, pray that it's still there."

~

ELA WAS PREPARING to write to Spicewell again, asking him to have someone investigate the map seller and hunt for Beatrice Panton's Bible, when he surprised her by arriving at Gomeldon.

"I'm on my way to spend a few days with your mother, and it was barely out of my way to stop here and visit you," he said, after he'd climbed out of his covered carriage. "May we speak somewhere privately?"

Ela took him into a small room where she'd set up the ledgers and where she stored her supplies of ink and parchment. There were two chairs, and she invited him to sit in one, then closed the door.

Spicewell leaned back in his chair. "Drogo Blount has no heir."

"But he spoke of a son. At least I think it was a son. Maybe it was a daughter?"

"His wife died giving birth to a boy but the child perished

too, nine days later. Both deaths are noted in the parish records. A local friar told my man that Drogo Blount went quite out of his mind at the double loss and was not the same man again. His parents are both dead, and his only surviving sibling is the imprisoned Thomas Blount."

"Who is soon to face a judge here on earth and then again in heaven."

"You're sure he'll hang?"

"He murdered a man. Hilda witnessed it and she's alive to testify against him, no thanks to Drogo and Morhees."

A sudden thought occurred to her like a blow to the head. "Hilda's pregnant with Drogo's baby. If Thomas Blount, as an illegitimate son, might have inherited the manor, could Hilda's child inherit it in his stead?"

She felt her heart beat faster as Spicewell stared at her with his pale blue eyes, trying to make sense of her garbled words. If Hilda's child were to inherit the manor—with her to keep it in the meantime—it would make Hilda a far more attractive marriage prospect than she'd be as a penniless, unchaste servant girl whose parents had disowned her.

Spicewell rubbed his chin. "You're sure the baby is Drogo's?"

"As sure as I am that my children are my own. I scolded her only days earlier for creeping out to meet him. The night he was killed she lay under him and his blood sprayed over her naked body."

Spicewell blinked. Ela crossed herself, appalled by the awful image she'd just brought to life. "Please excuse my blunt words."

"With a countess to vouch for her, she may well have a case."

"Please apply my coin to the pursuit of it," said Ela, suddenly cheerful.

"How will an ignorant young servant girl run a manor

any other way but right into the ground?" he asked doubtfully.

"She has friends in high places," said Ela with a slight lift of her brow. "I've schooled my daughters in the management of a household, and I can teach Hilda as well."

"But it's not just a household." He looked skeptical. "There will be sheep and crops and the logistics of bringing them to market."

Ela tilted her head, more amused than annoyed. "And who do you think manages those matters when all the men are away fighting?"

"The steward?"

Ela sighed. "If she inherits the manor I will make it my duty to find her a suitable husband to help her manage it."

"Very sensible. I shall pursue her claim."

"I thank you. If it sits empty too long de Hal may claim it for himself or even for the king, to curry favor."

"I shall proceed with all haste. As soon as I've enjoyed your mother's hospitality," he said with a smile. "If you'd like to join me there I can offer you a ride in my carriage. I feel confident it would delight her."

"Oh, no, thank you. I have much to attend to here." His suggestion perplexed her. She hoped he wasn't looking to put their relationship on a more personal footing since she valued Spicewell greatly as an ally in the business of law. "And there's another matter you might be able to help me with."

"It would be my pleasure." He smiled, revealing yellowed teeth.

"Thomas Blount borrowed a Bible from Mistress Panton and sold it to a map seller behind St. Bride's in London. It's a treasured gift from her late husband and also a fine piece worth a good deal of money. Might one of your associates be able to hunt it down?"

"I shall have my man make enquiries. Does it have any distinguishing features?"

"It's bound in green leather with a gold cross tooled on the front."

Spicewell scratched some notes in a little bound notebook he carried. "If it's found would you like him to buy it? I don't have the legal authority to seize it as stolen goods."

Ela considered. It was far from her duty to pay for the return of Beatrice's Bible. But if it wasn't seized at that moment it might never be seen again. She thought again about the roomful of gold it would take to build the monastery in her husband's memory. Surely this was a brick in the same edifice?

"Yes. If it can be found, please instruct them to buy it and deliver it to Mistress Panton with my good wishes."

They bid each other good day. Ela was startled—and not well pleased—when his lips rested on her fingers a little too long at the goodbye.

Despite his vigor and sharp mind, Spicewell must be nearly thirty years her senior! Perhaps he felt that her high rank and great fortune might come to grief in the hands of a mere woman.

It was also possible that her meddling mother might have put the idea in his head. She'd have a quiet word with her next time they met. If she'd sown the prospect of marriage in his mind, she'd have to uproot it.

~

Lincoln Castle, St. Swithin's Day, 1226

The day after Will's wedding Ela rose early to break her fast before the crowds of drink-damaged revelers could raise themselves from their beds. She'd been given a lovely chamber with a view over the surrounding countryside and French silk tapestries on the walls.

The wedding had been a lavish affair, well attended by nobles from all over the kingdom. Will had stayed sober enough to dance with his bride and carry her off to her bedchamber without swaying. Mostly she was relieved the whole affair was over.

The great hall was mercifully quiet. The servants were bringing out the first dishes of the day to lay on clean white tablecloths that would soon be blotted with cake crumbs and spilled wine. Ela picked up a plate and helped herself to a piece of a delicious-looking berry tart.

"The early bird catches the worm."

Ela spun around at the sound of a strident female voice behind her. Nicola de la Haye, her veil and wimple crisp and white as snow on a mountaintop over her plain brown gown, swept toward her.

"Good morrow, my sister," said Ela warmly. She hoped to make an ally of the woman her late husband had skirmished with many times over the years.

"Sisters! Good Lord preserve us. At my age I shall be your aunt." Nicola peered down a great nose that could most politely be described as aristocratic. "Do sit down."

Ela didn't know Nicola's age but suspected her to be at least three score years and ten. "I shall forthwith consider you to be my aunt Nicola." She sat in the carved chair Nicola indicated.

"I shall do my best to endure it." She sat next to Ela with a supercilious smile. A servant hurried over with a plate of food for her. "Thanks be to God those foolish children are finally married and we can breathe a sigh of relief for them and for ourselves."

Ela was surprised. "Did you think the king might have other plans for them?"

"Kings, like all men, are subject to whim and pique. Frankly I'm exhausted by them. After promising it for years I plan to finally retire as castellan of Lincoln."

"So soon?" Ela wasn't sure she liked this. Will was hardly ready to take over.

"Don't worry about your boy. I shall make sure he's groomed for the role and no doubt he'll be sheriff one day, just like his father. When the time is right."

Ela felt a trickle of relief. "He has some maturing to do."

"I presumed as much. I supposed that if he were ready to command men, you'd have put Salisbury in his care already."

"That might have prevented me being swept out of my home," Ela said softly. She felt she could be quite blunt with Nicola. "Did you really offer to surrender the keys of this castle to King John?"

Nicola laughed. "Not in quite the way it's described, but let's say we came to an understanding. And he got his revenge by installing your late husband as a thorn in my side."

Ela's wine soured in her mouth. "My husband was a good man." She felt duty bound to defend him, even as she hoped to make Nicola her friend.

"He was a fine man in every possible way, my dear. I'm sure you miss him keenly. He was always such good company, too. So entertaining that I hardly minded him commanding my troops from within my halls." She winked. Ela didn't know what to make of her. "But you must get your castle back. For yourself as well as for young Will."

"I intend to. I'm priming King Henry with rich gifts. I fear his justiciar is my biggest obstacle."

Nicola leaned in. "Rumor has it that he poisoned your husband. Is it true?"

Ela's stomach clenched. She didn't want this gossip heard leaving her lips. Hubert de Burgh was dangerous. She could find herself accused of treason and twisting in an iron cage dangled from the walls of Salisbury Castle if she wasn't careful. "He did take ill suddenly."

"De Burgh will get his comeuppance. You mark my words." Nicola poured herself a cup of wine. "In the meantime you're doing a splendid job of securing the fortunes and rank of your husband's wards to your own family and I commend you for it." She raised the cup.

Ela nodded her thanks, unsure if this was compliment or reproach.

"I was seated next to Will last night, as you know, and he told me the murderer you caught was just convicted at the assizes."

"Indeed he was. Since he killed a man who once saved my husband's life I'm glad he'll meet his last judge." Blount was to hang before Lammas. Morhees unfortunately still evaded capture. He'd either left the country or gone underground. But she had feelers out from coast to coast. It was only a matter of time.

"And Will told me an extraordinary story about how the dead man's unborn bastard is going to inherit a manor." Nicola arched a silver eyebrow. "I suspect he was rather too far in his cups. I've never heard of such a thing."

Ela winced, as always, at the cruel word. A child was always innocent, even if its parents weren't. "In the total absence of a legitimate heir or any next of kin I'm working to convince our sheriff that the baby is the rightful heir. It requires a lot of expensive legal work that made even my lawyer mock me for extravagance."

"Some men think we women only enjoy spending money on furs, fine fabrics and pretty trinkets. There are other more satisfying pleasures to purchase with our silver."

"True." Ela's coin had purchased the return of Beatrice Panton's precious Bible—at a bargain price based on its dubious provenance. She'd received a grateful letter from Beatrice thanking her for her kindness and for saving her from a potentially disastrous marriage.

Ela took in a deep breath. People had trickled into the hall and several joined them at the table. She smiled at them in greeting before turning back to Nicola. "What do you plan to do with your days once you retire as castellan?"

"Why the same as I've always done." Nicola smiled sweetly and picked up a tiny cake. "I shall spend my days in prayer and at my needlework." Ela almost glanced away too quickly and missed her wink.

THE END

For information about upcoming Ela of Salisbury mysteries, please visit www.stoneheartpress.com.

AUTHOR'S NOTE

While I was initially intrigued by Ela Longespée because she was sheriff of Wiltshire, I soon discovered that her path to that role was not strewn with rose petals. In fact, shortly after her husband's sudden death, Simon de Hal was installed as sheriff and Ela was forced to leave her castle. She did not manage to regain the castle or the role of sheriff until she paid a substantial "fine" to King Henry III in 1227. I could vividly imagine her frustration at being sidelined and the trouble and effort she went to in order to fight her way back to the role she considered rightfully hers.

Ejected from her castle, Ela would have moved to one of her manors. We know that Ela owned a number of manors, including Lacock, Hatherop, Bishopstrow, and Heydington, which were donated to the religious houses she founded. I imagined Ela wanting to be as close as possible to the castle in Salisbury, so I took the liberty of installing her in an imaginary manor at Gomeldon, which is a village near the old castle mound.

In 1226, when a wealthy heir or heiress was orphaned, they were assigned as the ward of a powerful noble. This noble then enjoyed the profits from the child's estates until they came of age. William Longespée's will reveals the high value of the wardships he'd secured. This led me to imagine Ela rushing to secure these fortunes by marriage before they could be snatched away and given to another noble after her husband's death. William II and Isabella Longespée did indeed marry two of these wards, Idonea de Camville and William de Vesci, in alliances that were probably planned since they were young.

When we think of the Middle Ages, we often imagine people living their whole lives in a ten-mile radius, never traveling farther than the local market. While this was true for many, Ela and her circle lived in an international world, enjoying wine, spices, fabrics, jewels and books imported from Europe and beyond—even opium from Ghandhara, or Kandahar, as we know it today. Knights traveled to the Continent and the Holy Land to fight for their king, and a wealthy man or woman might own estates on the Continent as well as in England, or might undertake a pilgrimage to a far-off holy site. A noble like Ela would travel readily to visit friends and family or to call on the king at one of his many residences. Although the journey from London to Salisbury would have meant many hours on the road, Ela and her entourage would have been used to the rigors of travel much as we endure tedious drives and plane flights today.

I'm grateful to the Internet for putting history at my fingertips, so I can find and read obscure sources and look at images of the coins Ela would have held in her hand. Once again, *Annals and Antiquities of Lacock Abbey* (1835), written by William Lisle Bowles, working with genealogist John Gough

Nichols, was a valuable resource of information about Ela's life and family. Bowles included the intriguing story—gleaned from the *Book of Lacock*, written during Ela's life at the abbey she founded—of Ela being rescued from exile in Normandy by dashing young knight Sir William Talbot, who would go on to be a longtime member of her household. I'm also indebted to Roger of Wendover for the vivid account of his times in the contemporary *Flowers of History* and to King Henry III for keeping such excellent records, including his extensive Fine Rolls.

While some of the people in the story are real—including Ela and her children, her mother, Bill Talbot, Simon de Hal, Nicola de la Haye, King Henry III and Hubert de Burgh—many of the others are invented. The mysteries Ela solves in this book are entirely a product of my imagination.

If you have questions or comments, please get in touch using the email form at www.stoneheartpress.com.

SERIES BOOKLIST

CATHEDRAL OF BONES
BREACH OF FAITH
THE LOST CHILD
FOREST OF SOULS
THE BONE CHESS SET
CLOISTER OF WHISPERS
PALACE OF THORNS
A SURFEIT OF MIRACLES
THE D'ALBIAC INHERITANCE
UNHOLY SANCTUARY

AUTHOR BIOGRAPHY

J. G. Lewis grew up in a Regency-era officer's residence in London, England. She spent her childhood visiting nearby museums and riding ponies in Hyde Park. She came to the U.S. to study semiotics at Brown University and stayed for the sunshine and a career as a museum curator in New York City. Over the years she published quite a few novels, two of which hit the *USA Today* list. She didn't delve into historical fiction until she discovered genealogy and the impressive cast of potential characters in her family history. Once she realized how many fascinating historical figures are all but forgotten, she decided to breathe life into them again by creating stories for them to inhabit. J. G. Lewis currently lives in Florida with her dogs and horses.

For more information visit www.stoneheartpress.com.

Published 2019 by Stoneheart Press
11923 NE Sumner St
STE 853852
Portland, Oregon, 97220,
USA

Cover image includes: detail from Codex Manesse, ca. 1300, Heidelberg University Library; decorative detail from Beatus of Liébana, Fecundus Codex of 1047, Biblioteca Nacional de España; detail with Longespée coat of arms from Matthew Parris, *Historia Anglorum,* ca. 1250, British Museum.

Printed in Great Britain
by Amazon